EARTHKING

EARTHKING

THE EARTHKING CHRONICLES: BOOK 1

Christopher C. Hall

Cover Art by Mike Yakovlev

ISBN: 0996604804
ISBN 13: 9780996604802
Library of Congress Control Number: 2015914261
Piper Books, Intercourse PA

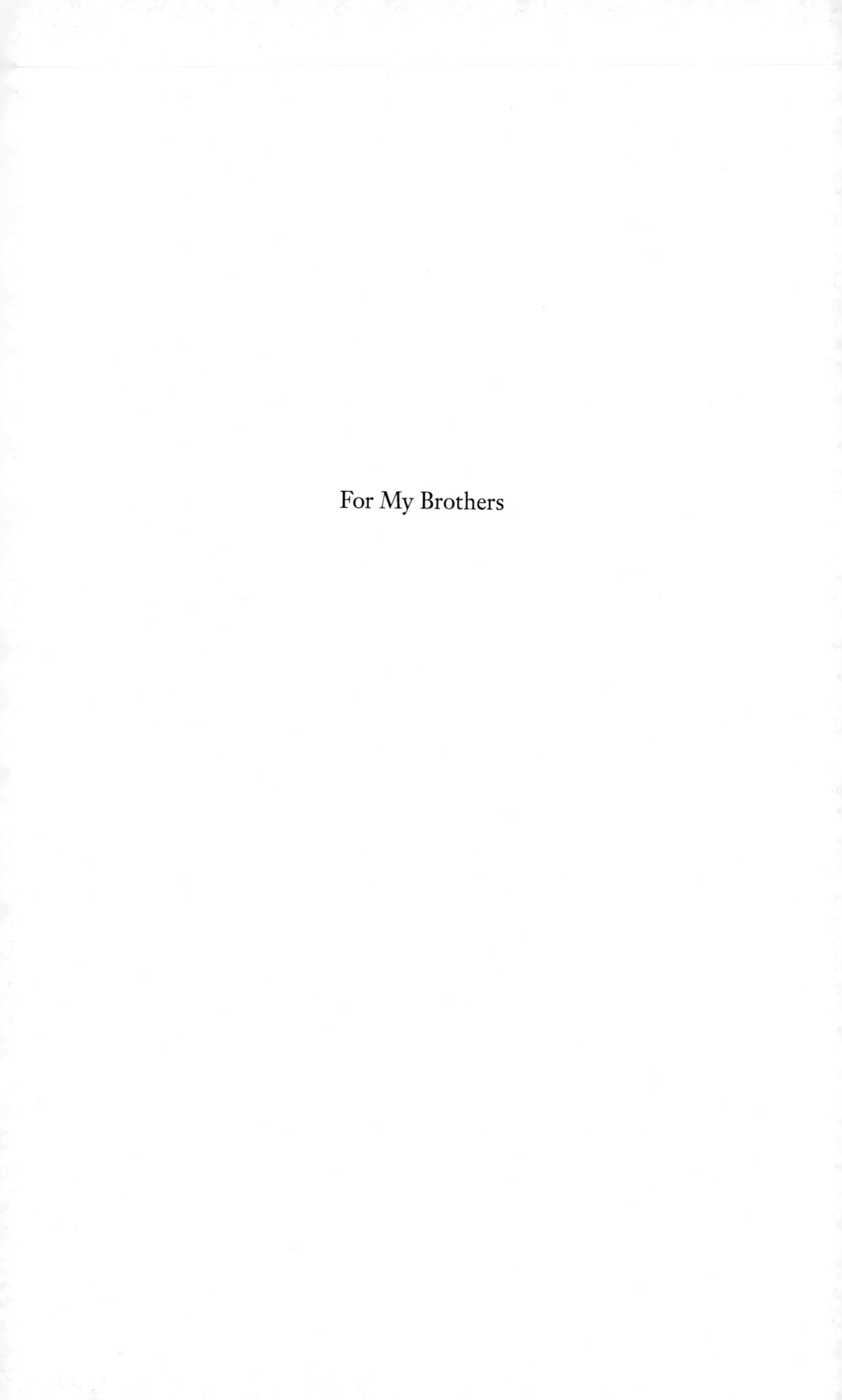

For My Brothers

CHAPTER 1

THE MISSING RIDER

—∞—

EVEN FROM HIGH ATOP THE Western tower Col could tell something had gone terribly wrong. With one eye squeezed shut he peered over a nocked arrow and watched a lone horse emerge from the wood below. The steed shook the brambles from its mane. The saddle on its back fell awkwardly to the side.

Col dropped the bow and swung the quiver from his shoulder. He raced down the tower steps leaving a flutter of torchlight in his wake.

He toppled a basket of rolls as he sprinted through the kitchen but only managed to yell a "Sorry!" over his shoulder as the cook stooped to retrieve them. In the yard, riders appeared from between the trees. His older brother, Tonn, was among them.

Col stared at him in surprise. "I would've placed money that was your horse," he said. "Who was it then? Which one of you was bested by his mount?"

A pointed glare from Tonn stopped Col short. There was no laughter, no jeering among the men. This was worse than a broken leg or a twisted knee.

From among the riders, King Tephall stared into the crowded shadows of the forest. "The horse is Nabal's," he said. He motioned to the nearest stablehand, "Take the steed inside and clean him up."

The servant nodded and took the horse's reins, leaving Col to see what the others already had.

The horse's flank was smeared with blood. Its coat was stiff and sticky from the spill.

"Etau," the king spoke to the Captain of his guard. "Take the riders back into the forest." King Tephall pulled the big man close. "Find my friend and bring him home. Tonight."

Etau and his men turned back to the woods. Tonn made to follow but the king stopped him. "Not you, son. Go inside and keep your brothers busy."

A plea spread over Tonn's puffed cheeks and down his wobbly chin, but the king would not be swayed.

"Fine," said Tonn. He spun his mount and caught Col staring at him. "Come on, worm. Back to the castle."

"Your first ride in the bear hunt and someone gets killed. That can't be a good sign," Col said.

"Shut up!" Tonn's foot struck Col's shoulder and sent him to the ground. "They'll find him. Nobody's better than Etau."

Col and his brother went back to Ten Rocks, their father's castle. It was an immense, towering structure perched over a sprawling lake so deeply blue it was nearly black. On clear nights when the moon mimicked the sun, like a child dressing in his father's armor, Ten Rocks seemed to grow like a stone giant threatening to drink the lake dry. But most of the time it was simply home. The only home Col and his family had ever known.

Etau and his men searched until the dying light afforded them no more time. The party returned through the two stout oaks that formed the entrance to the western wood. Each man wore the same look on his face as the path behind them disappeared into the gloom.

They gathered that night in the feasting hall. Ornate tapestries hung between heavy cedar columns and an immense hearth at the far end filled the room with somber light. Tephall's board showed a hearty spread but the men had little appetite.

Caménor, the king's brother, spoke, "To hunt the bear only to find it's the bear that is hunting you? It's a shame to lose Nabal in such a manner."

"You give up too easily, brother. There is still hope." King Tephall's deep voice echoed through the hall. The tapestries seemed to ripple from its force.

"Of course. I didn't mean to cast hope aside so soon. I'm sure the morning will bring better news."

"It's been a long day for all of us," Tephall said. "It's time we found our beds. We'll resume the search with the sun." Tephall emptied the remains of his cup. "Etau, I want more men for the search tomorrow. He's injured, at the least, and the longer he's out there the worse off he'll be."

"Of course, my lord." Etau's smooth voice belied the great barrel from where it came.

As the hall cleared, Tephall beckoned his sons. Col yawned as he neared.

"You boys are to keep to Ten Rocks for now. At least until we find Nabal and put down this bear."

"But—"

"I've made my decision, Colmeron."

Col bit his tongue.

"Tonn, I trust you'll make sure he respects my wish."

"Of course, Father," Tonn said.

At sixteen, Tonn was the oldest of the king's three sons. He was the NéPrince, first in line for the throne. Col was only two years behind him with the youngest, Mino, a full six behind that.

"One more thing." The king placed a hand on their shoulders. "I don't want Mino being told about any of this. Your brother has enough nightmares as it is. Keep him inside and occupied."

"I'm not going to babysit the brat. That's what his nurse is for," Col said.

A knot formed in the king's brow. "To bed now. Both of you."

The two boys left their father alone in the heart of his great castle.

Col went to his room, stripped down and burrowed deep beneath his covers. Beyond his cloth shelter he heard his home fade to the deep stillness of night.

It was a shame to think Nabal could be dead. Col would miss his stories.

At night the world beyond Ten Rocks' walls was an arena of dangers. Here in his room, though, nothing was beyond Col's control. His clothes still lay in a pile where he'd left them. His books were still haphazardly stacked on his desk and the misshapen dagger he'd carved when he was ten still hung impotently over the hearth.

The first beams of day slipped through the curtains where the cloth had worn thin. Col's nose twitched. He opened his eyes, stretched, and dropped both feet to the ground.

Footsteps sounded in the hall as he pulled on his shirt. He opened his door and saw Caménor disappear at the end of the hall. Why wasn't he searching for Nabal with the others?

Col slipped from his room and fell in a few yards behind his uncle. He stayed there, unnoticed, until he passed a window and saw a fat figure slinking toward the forest. Catching Tonn disobey their father was too good to pass up. He let Caménor escape and went after his brother.

Outside, crisp frost snapped underfoot as Col rushed past the stables. Tonn disappeared into the trees. Col quickly closed the gap. He stopped a few yards short and crouched low to watch.

Tonn swiped at the bracken with his sword. Col threw a stone to Tonn's right. Tonn jumped and swung toward the sound.

Col took another stone and cleared the dirt from its edges. This time he aimed for the back of Tonn's head. The rock sailed true and struck Tonn behind the ear.

The older boy yelped. Col tried to conceal his laughter but it spilled past his lips and he gave up trying to hide.

Tonn lunged at him. "You!"

Col ducked to the side. "Put your sword away. Are you trying to kill me?"

"Are you trying to kill me?"

"You're not supposed to be out here."

"Neither are you, worm. And you can't tell father without getting yourself in trouble, too."

"I don't care."

"Of course you don't. When do you ever? Now, leave me alone. I'm busy."

"I can see that. Those weeds would only keep growing if it wasn't for you."

"Shut up. I've got things to do." Tonn disappeared into a crease in the hills.

Col slid after him. "Like what, get yourself killed?"

"You talk too much. Do you know that? Go home. You're going to get us both in trouble!"

"It's a nice morning. I think I'll stay here," Col said, "What are you doing anyway?"

"I'm looking for Nabal."

"Why? Etau and the others will find him."

"I was supposed to be with him yesterday. We got separated."

"So it's your fault he was eaten by a bear?" Col poked a finger at him.

Tonn balled his fists and turned on him. "It's not my fault!"

Col was almost afraid but not near enough to stop teasing Tonn. "Of course not. It was only your first hunt and his ten thousandth. Good job getting an experienced hunter killed, big brother."

"He's not dead. He's just lost."

"Of course. I know I tend to lose a bucket of blood every time I get lost, too."

Tonn glared at him.

Col could tell when he'd pushed Tonn to the edge. His cheeks puffed, more than usual anyway, and flashes of crimson lined his forehead. Seeing those signs now Col eased up. "Alright. Let's go find him."

"Fine. Just keep quiet. There's only so much of your blabbering I can take before I leave you out here."

"You know there's a killer bear out here, though, right?"

Tonn pushed on without answering.

"I just wanted to make sure you had that in mind while dragging your little brother out here."

The two pressed deeper into the wood. Trees still blazing with Autumn's vigor crowded around them. The further they went the more Col wished he'd eaten breakfast.

Nearly two hours passed before Col finally spoke up. "I don't know where we are, Tonn, and if I don't know I'm sure you don't have a clue."

Tonn stopped. He slid his sword back into its scabbard and stared at Col. Col didn't know whether to laugh or take a step back.

"If you're so worried why don't you just stay here?" He shoved Col to the ground.

Col jumped up with fists clenched, but before he could swing he saw blood on his arm.

Tonn saw it too. "I didn't do that. You're just clumsy," he stammered.

Col turned his arm over. "It's not mine. Look," he pointed to a patch of ground where red splashed across bending ferns.

"It's probably from an animal. A deer, maybe." Tonn's hand fumbled for his sword.

"Do you think so?"

"I don't know."

"What if it's Nabal's?"

Tonn looked at the blood and tightened his grip on his weapon. He swallowed hard. "Let's find out."

They followed the erratic trail of blood, but it was slow going and gruesome with only a drop here or a smear there. They stopped in a small clearing to regain their bearings.

"What do we do now?"

"I don't know, Col. Why do you think I always have the answers? Try thinking for yourself."

"You're older. You're supposed to know more than I do."

To their left, beneath a spent honeysuckle bush, Col spotted an unnatural lump of fabric. "Tonn," he nodded toward the sight.

The two boys slowly approached.

Nabal lay twisted in a mess of leaves and thorns. A deep gash ran from the top of his bald head to his chest. Blood spilled past the corners of his mouth and soaked the shoulder of his tunic.

"Do you think he's dead?" Tonn asked.

"It looks like it."

"What happened to him?"

"Isn't it obvious?" Col said.

"I'm sure Etau and the men will be along soon. We'll be alright."

Col watched in fear that the body would move at any moment. "Tonn, give me your cloak."

"Why? It's not my fault you didn't bring one."

"I need something to cover him with."

"Oh." Tonn loosened the silver clasp at his neck and handed Col the cloak. "I don't want to see him either."

Col draped the gray cloth over the body. As he pulled it across the mangled face something stopped him. Nabal's arm lay twisted near his head. Each finger wore a valuable ring but the third finger on his right hand was noticeably bare. A band of pale skin with blood on either side showed where a ring had been until recently.

Col looked back at his brother. "We aren't the first ones to find him. Somebody else has been here."

CHAPTER 2

A NIGHT IN THE WOODS

Tonn's cloak concealed most of Nabal's body. The grisly parts, anyway. Col sat a few yards away. "I don't want to spend the night here," he said.

"Just sit there and be quiet," Tonn said. "Etau will be here soon."

"I hope he finds us before someone returns."

"This again? The ring probably slipped off when the bear was attacking him. No one would find him and just take one ring. Nabal had half a fortune wrapped around his knuckles. It's probably in the weeds somewhere."

Col wanted to believe him, but he couldn't shake the feeling his brother was wrong. He tried not to look at the body. Instead, he stared into the fire.

"Why don't we find our way back now?" He asked. "We can lead Etau here later."

"I'm not leaving Nabal," Tonn said.

"What does it matter? He's already dead." Col rolled a twig between his fingers. "You didn't bring anything to eat, did you?" The twig snapped.

"No," Tonn dropped an armful of dried leaves onto the fire, sending fresh billows of smoke through the treetops. "But Etau will be here soon."

Col closed his eyes and yawned. "I don't want to spend the night here."

"We won't."

Col leaned his head back and drifted into a nap. The hushed waving of the flames turned into the tumble of the sea and Col's mind was no longer in the forest.

He floated easily over the endless blue of the sea. He was tossed over trough and crest until the water began to roil beneath him. Something stirred far below. Col tried to swim. He flailed his arms and legs in a desperate attempt to escape but a pressure grew under him until he felt he might be torn apart by it. Flashes of heat washed over his face and pulled him from the sea. He awoke to darkness and torchlight.

Tonn stared into the growing night, sword in one hand, branch aflame in the other. He spun wildly and Col felt heat spit from the torch.

"What are you doing?" Col said. He pulled himself to his feet.

"Stay still. There's something out there."

"What is it?"

"I'm not sure. I was getting more wood. When I looked into the trees, something looked back at me. Something big."

"Whoever took that ring is still here, watching us. Give me the torch."

Tonn tossed him the brand then gripped his sword with both hands. "I don't want you to be afraid, Col. It'll be okay."

"I told you we should've left."

"And I told you I'm not leaving Nabal. Father will be here soon. Everyone will be looking for us by now."

Col wished he had his brother's faith. Soon the forest would be soaked in black and their little fire would be all that stood between them and it. No one would find them then.

"We know you're there," Col said. He tried to hide the quiver in his voice. He waited and watched, holding his breath and listening for the someone that lurked beyond their light, but nothing moved, no one made a sound.

Night fell and the brothers' world shrank to a circle of pallid light. The two of them moved back to back as they gathered more wood for the fire.

Col stoked the flames and sat with his back to a tree. He was tired. Tired of being away from his bed.

And the kitchen.

His stomach loudly protested its neglect. Col could only respond with thoughts of roasted meats and berry pies, soft cheeses and steaming loaves of bread. He turned his face to the flames. He may have doubted Tonn's decisions but he was glad for his older brother's vigilance. He looked through the leaves and past the trees around him. He tried to see anything that might intrude upon their shelter of light. Col's tension eased as Tonn moved unceasingly across their camp with his sword at the ready. Though he didn't mean to, Col soon fell asleep.

Dawn climbed through the trees and woke Col with warm fingers of light on his skin. He rolled to his knees and stood, groaning. Princes were not made for such nights.

"Tonn," he called. Their fire had burned to coals, with only a flame or two popping like a surprised groundhog from its hole. Despite Col's fears, Nabal still lay unmoving beneath Tonn's cloak.

Col called for his brother again. He was gone. Col scrambled for a branch, a stone, anything with which he could defend himself.

The hair on the back of Col's neck stood suddenly as a low growl sounded from beneath the briars.

Col slowly turned, fighting the urge to close his eyes. The brush erupted in a flash of teeth and fur. Col tumbled backward and his shoulder caught an errant stone. He cried out as much from pain as from fear. His terror quickly faded, though, as his face was bathed by a long, coarse tongue. His eyes focused to see the furrowed brow of his father's favorite hound. Col threw his arms around the hound. He'd never been so relieved to see a dog.

"If you're here Father can't be far off. He's close, isn't he, boy?" The dog's tongue wagged in time with his tail. "That still leaves Tonn missing." Col held the muscled hound close.

The dog bellowed and a moment later three men rode into the makeshift camp. The first was Etau. The ridges of his sculpted armor shimmered like dew in the morning light. Caménor came next followed by a weary, yet sturdy, Tephall who held a snoring Tonn in front of him. Col looked up at his father. The king's eyes showed fury and love all at once.

"I was only following Tonn," Col said.

"You were both told to stay in the castle and you both disobeyed me."

Tephall turned to the other men. "Caménor, take Colmeron back to the castle. Etau, see to Nabal."

Col gave the dog a final scruff before Caménor reached down and hoisted him into the saddle.

Col settled in, secure at last from an unseen terror. "How mad is Father?" He asked Caménor.

"I wouldn't say he's mad," Caménor's voice was soft and reassuring.

"He's relieved. We all are. His oldest friend and two of his sons were missing. The sun couldn't rise fast enough for any of us. No, he's not angry. Although, I wouldn't plan on either of you leaving Ten Rocks any time soon."

They caught up to Tephall and the the rest of the searchers. Etau brought up the rear with Nabal's body slumped in front of him. The horse jostled through the brush causing the dead man's arm to fall free and Col saw again the ringless finger.

"Uncle Cam?"

"Hmm?"

"What do you think killed Nabal?"

"A bear seems likeliest but Ten Rocks sits among some of Arnoc's fiercest wilderness. It could have been a lot of things."

"Bears don't like jewelry, do they? I mean, a bear wouldn't steal something off of a body, right?"

"That's an odd question to ask, Col. Was something taken from Nabal?"

"No," Col lied. "I think the woods were just playing tricks on me last night. It's nothing."

"From the look of what that bear did to Nabal I'm surprised he even has his skin left on his bones. A bear is a powerful animal. It's strong enough to do a lot of things we wouldn't think of."

"I suppose you're right, Uncle Cam."

"Don't concern yourself with these things right now. Let's get you home to a hot meal and a warm bed."

Upon reaching Ten Rocks the servants' jubilation at finding the princes in good health was quickly lost at the sorry sight of Nabal's body.

Wembus, Etau's brother, helped him with the body. "Joy and sorrow taken in with one breath," Wembus said.

The brothers looked remarkably alike. Just as Etau was charged with the king's guard, Wembus was given charge of Ten Rocks as head servant. Both were men of considerable size, as if their family tree hid a lion somewhere in its branches.

Behind Wembus crept an older man. His back was bent from years of craning over a table and his white hair spun wildly from his head giving the sense that fingers were constantly pulling at it. This man, Healer they called him, grabbed Nabal's hand and squeezed the lifeless palm. "Hmm," he nodded. "Take him to my rooms. I'll prepare him," he nearly squeaked as the air wheezed from his lungs.

Wembus called two servants to him and together they carefully placed the body on a wooden stretcher.

Wembus turned to his king. "I'm glad to see you found the princes, my lord. It's good to have something to celebrate on a day such as this."

"We'll celebrate later, Wembus. Right now I want these boys cleaned up, fed, and put to bed. If they try to leave, you have my permission to chain them."

Col knew his father wasn't in a jesting mood. He meant what he said.

Wembus reached for Tonn but Tephall stopped him. "I'll take the NéPrince in. Take care of Colmeron."

Col snatched a fistful of dried venison on his way through the kitchen and chewed on it while he soaked in a hot bath. The muscles that had been so abused by the hard ground relaxed and any thoughts of missing rings or ghastly faces were pushed further away by the sumptuous meal that followed. He feasted on roasted quail and glazed sweetbreads along with honey filled tarts. Tonn must've taken straight to bed because there was no sign of him at the table.

After lunch, Col made his way to the Upper Garden. It sat high on the eastern wall overlooking the lake. Elm trees that began their growth long ago gave shelter throughout the sprawling patch. Great care was taken to groom the flowers and bushes whose colors burned like fire. Ten misshapen stone pillars stood in odd formation in the garden. It was for these stones that Ten Rocks was so named. Caménor said the Earthkings had put them there when the foundations of the castle were laid. Col had always wondered why they were there, though. He and Tonn had spent many days making up stories about their origin. They marked the entrance to a secret stairwell that led to great treasure. They were the remains of ten faithful guards who were turned to stone so they could ever watch over the castle. Or maybe they served as a gateway to another world. Whatever the truth was, the stories Col and Tonn told had filled endless afternoons.

Col followed a winding footpath through a layer of fallen leaves. He went to the garden's far edge and climbed over the waist-high wall. The drop was nearly straight down the cliffside but a small ledge pushed out from under the wall. He sat there and let his feet hang over the long fall to the rocks below.

He heard footsteps behind him. These were joined a few moments later by more steps, slow and halting.

"What is it?" Caménor said.

"I'm sorry, my prince. I need to speak to you before I see the king," the Healer replied.

"Speak then."

"I don't believe Nabal's death was a mauling, my lord. Something about his remains was... amiss."

"What are you saying?"

The Healer paused before speaking again. "Nabal's death was brutal and violent but I believe it was done that way to hide the true reason for his demise."

"What would his death benefit anyone?"

"His tongue was taken. Torn out by the root."

Caménor breathed sharply.

"What should I tell the king?" the Healer asked.

"Tell him nothing other than that his friend and advisor is finally at peace."

"Do you think it could really be them?"

"Of course not. Nabal's tongue was always wagging too much. I'm sure the bear tore it out along with the rest of his face."

"There was one more thing. It may be nothing but I thought you should know. His signet ring was missing from his hand. The knuckle where it was worn was crushed."

The Healer left. Col's legs were starting to hurt which made his seat feel smaller and the drop seem even further. He tried to keep still. He had the sense he had heard things he was not meant to hear.

Caménor stood right above Col, his hands on the wall. If he looked down Col was discovered. He looked out over the lake instead and spoke quietly to himself.

"Have the Three returned?"

CHAPTER 3

A FAREWELL

Three Days Earlier

Mino squirmed on the step in front of Col while Tonn grunted his own impatience behind him. The three princes stood in the passage to the upper garden. They waited, though not well, for their introduction. A great wreathe of bright, crisp leaves adorned the passage's gaping mouth and the smell of cool Autumn nights filled the space.

Col hated waiting. Especially when it came to his brothers. Finally, the announcement was made and the procession began.

Mino ran in and nearly stumbled over his own feet upon his entrance to the festive garden. A channel in the perimeter wall was filled with flames leaving only the sound of the tide as evidence of the waters below. Long wooden tables filled the yard. Lanterns hung from the branches and shed a calm glow over the garden.

Col slowed suddenly and Tonn crashed into him with a grunt. Col smiled and continued on.

The gathered guests — champions of the hunt, visiting lords and regal ladies — applauded as Col stepped from the ever-yawning tunnel into the warm light.

He knew it mattered little to them whether or not he was there. They weren't here for him. He took his seat between Mino and Caménor as Tonn came into the crowd's view.

King Tephall stood and addressed those in attendance. "Ladies, gentlemen, loyal subjects, I give you the man who will one day sit on my throne -the throne of my father and all the fathers before him, the throne of Arnoc - my son, the NéPrince Tonn!"

Tonn walked with slow, deliberate steps to his seat, head held high. The crowd cheered. Tonn beamed.

Mino wriggled in the chair next to Col.

"Sit still, will you?" Col poked him. "This party is stupid enough without you annoying me."

Mino's fresh face scrunched into a sneer. Col glared back. If Tonn wasn't bossing him around, Mino was bothering him. As the youngest, Mino could do no wrong. He could pout his way out of any reprimand because he was the baby, the only one who had never known their mother. Col was only six when she died but nobody seemed to care that he'd lost her, too.

A bell rang and the first course was served: meat pies baked in the shape of bears. Tonn didn't bother waiting for anyone else before breaking the tender crust with his knife.

"I hope our dear brother enjoys his pie," Col said to Mino. "I'm sure it'll be the only bear he gets."

"What do you mean?" Mino said.

"Tomorrow is Tonn's first ride in the great bear hunt. Or did you think we were here for you?"

"I knew that! And I'll bet Tonn gets the biggest bear of all."

"We'll be lucky if he comes back with his pants dry." Col waited for Mino's response but the boy was busy stuffing his mouth as trays of fresh breads, roasted vegetables and spitted pheasant stuffed with herbs and bacon were set on the tables. Col may not have been enthusiastic about the cause for this celebration but he had to admit the food was worth his older brother's overweening pride. At least for tonight.

As the final course finished Etau wiped his mouth and checked his shirt for crumbs before standing to speak. He looked to the king, who nodded his approval.

"Every year a crew of our bravest men take to the forest for the hunt," Etau began. He stood head and shoulders above most men and his voice carried well through the garden. "I am happy to say that our NéPrince will be joining those venturesome ranks tomorrow and I know he will make us all proud."

King Tephall stood and thanked Etau for his kind words. "Even the Captain of my guard, a champion of the hunt himself, knows that our NéPrince is destined for glory!" The crowd applauded enthusiastically. Col fought the urge to laugh.

"Such a day awaits you, my son. But first, I'd like to ask my advisor to honor us with a story." The king turned to Nabal. "How about it, old friend? Remind us why we hunt the great bear."

A small man, extravagantly dressed, stood from beside the king. Nabal had no hair, neither on his face, nor his head. He held his hands up to still the crowd's applause. The rings adorning his fingers gleamed in the light. "Of course, my lord. To serve the king is ever my pleasure."

He moved in front of the fire and pulled his dark cloak tightly around him. His eyes glimmered and he opened his mouth to let the story come forth.

"Long ago, before the world was as we see it now, Arnoc was a wild and untamed land, dangerous as the sea in a storm. It was in those days a man named Derid walked the path that would lead him home. But as Derid roamed the forest, he was soon lost. He pushed on, knowing he would make an easy meal for any of the terrors that dwelt in the forest's shadow, but home could not be found.

He searched for any sign of the trail, but a swirling mist swept over the ground and huffed itself into a heavy fog. Derid ran blindly on, certain that death was at his heels, until fear and exhaustion claimed him. He collapsed and heard the muffled steps of predators surrounding him. He knew he would never rise again.

Such a fate was not meant for this man, though. He woke to a calm forest. Thinking he was at last born into the world beyond he did not bother to stand. He lay atop a high hill. His head rested on the root of a tree whose leaves swam in a cool morning breeze. To his right was a clear spring.

He crawled to the pool and scooped cold water to his lips. It tasted like no water he'd ever drank and filled him with new strength. He took one last satisfying mouthful and lay against the tree. Another tree, nearly identical to the one at his back grew on the other side of the spring. The two trees, the spring, and Derid were the only things upon the hill overlooking an endless canopy of green. There were no furrowed lines of fields, no smoke curling through the branches, no roads snaking between the hills, just the wild as far as he could see.

As Derid despaired, a strange leaf tumbled over his shoulder and into his lap. He took it and held it to the light. It was deep blue with traces of red through it. Holding the leaf brought an odd temptation. He tore it in two and put half to his lips. His mouth watered at the tart flavor and he quickly ate the leaf. The branches above shuddered and sent more spinning to him. He found two more colors: deep red and smooth gold. The red was firmer than the blue but had a heavy fragrance that reminded him of smoke while the yellow was just as filling with a warm, nutty flavor like fresh bread.

After he'd eaten his fill he set out in search of home. He travelled through the day only to succumb that night to the same blinding fog and wake again the next morning with the spring beside him and the trees above.

Day after day Derid searched until eventually he stopped searching. The hill became his home. He found shelter under staunchly arching roots and a kind embrace in broad limbs above. The trees fed him and the spring was ever there to quench his thirst. He watched the valley below move through the seasons but the trees on his hill remained the same.

One morning, as the stars were still fading, Derid was pulled from his sleep. The tree shook and leaves crashed on the water. Derid dropped from his branch to find an enormous bear tearing at the trunk with its long, razored claws.

Filled with rage, Derid lunged at the bear. The beast fell back with a roar and threw the man from itself. The bear rolled to its feet and charged, but Derid leapt from its path as it rushed past. He threw himself onto the bear and beat at it furiously. His fists were like hammers constantly striking. The bear howled and rolled over, trapping Derid beneath its massive frame. Still, Derid would not relent. He thrust his arm up and tore through the bear's thick hide. Fur, flesh and sinew gave way. He felt the warm, slippery rush of the bear's insides and took hold of its heart. As he squeezed, the bear spoke.

"Enough! I surrender."

Derid froze.

"Spare my life and I will give you all the land you see here."

Derid pulled his arm from the bear's back. They stood and faced one another, though the bear stood a great deal taller than Derid.

"You fought to protect this land's greatest treasure and you showed mercy where it was not warranted. In return I give to you this land and all that is in it and you shall be its king." At this the bear dropped on all four paws and never again rose up in the presence of the king.

The next day King Derid met the first of his people. They came from the forest below, a heavy fog at their backs. It was his family, wife and children exactly as he'd left them. Soon, more people found their way to King Derid's kingdom. Derid cared for the land. He named it Arnoc in honor of the great bear. It is the land of our fathers and the land we call home."

Nabal's words settled over a rapt audience. Not everyone was enthralled, though. Caménor erupted from his seat and looked to the king. "Why do you let him spin such twisted tales, brother?"

"There's no harm in a story, Caménor. Please, sit down," the king said.

"You know what danger lies in changing the past, Tephall."

"Of course the king knows these things," Nabal said. "He is wiser than you give him credit for. You do not know the burden of that crown. How could you? Our king sees truth where it may be found. Or do you doubt him?"

"I doubt only the people he chooses to trust."

"You doubt his judgement, then?"

"Enough," the king said.

"I agree," Caménor said. "I've had enough. I have someplace I need to be," he turned to Tonn. "I pray you'll have good fortune on the hunt tomorrow, nephew."

Nabal turned to the crowd. "I must beg your forgiveness for the interruption. Our tale is not quite at its end. You see, it is from the noble King Derid that our own king, Tephall, descends and it is to celebrate this kingdom's birth that we hold the great bear hunt each year. And we are privileged to be here to celebrate such a momentous event with our someday king, Tonn.

"NéPrince Tonn, it would be my great honor, with your father's blessing; of course, to ride with you on the hunt."

Tonn looked to his father, who smiled back. "It would be my pleasure, Nabal," Tonn said.

"Excellent. I'm sure it will be a memorable day for us all."

Nabal was put to rest two days after his body was found. The evergreens stood sentry in the burial yard, their unchanging tone a testimony to their faithful watch over the forgotten and the soon to be. A chill wind swept between the stones and Col shivered as his father ended the ceremony.

"...from the earth we rise and to the earth we fall, forever to keep watch over the world we once made home, a world we all make home. Rest now and keep your watch, old friend."

The funeral over, the three young princes returned to the carriage and wrapped themselves in fur. They sat quietly and waited for their father.

The king had always been a strong man but today Col thought he saw his father flinch. It had been years since Col could remember him as happy but this day he seemed to bear a further burden. Col watched him through the carriage window. The king stood alone before the mound of earth where his friend lay. He held his arms behind his back and looked over the cemetery.

"What's taking so long?" Mino said.

"Father's saying goodbye to Nabal, Mino. Give him a few minutes," Col replied.

The boy sighed and sunk further into the furs.

"That's not what he's doing," Tonn said.

"What do you mean that's not what he's doing? We're at a funeral. What else would he be doing?" Col said.

"He's trying not to look at mother's grave. He knows when he turns around he'll have to see it."

"This is where my mother's buried?" Mino asked.

"Yes, Mino. This is where *our* mother is buried," Tonn said.

Col watched his father closer. "Why wouldn't he want to look at her grave?"

"He doesn't want to look because he misses her. I don't think he's come here in years."

"Do you ever think about her, Tonn?" Col asked.

"I think about her in the Spring. That was when she was happiest, when the Winter months were gone and everything was new."

"Sometimes I can't sleep," Col said. "That's when I miss her the most. That's when I can almost remember her face. I can almost hear the lullabies she used to sing to me."

"I never got to see her. I never got to hear the lullabies," Mino said.

Col hated it when Mino talked about their mother. Women often died during childbirth but it wasn't supposed to happen to Col's mother. There wasn't even supposed to be a third child.

Besides, Mino had Brenna, his nurse. She was as much a mother to him as anyone could be. What did he care?

The king turned and Col thought he saw his father's eyes catch for a moment on his mother's grave. And for an instant Col saw that he was not just a father and a king, a tower of strength and discipline, but that he was also a man, a man who had given much and lost much.

Tephall stepped into the carriage and sat between his sons. The driver clucked his tongue and snapped the reins. The carriage lurched forward. The turning wheels made hardly a sound. To Col's surprise they didn't stay on the road to Ten Rocks. Instead, the carriage rolled slowly through the streets of Preet, the village below the castle.

Preet was a small town burrowed among the wilds. Ten Rocks perched in one of the more remote corners of Arnoc while most of the kingdom's larger villages and its few cities were closer to the sea. Neither Col nor his brothers had ever even seen the sea, though it had once been central to the kingdom's trade.

Col usually felt a surge of excitement when he visited the village, but that convivial spirit was lost behind the clouds today. He would have much rather been home beside a warm fire with something good to eat. He watched the storefronts and shuffling passersby as the carriage rolled further on. They passed through the square and around the statue of Col's grandfather. It was starting to crumble around the edges. A blackbird scratched at its shoulder.

The driver guided the carriage down a farm lane and into a small yard. A single horse was tied to the fence at the far end of the yard. It was a large, well-muscled horse that Col immediately recognized as Etau's.

"Tonn, I want you to come with me," the king said. "Col, stay with your brother."

"He's asleep. Can't I come, too?"

"This doesn't concern you."

"But it concerns Tonn?"

"We won't be long." The king shut the carriage door and walked to a squat, sturdy house. Its thatched roof was well kept and its walls showed no signs of stress. Col had never seen the place but his father was at ease walking through the door. Tonn followed and looked as confused as Col was.

Col leaned back and listened to the shuffle and shiver of the horses. The easy rhythm of the driver's snoring came a few minutes later.

Col reached for the door. He slipped the latch but sat back as another rider approached.

Caménor dismounted, tied off his horse and hurried inside. He let the door close behind him but failed to shut it. The door slipped open.

Col stepped carefully to the ground and crept up the path. He crouched beside the door and thought to eavesdrop but there were no voices coming from inside.

He peered inside to find an empty room. He pushed the door wide. The house was one large room and held only a rough hewn table. There were no other doors, no windows and most bewildering of all, no people.

CHAPTER 4

SECRETS IN THE SHADOWS

Col searched the empty room. He scoured for a crack of light, a hidden door, anything to let him know where everyone had gone.

A gust of wind pulled the door toward its frame. Col looked at the back of the door. Something was different about it. He reached out and felt a thin length of twine tied tightly to a hook. It stretched between the hinges to the corner of the room. Then it just disappeared. Col pushed the door all the way shut. Something scraped behind him. A thin light emerged from the floor and cleared the dark in the middle of the room. The corner of the table pivoted on a hinge in the floor to reveal a small hatch when the door was shut. A narrow ladder descended into the ground.

The fickle light of torches climbed the rungs along with familiar voices. Col leaned over the opening and listened as his father spoke from below.

"Tonn, I need you to tell Etau and your uncle what you told me you saw in the woods that night."

There was a pause before Tonn spoke. "Col was asleep and I was keeping watch — like you taught me, Etau — and I saw something in the trees. It was looking at me. I could see its eyes looking right at me."

"What was it?" Caménor said.

"I don't know."

"Owls have eyes like that," Etau said. "They sit in the trees at night and watch for prey."

"Do you think it could've been an owl, son?"

"I don't know. Maybe?" Tonn didn't sound sure of anything.

"Why are we here, Tephall?" Caménor said. "This could have been discussed anywhere."

"Something's not right. It's not just what Tonn saw. Nabal's ring was missing. Taken. My ring. A token of favor from the king."

"It could have been lost during the ride back to Ten Rocks," Etau said.

"It was missing when we found him," Tonn said. "Col noticed it right away."

"His tongue was torn out, too. The ring, the tongue, someone watching my sons as they guarded Nabal's body. I don't believe this was as simple as a mauling."

"His tongue?" Caménor didn't sound pleased that bit had been shared with the king. "You think *someone* did all this?"

"His tongue was taken," Etau said. "Perhaps *someone* was unhappy with his words."

"It's possible, but that's a vicious response for words. No, I fear something bigger is at work," the king said.

"It could be Greenkind," Etau offered

"The Greenkind haven't been seen in a hundred years. They're more superstition than threat these days," Tephall said. "Any other thoughts?"

"If there is something bigger happening, something yet unfinished, we'll find a weak link. No conspiracy is without its doubter," Etau said.

"Who do we begin with?" Caménor finally said. "There are still too many unanswered questions."

Col stared breathlessly down the opening. He had an idea where to start.

"Prince Caménor is right about one thing. We need to know more before we can take action," Etau said. He continued on but his voice quickly trailed off.

Col tipped forward, straining to hear, but the gathering had gone silent.

A hand shot up and grabbed him by the scruff of his shirt. Ladder rungs blurred past and suddenly he was on the floor of the small chamber.

"Colmeron!" The king loomed over him as Etau let go. "I told you to stay with your brother."

"I'm sorry, Father."

"Sorry Etau heard you breathing all the way down here, you mean?" Tonn said.

"Leave him be, Tonn," Caménor said. "Maybe he's got something to offer. What do you think, Col? You'll be the brother of the king someday. What insight might you have?"

Col stared at his uncle. He thought to speak to say what he knew but realized he knew nothing. Not enough, at least, to say anything.

"Silence is the wisest answer for you right now, son," the king said. "Etau, tomorrow I want you to take some of the men and return to where Nabal was found. The NéPrince will go with you. I want answers. Caménor and I will speak with my spies in Preet. Garren may know something of use."

"What about me?" Col said.

"You'll stay at Ten Rocks. This was never meant to be your affair. And if you disobey me again there won't be a sympathy on earth that will keep you from punishment."

"I understand," Col said with his eyes to the ground.

Caménor and Tonn disappeared up the ladder.

"I'd like to have a word with the young prince, my lord." Etau said.

"Of course. Maybe you can get a seed of sense to take root in him." King Tephall smiled at his Captain before leaving them.

Col stood straight. He pushed his shoulders back and chest out. "What is it, Etau?"

"You're much more observant than people realize, Col. You have a way of hearing things that aren't meant to be heard and finding things that weren't meant to be found. It's a very useful talent."

"I've often thought the same thing."

"I think you can help in the search for answers while still obeying your father. I'd like you to keep an eye out for anything suspicious at Ten Rocks. Look closer at anyone who may be hiding anything. Do you think you can do that?"

Col set his jaw while he pretended to ponder Etau's request. "I'll do it."

Etau gently set his hand around the back of Col's neck and grinned wide, "I knew I could count on you."

Col felt a swell of pride at the big man's approval. He knew what he needed to do and with his father and Caménor going back to Preet in the morning he knew he needed to act soon.

That night as the hearths were lit to keep the Autumn grey away, Col followed a winding hallway until he reached the heavy wooden door to Caménor's chambers. Col had spent many Winter nights laying on the thick rug listening to his uncle tell stories of what his father was like as a boy.

He found the door closed which was unusual. He knocked twice and waited. Feet shuffled inside the room. The latch clicked and a tired face greeted him.

"Col? What are you doing here?"

"I'm sorry, Uncle. I didn't realize you were sleeping."

"No, it's fine. Come in. It's been a long day. It's been a long few days, in fact." He ushered Col inside. Tapestries, stiff with the years, draped over the room's block walls. Caménor's simple bed sat in the far corner, its covers twisted upon it. He stoked the fire and brought it to life with a new log.

The room brightened and Col's shoulders eased with the light.

Caménor leaned back in a plump old chair. "I'm not sure I've got any stories for you tonight, Col. Though I feel I could use one myself."

"Is something weighing on your mind, Uncle?"

"Oh, nothing you need to concern yourself with."

Col took his customary seat on the rug and looked at the haggard man. "I've been wondering about something."

"Hmm?"

"The other night, at Tonn's party, why were you so angry with Nabal?"

"Oh, that. I was hoping nobody would remember my little outburst. I guess it's not the first time I've let my anger get the better of me."

"Prince Caménor and his temper are well known."

"Thank you for that, nephew."

"Father always says I was born to keep him humble. I don't see why I can't do the same for you. Now, why were you so upset with Nabal?"

"Nabal was a wonderful storyteller. Unfortunately, he had a habit of changing the story to suit the listener's ear. Which isn't always a bad thing. Being able to adapt was one of his strengths. Some stories, however, shouldn't be changed, because when you change them they lose their meaning. Especially if a story is true."

"You mean Derid's story?"

"It's the basis of our lineage. It's our history. It's sad you don't know it. Too few do these days. But it didn't happen the way Nabal told it."

"How did it happen?"

"Nabal was faithful to the story up until the fight with the bear. Derid fought the bear and won the battle because of the strength he had gained from eating the leaves and drinking from the spring, but the bear didn't beg for mercy. Derid killed it with his hand wrapped around its heart. He rolled the beast from himself and crawled to the spring to wash off the blood. As he reached for the water he saw something that stopped him. A man stood at the water's edge. His face showed the lines of time, while his eyes seemed to know time not.

"He looked down at Derid 'Thank you for taking care of my garden,' he said.

'Your garden? I've never seen you here before.'

'I see you, though. I come here every night to see how the garden is faring, to see how you are faring.'

'Why have you never shown yourself before?'

'I waited until you were ready. I brought you here, you know. I needed to find someone who would care for these trees, someone who would fight for them.'

'I've spent years away from my family! You took me from my home!'

'Sacrifice is never easy and greatness never comes without a cost, but you will be rewarded. This land is now yours. You will be a king. The land is yours to command. Tell a rock to move and it will do so. Speak life to a tree and it will grow.'

"Derid leaned back in astonishment and the ground rose to meet him. The man was gone. Derid looked at the still form of his fallen foe and the earth opened beneath it. The bear disappeared and the ground knitted itself back together leaving only the blood stained grass as evidence of the battle.

"The next day, Derid awoke to strangers in his garden. Strangers but not enemies. They huddled together, afraid they had been caught trespassing. He greeted them and welcomed them to his kingdom. But it wasn't long before he realized they weren't strangers at all. These were his children along with their families. They'd grown in the years he had been away.

"'Where is my wife?' Derid asked after he revealed himself.

"'Our mother passed three nights ago,' said the oldest. 'We were walking from the burial yard when we became lost in a fog.'

"Derid grieved for his love and named his kingdom Arnoc in her honor. That day King Derid raised a house of stone and branch for his family. It would be the beginning of the great city of Entaramu, the city of the Earthkings. Derid was the first of the Earthkings."

Col sat engrossed by his uncle's telling, nearly forgetting why he'd come to Caménor in the first place. "Who was the man Derid met?"

"He is the one we know as Orum. His was the unseen hand that shaped the earth. Nabal's change may seem trivial but it robbed the story of its true meaning and Orum of his due."

"And that's why you were so angry? What could you do about it?"

"I don't know. Nabal was dead before I could decide what to do. I suppose I should have talked to your father in private rather than lash out."

This wasn't the confession Col had hoped for.

"Do you want to know what I really think about Derid's story?"

Col sighed. "Sure." He was getting nowhere.

"I don't think it was a bear that Derid fought. I think it was something far worse."

"What was it then?"

"I think it was one of the Kheva Adem."

"Kheva Adem?"

"Yes. The Kheva Adem were the enemies of the Earthkings for thousands of years."

"What were they?"

"They were monsters, terrible hulking beasts that stood nearly twice the height of a man. Horns twist from the rear of their head and down their back." Caménor's hands moved in enthusiastic description as he spoke. "It's easy to see how one of the Kheva Adem could have become a bear as the story was told over time."

"Oh." Col had wanted some proof of his uncle's treachery. Instead, all he'd gotten was a deranged family history and a monster from a bedtime story.

"I hope you take an interest in our heritage, Col. I'm sorry to say that over the generations it's been relegated to superstition. The Earthkings, Kheva Adem and the Noflim, Orum - they're all seen as stories now."

"Noflim?"

"Oh, yes. There's a lot more to tell. For now, though, my bed is calling me."

Col stood and felt the blood rush to his feet. He'd find the answers he needed one way or another. "Good night, Uncle Cam."

"Good night, Col. Rest well. I hope for all our sakes this bad dream comes to an end soon."

Returning to the forest put a pumpkin sized knot in Tonn's stomach. It had been days but the tension still gripped him. He was glad to have Etau with him, though. If there was anyone he felt safe with, it was the Captain of his father's guard. The man was a living statue.

So why did he still feel so anxious?

Tonn's legs stretched on either side of the saddle. He didn't want to walk here. He'd spent too much time circling their camp that night. The fire pit still held the ashes. Though the coals had been sifted, most likely by a passing fox, Etau and his men searched the brush. The tips of their spears shuffled the leaves to find what little remained of the blood trail.

Tonn's mount clapped the ground with her hoof. He patted her flank, trying to soothe her, and looked into the dim grey above.

Etau approached. "It was a brave thing you did that night, keeping watch over your brother and a fallen friend. I don't know many men who would do such a thing."

Tonn fought to steady both hand and voice before speaking. "Thank you, Etau. I didn't see that I had a choice."

"It won't soon be forgotten, I assure you."

Tonn scoured the trees for any clue that might avail itself. At least that's what he wanted Etau to think. He didn't want to be here where half naked trees stood in silent watch. He tried to tell himself his mind was playing tricks in the shadows, but it wasn't working. He'd seen something in the branches that day. And it wasn't an owl.

He fought the urge to look behind him. If he was going to lead these men someday he needed to show that fear had no hold on him.

A crow flew overhead. Its shrill caw fell through twisting branches. Tonn's hand moved to his sword. His horse came to a stop at an old road that disappeared in the horizon. He listened for any sound of his companions.

He moved silently onto the road. The trees on either side reached overhead to clasp one another. Still waiting for the riders he began to catch a faint, rhythmic hiss. He pulled back on the reins and listened.

"Hheeeessss..." It was louder this time, followed by a quick snort.

Tonn pulled his sword hard from the scabbard, nearly breaking his belt. The methodic rush of air didn't stop this time. It grew louder, closer, until it was right behind him. He wanted to turn around, wanted to see that there was nothing there, but he couldn't move. His sword was a useless weight in his hand.

A rush of hot air swam down his neck. The sword fell from limp fingers. Something brushed against the side of his neck, something rough, cold. And then the shadow beside him spoke, "Twice you've crossed my path and twice you'll live. Will you try for a third?" The shadow lingered before retreating.

"NéPrince Tonn!" Etau's voice boomed from the path ahead of him.

Tonn focused and he saw his protector riding toward him. He jumped down and grabbed his sword from the short grass.

"Is everything alright, my prince? I turned around and you were gone."

"I thought I saw something. Did you see… anything?"

"I saw only you falling asleep in the saddle and your sword falling to the ground."

Asleep? Tonn hated for Etau to think of him as anything less than his someday king.

"It's been a hard day."

"Have we found anything yet?"

"No, our search has yet to turn up anything useful."

"Tell the men we're finished here. This place holds nothing but curses."

"Yes, my prince." Etau pulled hard on the reins and turned for home. Tonn followed, willing every muscle to be still and allow calm to return to his face.

The option of leaving had been taken from Col, giving him only one way to feel free.

He grabbed a heavy cloak and passed through the archway to the spiral stairs of the Western tower. He rounded the first turn and nearly collided with the elder prince. Tonn haplessly put one foot in front of the other. Col stayed back and watched Tonn move up the stairs in short bursts. He put his shoulder under Tonn's arm. Together they reached the top. Col shoved the hatch open and Tonn stumbled out ahead of him. The night air blew cold atop the tower and the aged structure rocked in the wind. Two marble benches sat in front of the parapet circling the tower's peak. Col stretched himself out on one and pulled the thick cloak tight around him.

Tonn stood against the wall with his face to the forest far below. "I know you're there!"

"Of course you know I'm here. I helped you up the stairs. I think you were in the saddle a little too long today."

"I wasn't talking to you."

"Ah, a private conversation. Should I leave?"

Tonn's face looked suddenly very serious. "No, please don't. I don't want to be alone."

"Is everything alright, Tonn?"

"Nothing you need to worry about."

Col was beginning to tire of people telling him that.

Tonn turned back to the west and spoke, lower this time, the wind weighing his words down. "I know you're there, stalking through the trees. Waiting for me to come back. Waiting for that third chance, but you'll wait forever. I've got a whole kingdom at my feet. I don't need these woods. Just know this, when I take the throne I'm going to have it all burned!" He threw his hands into the air. "I won't leave a single tree for you to hide behind." His voice grew louder. "Then, if the flames haven't claimed you my hunters will find you and give you the fate you think to give me."

"I don't know who you're talking to but I'm sure they're trembling," Col said.

"You wouldn't understand."

"I think you need to go to bed."

"These woods are old, little brother, You don't know what's out there."

"Sure I do. There are bears and foxes and birds and little rabbits and every now and then a prince or two. How did the search with Etau go? Did you find anything?"

"No," Tonn said, the bluster gone from his face. "but something found me."

"What do you mean?"

"I saw something in the trees that day and, today, when I was alone, it found me. It spoke to me."

"What did it say?"

"It doesn't matter." Tonn pulled the hatch open and looked down the stairs. "Those woods aren't safe, but I don't want you to worry about it. I'm going to take care of it." He stumbled down the step and threw empty threats at the ever winding stairs.

Col looked out over the forest. He didn't know what was out there but he was less concerned with it than with what might be beneath his own roof. He would find what he needed soon enough. He just had to keep a sharp eye and a ready ear.

Col lay back on his bench and stared up at the stars. Their distance didn't seem to matter on such a cold, clear night. He put one hand behind his head and, with his finger outstretched, he traced the stars with the other. He was trying to spell his name when the last three stars he'd connected vanished. Only the inky void remained. The darkness moved and caught a glint of moonlight. A small man stood over him.

"Don't stop your searching, dear prince." Nabal's pale face looked down at him. Stitches still held his wounds shut.

"If only we'd known…" He brought a cold hand to Col's cheek. "But there was nothing you could have done to save me and I fear you won't stop what is yet to come."

Col tried to turn away from the stiff fingers.

"Oh, yes. There's more. I saw it all too late. But you, young prince, you still have a chance to help." Nabal pulled his hand from Col's cheek and showed him the naked finger.

"Go to his room. Find the ring." Something moved behind Nabal. It crawled along the wall and perched atop it.

"There is little time left. Go now!" Nabal said. He stepped back and disappeared into the night.

Col stared at the wall. There was still something there.

A hand on Col's shoulder shook him awake. Wembus stood over him.

"Come now, Prince Colmeron, let's get you to bed. It's too cold for you to be falling asleep up here."

Col sat up. The stars were all back in their place.

"Wembus, have my father and uncle returned from Preet yet?"

"Not until tomorrow. Is everything alright?"

"Everything's fine. I'm just cold. I'll see myself to bed."

"Very well."

Minutes later Col quietly entered Caménor's room. He looked through the wardrobe and scoured the pockets of every shirt and pair of pants but found nothing. Beside the bed was a small table with a single drawer. He slid it open and cleared away a sheaf of wrinkled paper to reveal a small wooden box. He tipped the lid and pulled out a velvet pouch. He pulled open the pouch's mouth and shook the bag over his hand. A silver ring dropped into his palm, its band swathed in blood.

CHAPTER 5

A FRAGILE PEACE

Col didn't spend the night thinking what he would tell his father. That would be easy. Instead, he wondered what his mother would think. Would she be proud of him? Or would she have kept him from all this? She'd been the one to chase his nightmares from the room. But she was gone now, and it was Col's turn to drive the monsters away. In his hand was all he needed to bring peace. He laid down again and tried to sleep.

He woke early with the ring clenched in his hand. He set it on his desk while he dressed then put it back in its pouch and secured that to his belt. Now all he had to do was wait for his father.

He stood at the window above the courtyard. He watched the gaggle of traders coming and going. They were lost in their own world of haggle and sale, unaware of the intrigue so close at hand. Col envied their ignorance.

The crowd cleared the gate and six soldiers entered the courtyard. The points of their spears jabbed the air. The king and Caménor came close after. Caménor's fingers combed through his short beard.

Col went to the throne room to wait for them. A moment later his father entered the intimate space with Caménor still at his side. Wembus trailed behind them and took their cloaks.

Col took a deep breath. "Good morning, Father."

"Ah, Colmeron. You're awake early. I trust you kept to the castle while I was gone."

Col reached for the pouch on his belt and opened his mouth to speak.

"Wembus," the king continued. "Did my son obey me for once?"

"Yes, your majesty. He even helped the NéPrince Tonn."

"Well, perhaps things are beginning to look up."

"How was my lord's meeting in the village?"

"Fruitless, I'm afraid."

"Father, there's something I need to show you," Col tried to interrupt.

"Caménor, send word to Garren that his spies are to focus on the Greenkind border. If they're still there I want to know."

"I'll see that it's done," Caménor said.

"Father!"

"What is it, Col?"

"There's something I need to show you."

"Well? Go on, show me." King Tephall tugged his robes forward and sat down.

"Hold out your hand."

The king extended his hand. Col pulled the ring from its pouch and placed it in his father's hand.

King Tephall's face hardened. "Where did you get this?"

"I found it."

"Where?" The king's voice rose.

"I found it in Caménor's room."

Caménor stood silent, arms at his side, eyes staring coldly ahead.

"Is this true, brother?" the king said.

"No."

"My son says otherwise. What reason would he have to lie?"

"I don't know."

"Who am I to believe, my son or my brother?"

"I ask you to believe the truth, Tephall."

"The truth? Nabal's blood still stains his ring. That is the truth!" He flung the ring at his brother. Caménor flinched as it flicked against his chest.

"Answer me plainly. Did you kill Nabal?"

"No."

"Guards!" the king called. Etau answered the call with three men in tow. "Lock my brother in one of the empty quarters. I want sentries outside the door at all times."

The guards seized Caménor. He strained against them and roared in protest. "Let me go! Get your hands off of me, you fools!"

"Etau," the king said. "I want you to search his rooms."

"Listen to me, brother," Caménor said. "I didn't kill him. You know me, Tephall."

The king looked at Etau. "Take him away."

"Let me go! It's only going to get worse! There's more to this!" Flecks of spit caught in his beard as they pulled him from the room.

Col sighed when they were finally gone. Wembus picked the ring from the floor and gave it back to the king who rested his head in his hand.

"I'm sorry," Col said.

"You have nothing to apologize for, my son. You've done a good thing today."

Col's fingers drummed hastily while he waited for his lunch. The air was vibrant with the news of Caménor's arrest and Col beamed with the attention it brought him. He had done his part and done it well. Now it was up to Etau and his men to shake loose any conspirators. And to find out why the murder had taken place at all.

Wembus set a steaming bowl of stew in front of Col. Two more were placed beside him.

"Where's the bread?" Col said.

"Martle's just pulling it out of the oven now. He said no hero would be eating stale bread while his hands could still knead dough."

Col smiled and breathed in the heavy aroma of tender beef, soft potatoes, mushrooms and beans. A moment later Wembus returned with a basket of warm bread. Tonn and Mino followed him in, drawn by the wafting steam from the fresh loaves. They sat down at the other bowls. Mino wasted no time tearing his bread apart and dipping it in the stew.

Wembus sat across from Col and took a roll. "You've caused quite a sensation today."

"I did what needed to be done," Col said.

"How did you know to look in your uncle's room?"

"I have a way of finding things that aren't meant to be found." Col took another bite.

"Indeed he does." Etau said, entering the room. He gave Col a slap on the back and sat next to Wembus. "Our prince sees past the lies that shroud men's hearts and to the truth that has saved us all."

"What did he do?" Mino said with a cheekful of bread.

"Haven't you heard, young one? Your brother searched out the fiend among us. A murderer has been caught today and we will all rest a little easier tonight."

"A murderer? Who was it?"

"It was Uncle Caménor," Tonn said. "Col exposed him to father. You really don't pay much attention to anything do you?"

"Uncle Cam never hurt anyone. Why did you do that, Col?" Mino said.

"I did it because it was the truth, Mino. You should be thanking me, not questioning me."

"But he's our uncle."

"Even family can't always be trusted, young prince," Etau said.

"Do you really think so, brother?" Wembus said.

"Envy can be a powerful enemy, Wembus. Nabal was closest to the king and had the ring to prove it. That was something Caménor never had. I'd say it was a bitter root that put murder in his heart. I'd wager there wasn't even a bear anywhere near Nabal."

"You think the prince did that on his own?" Wembus said.

"A murderous heart can make a man do many things. Awful things."

"What if he didn't act alone?" Tonn said.

"Something tells me we've cut the serpent off at the head," Etau replied.

"You are going to keep looking, though, right? What if something else is still out there?"

"Still seeing shadows, NéPrince?"

"Of course not." Tonn fidgeted in his seat. "Like you said, the killer was caught."

"Glad to hear it. Now, if my lords will excuse me I must be about the king's business," Etau said. He gave Col a knowing wink and left them.

Wembus remained at the table and watched Tonn, whose spoon continued to stir his untested stew. "The princes must be thirsty. I'll get you something to drink."

Once he'd left, Tonn let his spoon sit in the bowl and put his bread back in the basket.

"Why aren't you eating?" Col said.

"I'm not hungry."

"Why not?"

"Do you really think Caménor did that to Nabal? You saw the body. Could he have done that?"

"Everyone knows he's got a temper. Have you ever seen him in a rage? Besides, I found the ring, Tonn. What more do you need?"

"Something better than that." Tonn pushed himself from the table and left.

"What's wrong with him?" Col said.

Mino looked up with a mouthful of potato and shrugged.

Tonn walked past the royal stables and down the barren, sloping field separating the castle from the western woods. A bow was slung over his shoulder and a quiver on his back. The torch in his hand kept the nip from his face but the rest of him had gone numb. In the two days since Caménor's arrest Tonn had become certain of the path before him. While Col was hailed as a hero, Tonn knew a greater threat still lurked.

He looked back to make sure he wasn't being followed. He heard only the distant stomp from the stable.

He held his light up in the deepening dusk and pulled the small sack of tinder and kindling he'd hid in the quiver. He stood between the mammoth oaks that served as a gateway to the woods. They'd withstood the burdens of time and seen generations of men rise and fall like the sun. And tonight they would witness another season pass.

The wind rushed past as he picked a spot among the leaves and rotting wood and prepared the kindling. He kicked the brush closer and set the torch to his low monument of defiance. The tinder caught and he gently blew on the burgeoning flare. The kindling quickly took and Tonn stood triumphantly. He had only to let the flames be free. Once the forest was gone he would finally be safe again.

As he stepped away the wind huffed and scattered the burning twigs among the evening frost. He frantically tried to gather them back, but it was too late. His work gave a final burst of red before black stole it away.

Standing at the edge of the wood with darkness falling and his fire gone a sense of dread crept over him. He threw the dead torch into the trees and ran from the great oaks. Once he'd achieved the safety of the open field he turned back to the woods and offered a final sneer of contempt.

—~~—

Though he never revered his father as the people did, there was something about seeing the king on the throne that made Col nervous. For the first time, though, Col felt he had earned the right to be here. And he relished the feeling.

"Your uncle would like to speak with you," the king said.

"I don't have anything to say to a murderer."

"Don't be so hasty in your judgement, son."

"Are you saying he didn't kill Nabal?"

"No, but a man accused of such a crime should be able to face his accuser."

"We have proof of his guilt, Father. Doesn't that speak for itself?"

"It doesn't tell everything."

"Have you spoken to him?"

"Yes. And now you should, too."

"I don't want to."

"I'm not asking you, Colmeron."

Col felt the stab at his pride and took a moment before responding, "Fine. I'll speak to him."

He ventured to the small room in the bowels of Ten Rocks where Caménor was being held. He didn't like this part of the castle. It always scared him as a child. He was never at ease when he was below ground. The ceiling seemed to creep lower and lower and the walls were always wet.

Two guards waited outside the door, but paid no attention to the shouts coming from behind it.

"I'd like to speak to him," Col said.

"Are you sure, your highness?" one of the guards said. "He attacks us when we open the door."

"He threw a chair at my head," said the other.

Caménor's shouts echoed through the door. "...truth were bread you all would have starved to death by now!" Wood splintered as something cracked against the wall.

"He's broken another one," said the first guard.

"Caménor," Col said through the door.

The shouting stopped. "Col?"

"Open the door," Col said to the guards. The heavy iron key clanked in the lock and the door swung open.

"Come in," Caménor said.

A small fire wavered in the shallow hearth while a solitary window looked out on the feet of any who passed. Around the room were strewn remnants of a few chairs, a desk and what looked to have been dusty old curtains, their bottoms charred and tattered. Caménor sat in the corner with firelight washing over half of his face. His hair stretched wildly from his head and his beard looked like it had been pulled at for days. He stared at Col with dark eyes.

"What do you need, Uncle?"

"I need to ask you a question."

"Go on."

"Why me?"

"What do you mean?"

"What made you suspect me?"

Col hesitated.

"Don't you think I deserve an answer?"

"Why didn't you join the search for Nabal the day after the hunt?"

"You think I killed Nabal because I wasn't able to join the search?"

"Why wouldn't you have been able?"

"Nabal wasn't the only one injured on the hunt, Col. Something spooked my horse. I was able to regain control but I bruised a few ribs in the process."

"I also heard you talking in the garden the following day. You were so callous about Nabal."

"It's true. I never cared for the man but I wouldn't have killed him."

"You tried to hide the truth from my father about the tongue."

"I did. It's true. Do you know why?"

"No. It doesn't really matter."

"Yes, it does. We all serve something, Col. Men and women serve their passions, their hungers. Arnoc serves the king and the king serves Arnoc. Do you know what the Kheva Adem serve?"

"No, and I don't care."

"They serve the Noflim, three spirits; ancient and malicious who in turn serve their master. The Noflim can inhabit a person, but the tongues of men are powerful, too powerful for even a Noflim to control. The Kheva Adem tear out a person's tongue before a Noflim takes their body. Otherwise it might betray them."

"You think Nabal was a host for the Noflim?"

"No. Something prevented them."

"Why didn't you want my father to know?"

"I wanted to protect him from it until I knew for certain what was happening."

"Protect him? Don't be absurd!" Col was growing tired of his uncle's stories. "I've done as my father asked. I'm leaving now."

"How much power would the Noflim gain if they took hold of the king's advisor? We have an enemy that nobody believes in. Who would stop them?"

"Goodnight, Caménor."

"Wait!"

"What more do you want, Uncle?"

"What if I'm right?"

Col ignored the question and left his uncle alone once more.

After wandering through the castle for nearly an hour Tonn finally found the solitude he sought in the garden. There was no peace to be found within the walls of his own home. Even now, when the world slept, everything was in motion and he just wanted it all to stop. He'd been outshone by a worm and it gnawed at him like a scavenging beast. He leaned against the low wall and looked over the frigid lake. The dips and leaps of the water soothed him.

Soot still smeared his hands. He wiped them on his pants but the black remained. It was a reminder of his failure.

"Tonn!"

He jumped at the sound of his name. He looked around but there was no one else in the garden.

"Tonn!" The voice came from below.

"Who's there?"

At the water's edge a flicker of light caught on the rocks.

"Help me, Tonn!" It sounded like Etau.

"Stay there. I'm coming!" Tonn ran from the garden. He was mindless of his own commotion as he barreled through the halls. He reached the oversized doors guarding the courtyard. He lunged through a smaller door that nestled in the larger one. The air in the courtyard was still and cold. An empty fountain stood in the middle. Beyond that was the main gate. It was drawn shut for the night. He pulled at the iron crossbars to no avail.

"Open the gate!" he shouted.

Light flashed from the wall to his left where an elaborately carved wood panel was secured to the stone. It showed a four armed creature, covered with eyes, lurking behind a man between two trees. The eyes began to glow. Tonn had seen this image a thousand times but he saw something now that he'd never noticed before. A small gap had been opened between the panel and the wall.

"Hurry." Etau's voice echoed from inside the wall. Painfully, Tonn squeezed through the narrow rift and entered a small tunnel.

"I'm coming!" The lake's cold air wrapped itself around him like an embrace from lifeless arms. "Where are you?"

The pulsing of blood in his ears mixed with the lapping of the water. The light ahead grew bright and he ran toward it. The tunnel emptied beneath the moon and onto the silver ripples of the lake. A torch sputtered on the frozen edge.

"Etau?"

Hot air rushed over his head.

"Did you think we wouldn't see you?" It wasn't Etau. A hand wrapped around the back of Tonn's neck. Four long fingers closed over his throat and two laid over his cheek. Their tips dug into his skin and drew ruby drops. "Burn Arnoc to ashes and still we would remain. As we always have."

Tonn tried to pull away but the hand tightened.

"You were warned."

Tonn squeezed his eyes shut. A tear slid down his cheek onto the finger there.

"Poor, frightened little prince. We were always going to kill you." The fingers around Tonn's throat squeezed. "Are you ready to die?"

Tonn had always hoped that when his time came it would be after a long reign, when courage was a dream realized and death was a friend offering a kind hand out of a tired body.

Are you ready? The words lingered in his ears. He wasn't ready.

"No," he said. The word shattered the hard silence and surprised his foe. Its grip loosened and Tonn leapt into the freezing waters. He kicked wildly but the cold opposed him. There were no shouts or roars at his defiance, only a brilliant flash of color as he was driven under by a tremendous weight.

If he could only reach the surface and breathe he could fight. Tonn would emerge from the waters reborn, ready to become the man he'd always thought to be. He shoved against his attacker but was only pushed deeper into the frigid mud and sharp stone of the lake's bottom. He struggled to get his feet under him but the cold stole the strength from his limbs. He felt the weight upon him grow heavier. Then he felt no more.

CHAPTER 6

THE END OF WHAT WAS

—∞—

COL DIDN'T STRUGGLE AGAINST THE dip and turn of the tide that writhed endlessly around him. Even as he dreamed his body sank below the roiling surface he gave no protest. The light above disappeared until the cold and the dark surrounding him were all that remained. He drifted further and further down until he landed on the sea floor. His limbs dangled upward.

What would become of him? He couldn't stay here among rock and fish. He needed to feel the sun again.

The ground under him shook. Water rushed past as the stone beneath him hurled him toward the surface. The murky shape of a boat passed above. Towering stone walls filled the water around him. His chest pounded with the force. He screamed against the pain and pockets of air streamed from his mouth. The walls broke the surface with a terrific burst of froth and foam. He reached for the light.

A hand shook him from the dream. He was covered with sweat. The candle on the stand beside his bed had melted to its base.

"NéPrince Colmeron," Wembus said.

Col rolled over and rubbed his eyes. "What is it?"

"Your father needs to see you."

"Can't it wait until morning?"

"I'm sorry."

"Wait, what did you call me?" Col sat up. Wembus had called him NéPrince. "Where is my brother?"

"Your father is waiting for you in his rooms."

Col ran from the room with Wembus in tow. His father waited in the antechamber to his rooms. He gripped the back of his chair and used it to steady himself. A new fire had been lit. Wembus closed the door and stood silently behind Col.

"Your brother is dead," the king said.

Col struggled to speak but his lips were numb, cheeks flushed. His head felt suddenly light, as though it might roll right from his shoulders. Words were lost in the chaotic collision of sound and feeling and disbelief. He rubbed his hands across his face in an effort to clear the panic from his mind.

"He was found in the lake an hour ago," the king continued.

"How?"

"Drowned."

"Do you really think so?"

The king's grip on the chair tightened. "No."

"What about Mino?" Col said.

"Wembus, does my son still sleep?"

"Yes, your majesty. The prince is still safe in bed."

"Was it Caménor?" The name hardly escaped Col's lips when it was lost in the creak of an opening door.

"Caménor," the king ran to his brother. The two embraced. Caménor's tears stained the king's shoulder. They separated and the king cupped Col's face between two deep lined hands. "I have to send you away. You are the NéPrince now, our kingdom's next hope. It's not safe here anymore."

"No, you can't. Father, please."

"It's alright. You'll be in hiding. Caménor will watch over you."

"No!" Col jerked away from his father's hands.

"He'll protect you."

"Are you blind? How will I be safe with Tonn's killer?"

"Caménor's hands are clean. He couldn't have done it. I was with him tonight."

"He killed Nabal."

"I have been convinced of few things in my life, Colmeron. I knew I loved your mother and wanted always to be with her. I knew that my sons were a greater gift than I deserved and I know that my brother is not a murderer."

"I found the ring in his room, father. He took it when he killed your friend. He was jealous because he never had that token."

"He never needed one, Col. Blood is a far stronger token than any ring could ever be. I trust him. I always have. I never should have doubted him."

"You are blinded by grief, father. Simply because he was with you when Tonn-," he choked on the words. "That doesn't mean he's not guilty. He could have allies!"

"You're afraid, Col. It's alright."

"I'm not leaving you," Col threw his arms around his father and refused to let go.

"I can't protect you here, my son," Tephall said in a broken whisper.

"If I'm not safe here, where will I be?"

"You'll be safe with Caménor."

Col couldn't bear to look at his father.

"I'm sorry, Col," Caménor said. "We have to leave now."

Col refused to even acknowledge his uncle. "I want to see my brother."

"There isn't any time, Caménor said. " We need to be as far away as possible before anyone knows we're gone."

"I said I want to see him."

Caménor's tense gaze softened at Col's insistence. "Alright. I'll be waiting."

Col followed Wembus past rooms where men still slept in peace. He shivered as he walked by windows whose cracks let slip a chill like a spy behind enemy lines.

They reached the Healer's lab. They walked into the room where Tonn's body lay. A counter filled with various jars and stacks of books ran along three of the room's four walls. Tonn's body was on a large table in the middle of the room. He was naked from the waist up. His skin was pale and sallow. The Healer washed the body.

"The NéPrince wishes to see his brother," Wembus said.

"Of course, of course," the Healer said softly. "Forgive an old man his manners, your majesty. I'll leave you alone." He bowed as he backed out of the room.

A salve filled the cuts on Tonn's face and neck. Its pungent scent filled the room. Col touched Tonn's shoulder. The cold flesh felt so foreign. He let his hand rest there a moment. It was something he'd never done before. Tonn would have shrugged it off or pushed him away.

Now, all was still.

"You're not supposed to die, Tonn," he said. "You're my big brother. You're supposed to be here to look out for me. You're supposed to protect me. Like you did that night in the forest. I don't know how to be the big brother. I don't know how to be the NéPrince. That's supposed to be you, not me. What do I do?"

He looked at the unmoving face. It was familiar but vacant. The fine curve of Tonn's jaw shone clearly in the light. It was here that Col saw something he hadn't seen in many years and had, in fact, never thought to see again.

It was his mother.

He'd never noticed that so much of her remained in his brother's face. She'd been hidden behind scowls and uncertain grimaces. She was seen only in solitary moments. Tonn had held her more tightly than Col had ever realized and, here, in his final expression he let Col see her once more.

Col blinked over hot tears and kissed his brother's forehead. "Goodbye, Tonn."

He tried to hide his wet face from Wembus.

"It's alright," Wembus said. "I don't know what I would do if I lost my brother."

"It's never going to be the same, is it?" Col's mind was tearing itself apart in an effort to make some sense of what was happening.

"I'm afraid not."

"Why is this happening?"

"I don't know."

Col tried to dam the swell of tears with his sleeve.

"We have to go. Your uncle is waiting."

Col took a last look at Tonn before closing his eyes. He turned toward the door. "Let's go."

Caménor waited in the stables with two horses saddled and roughly provisioned. He motioned for silence. The stable boy still slept soundly in one of the stalls.

"Put these on," he whispered. He handed Col a bundle of old clothing.

Col stripped off his bed clothes and stepped into the rough pants. The shirt he pulled on was too big for him and the heavy leather vest hung low off his shoulders. He wrapped himself in the thick wool cloak and felt like a child playing in his father's clothes. At least he would be warm.

"I need a sword," Col said.

"I've got mine," Caménor said.

"At least give me a knife."

"Here," he handed Col a short curved blade.

Col took it without thanks and slid it under his belt.

Once dressed, he and Caménor joined his father outside. Two dusty mares shook themselves awake in the cold night air. The moon was only a shadow behind a veil of clouds.

"I look like a beggar in these," Col said.

"That's the point," Caménor said.

"The world will see what they will, but you will always be my son. Whether you are wearing a crown or are covered in mud," the Tephall said.

"How long will we be gone?"

"I'll send word once it's safe here."

"What about Mino?"

"I'm sending him elsewhere."

"It's time," Caménor said.

The king pulled Col to him and held him tight. "Know that I love you, Colmeron. Trust your uncle. He'll protect you. I'll see you soon."

Col pulled away and saw tears in his father's eyes for the first time that night.

"Goodbye, Tephall," Caménor said. "I'll keep him safe. I swear it."

The king stepped back and waited for them to depart.

"That one's yours," Caménor pointed to the uglier of the two horses. "Her name is Salee."

Col climbed into the saddle. Salee didn't take kindly to such an early rider.

"She'll wake more once we get going," Caménor said.

Col had never imagined what it would be like to leave his family or to abandon his home. He looked at his uncle and did little to fight the anger that rose inside of him. He felt the handle of the dagger at his belt.

Caménor clucked his tongue and his horse bounded forward. Col flicked the reins and Salee followed. They fled west to the woods and the memory of a night not long ago. Col feared he was only being tossed from one fire to another.

Heavy white flakes fell from a shrouded sky. The first snow. It caressed his face like a mother's hand, wiping his tears away. How long had it been since she'd been there to do that for him? He needed that reassurance more than ever. The ache of it all burrowed deep into his bones.

They passed between the great oaks and rode swiftly over the well worn path. The mares were old but knew the land well. They had no trouble moving over rock and root as snow drifted between the branches. The familiar quickly became strange.

Rounding a bend, they stopped suddenly. A solitary figure interrupted their path. He walked toward them.

"Our brother has fallen this night. Let us mourn together, my princes."

It was Etau. His sword was in his hand and shallow tufts of white lay on his shoulders. He'd been waiting.

"We mourn already, Etau, and our grief takes us away from here. Please, do not delay us any longer," Caménor said.

"Your king requests the company of his family. Come, let's return and honor both him and the fallen prince."

"We honor both the king and his son by continuing forward. Remove yourself."

"No." Etau spoke but his mouth remained still. "My duty, as ever, is to protect the NéPrince."

Caménor leveled his sword at Etau. "Who are you?"

"Is this a time for riddles, prince? I am Etau, Captain of the King's Guard, and I will not allow you to keep me from my duty."

"You are not our friend. You are a shadow filling corners of skin."

"You accuse me of such dark treachery, Caménor, when it was you who kept the ring after killing Nabal? Step aside and give us the NéPrince."

"Us? You betray yourself, Noflim."

Noflim? Now Col was sure he had been sent away with a madman.

Etau swiveled his gaze to Col. "Come here, Colmeron. He won't hurt you like he did your brother, I promise."

Col made to nudge Salee toward Etau.

"Col! Don't," Caménor cast a quick, pleading glance at him. His eyes were back on Etau almost instantly.

"It's alright, little prince," Etau beckoned. "I'll take you back to your father, back home."

Col hesitated.

"He killed your brother. You know he did," Etau's neck seemed to crane toward Col.

"Speak no more, spirit!" Caménor spurred his horse and slashed at Etau, but the warrior leaned away from the attack. He grabbed Caménor by the shirt and ripped him from the saddle.

Col had never seen him move so fast.

Etau wrenched the sword from Caménor's hand. He pinned him to the ground. He leaned in close. Neither man spoke but Col heard a voice. "Nabal fought, too. So we killed him. That left only you in our way. But one man has never been enough to stop us. We are Noflim, and we are your end."

Col moved to snap the reins to escape both Etau and Caménor. Before he could, a figure leapt from the shadows and tackled Etau to the ground.

It was Wembus. "Go!" he cried.

Col didn't move. He watched Wembus wrestle with Etau. Etau quickly overpowered him.

"I think you need to go back to cleaning your floors, little brother," Etau rolled to his feet.

"Do you think I don't know my own brother?" Wembus lunged at him, catching him in the chest with his broad shoulder. "Etau would never doubt family. Never!"

Caménor scrambled back onto his horse. "Quickly, Col!"

Col snapped the reins. Salee reared and bolted. He crouched in the saddle and squinted his eyes against the wind as the falling snow spotted his face. Steam spouted from Salee's nostrils. Her aged flanks billowed to the rhythm of her hooves. Caménor charged ahead of him.

The snow began to lay over the dark forest floor and the branches above grew sleeves of white as they fled. Their path soon broke onto an old road. Caménor pulled hard on his reins and spun his horse around. His eyes searched between the vacant branches.

"What happened back there?" Col demanded. "Why would Wembus attack Etau?"

"That wasn't Etau."

"Of course it was!"

"Not anymore. He's been taken by the Noflim.

"Taken?"

"There's no telling how long he's been their puppet, but that was not Etau. If you'd gone with him, he would have killed you, or worse, you'd have been taken as well."

"I don't believe you. Etau would never hurt me. How do I know you and Wembus aren't conspiring together?"

"Wembus, a conspirator? Have you lost your mind, Colmeron?" Caménor shook. "You don't believe me? Fine! Right now I don't care, but you're coming with me whether or not you choose".

Col had been told so many different things over the past few days he didn't know what to believe. His father trusted Caménor. Col believed that. For now that would have to be enough. He would go with Caménor, but not without reservation. "Where are we going?"

"South."

"This road goes west, not south."

"I know that, Col. This is the old King's Road."

The road hadn't been used in years. The trees had grown bold and encroached upon it. Col looked east, toward Ten Rocks, where Winter's hand was covering everything he'd ever known.

"We have to keep going," Caménor said.

"I know we do. Just give me a moment." He looked toward home one last time before turning back to the road.

CHAPTER 7

THE KING'S ROAD

—∞—

THE KING'S ROAD STRETCHED AHEAD. It gave itself neither to the left nor to the right. Giant boulders loomed like cliffs along the road's edge. They were the only landmarks Col had to note their travel. Hours passed and nothing changed. The falling snow covered their tracks nearly as quickly as they made them. The gray above and the white below were constant in their stark abundance. Maybe it wasn't Tonn but Col who was dead and Caménor was the spirit sent to hold him forever in the dim twilight.

Col was jolted from this trance when, with a shake of her mane and the raising of her head, Salee slowed and ambled from the road.

"What are you doing?" Col tugged on the reins. Salee continued away from the road and took him to the tumbling waters of a nearby brook. She stooped her neck and drank from the stream.

"We have to get back to the road, you stupid horse!" Col jumped from the saddle and his legs nearly gave way as his feet hit the ground. Salee kept drinking.

Col decided he could use a drink himself. He stretched and knelt to the stream. The cold water made his teeth hurt. He swallowed and looked at the sky with his eyes nearly as heavy as his heart. The clouds opened a small window and he felt the sun on his face.

Col turned to see Caménor following.

"Don't worry. I wasn't trying to run away." Col said. He shook the water from his hands.

"I know you weren't. She remembered this place better than I did."

"What do you mean?"

"Salee was your grandfather's horse. She's been down this road many times. She knows where she gets watered."

"Are you going to tell me where you're taking me now?"

"Not yet. I don't trust there aren't listening ears about. Here," he handed Col a chunk of bread and a lump of hard cheese. "Eat something. We've got a long ride before we camp for the night."

Col ate without tasting and swallowed without feeling.

They made their way back to the road and continued west. Col daydreamed in the saddle. His mind took him to a castle where Tonn was still alive and all of this was just a bad dream. It soothed him to think this, to see his brother breathing the crisp air again but any balm these thoughts offered was outweighed when he remembered the nightmare was real and he would never see Tonn again. He wondered for a moment why he would envision Tonn among the living but not his mother. Perhaps she had been gone too long. Perhaps her death could never be undone in his mind.

The sky ceased its sifting of the heavens and the sun dropped into the west. By the time they made camp for the night Col was sure his life had been a passing thought and the road was the only reality. The knot in his chest reminded him otherwise.

They went a hundred yards off the road. Caménor dismounted. "Clear the ground in front of that boulder," Caménor said. "We'll sleep there tonight."

Col kicked away the snow with his boot which only made his feet colder. He cleared a patch of ground large enough for both of them.

Caménor pulled a flint and tinder from his pocket. A burst of sparks and puff of smoke later and a tiny flame took hold of the kindling. "Warm yourself. I'll get more wood," he said.

Col stared at the fire. It grew in defiance of the dark Winter evening while Col only felt overshadowed by it.

"Is it safe to light a fire?"Col said.

"Even in Winter these woods are thick. We'll keep the flames low and the fire close to the boulder. That should hide it well enough until we have enough embers to stay warm by."

They built the fire higher at first and spread it out as the evening grew darker. Soon it was just a long pile of glowing coals. It gave off enough light to see each other and not much else. Col's body drank in the warmth.

He tilted his head back and stared up at the rock behind him. Its natural cracks and erratic lines were broken by something on its face. Col cleared away the dried moss with his hand to see, cut into the rock, a swirling circle with a tree on either side.

"What's that you've found?" Caménor asked, layering more wood onto the fire.

"I don't know. Some kind of symbol."

Caménor looked closer. "That, dear nephew, was once the royal seal of Arnoc. Many years ago."

"What is it?"

"It's the spring and two trees from Derid's story. I told you this road was old."

"Why doesn't anyone use it anymore?"

"It once ran to the sea which was where Arnoc's lifeblood was. Ports lined the shores and Entaramu, the great city of the Earthkings, rose from its waters. But Entaramu disappeared and Arnoc's kings moved to Ten Rocks. The sea became less important until this road was just a memory. Now there are other roads leading from more important places."

Caménor laid a few more branches along the fire. It stretched the length. Its heat reflected off the rock and created a haven amidst the cold. He spread his cloak on the bared patch of ground and wrapped himself in it. "Get some rest, Col. We have another long day ahead of us tomorrow. Take heart, though, we rest beneath the seal of the Earthkings tonight."

Col wanted to sleep more than anything, but he couldn't allow himself that luxury just yet. He couldn't stay awake forever but he could wait until his uncle slept. He wrapped his fingers around the dagger's handle and waited for the slow, deep breaths of sleep coming from his companion.

Once they came, Col rolled himself in his blanket. He shivered and hugged his knees to his chest to keep as much heat to himself as he could. He looked up at the seal on the rock above them and wished he could believe it was a sign of protection.

The next day passed much as the one before with the King's Road stretching ever before them. Caménor still held his sword at ready and kept his eyes to the trees whenever they stopped. Col was ever ready with his dagger and kept his eyes on his uncle.

Their meager portion of bread and cheese was soon gone. Hunger gnawed at Col. "How much farther until we reach someplace with real food?"

"We should reach the road's end by nightfall. From there it won't be long."

Col groaned at the thought of more hours on the perpetual road, but a few hours later the road ended suddenly. They stood with a line of trees at their back and snow laden hills rolling before them. Col was glad they'd made it but a pang of guilt came along with the new scape. How strange that he should want nothing more than to reach the road's end when doing so put home farther from him.

How was Mino handling his journey? Col wished he could be with his younger brother. He'd never been very protective of the runt but with Tonn gone Mino was all Col had left. And Col was all Mino had.

"Just over those hills there," Caménor pointed south. "is a bridge crossing a deep gorge. Once we're over it we should find shelter."

"Oh, to be warm and full," Col said.

"I pray so."

They bounded over the hills, virgin snow erupting in their wake. With no trees to hold back the wind, the tip of Col's nose was soon numb. His cheeks and ears soon followed. As they crested the final hill Col saw the gorge below but no means to cross it.

"Where's the bridge? There's always been a bridge here," Caménor said when they reached the chasm.

"Are you sure this is the right place?" Col asked. There were no moorings or stones arching in the air, not even a wooden post to show a bridge once existed here.

"Of course I'm sure this is the right place!" he nearly screamed. He growled and kicked the snow.

"I'm glad to see you're still in control of your temper, Uncle," Col knew the jab was risky but it was out before he could stop it.

Before Caménor could answer they were interrupted. "There you are!" An aged and weathered woman hobbled toward them with a gnarled staff in her withered hands. "My apologies for being late."

"Old woman, what happened to the bridge that was here?" Caménor asked.

"Oh, I'm sure it only wandered off for awhile." She waved her hand. "I expect it'll be back by morning. Come on, now. It's getting dark and these eyes don't work as well as I tell them they should. Let's get inside while I'm still able to find the door."

Col turned Salee after her but Caménor wasn't having it. "Is there another bridge? We need to cross by nightfall."

"That bridge is the only way and you won't see stone or brick of it until first light. It does this from time to time. There's no use waiting." She motioned for them to follow.

Caménor grabbed Col's arm and leaned close. "We don't know who she is. If I give the word be ready to run."

"Dinner should be good and hot by the time we get home," the woman said.

Col nodded to appease his uncle but the thought of a meal drew him toward the old woman like an Autumn leaf to the ground.

She shuffled through the snow at an agonizing pace. She stopped every few yards to sniff the air like a hound before turning in a new direction. If she was leading them to an ambush they'd certainly be able to see it coming. They soon gave up riding and walked with her, leading the horses by their reins. They came to a small thicket and just as suddenly as the old woman had appeared, so too did her home.

"Your horses will be fine in the yard. Winter looms but there's still plenty of grass for them here," she said.

The cottage that appeared from nowhere was larger than Col expected. The image of the old woman brought to mind small huts and dirt floors. The kind of thing Nabal would tell of in his stories, but what stood before him now was tidy and warm. A smooth, worn door hung sturdily in the center of a wide porch. Four heavy poles supported the porch's sloping roof. In front of a window sat a wooden chair with a low table beside it. An old pipe rested atop it. Firelight played behind the clouded window.

"Come in, come in," she said.

The wind snapped at Col's back and he nearly pushed Caménor into the cottage. He reveled in the warmth that greeted them. A kettle boiled over the fire. Its scent threatened to bring out the beggar in Col. Before he got near it the old woman chided him. "I'll take care of that. You sit down."

Col fell into a chair by to the fire. The seat was covered in tattered furs but was well worn and cradled his aching body. Caménor stood uneasily by the door.

A rough wooden table with four stools sat in front of the far window. In the corner behind it was a neatly made bed.

The old woman looked at Col. "You have the best seat I have to offer, young man," she said as she stirred the mysterious brew. "And while our young friend warms my seat would you be so kind as to hand me that bowl?" She looked at Caménor. "Yes, you there. The one with the wary scowl who's afraid to leave the door. You've got nothing to fear from an old crone like me."

Caménor handed her the bowl. She picked two long carrots and three rotund potatoes from it. She snatched a knife from atop the hearth and sliced the vegetables into the brew. She bent over the fire. Its heat gave a glow to the kind wrinkles lining her face.

"Our guests are quiet this evening," she said.

"My apologies," Caménor said. "We mean no disrespect. We've been riding for days."

"I should think that would be a greater reason to speak. Or not. Perhaps our guests bear a burden I cannot see. Maybe a little food and some rest will help to ease them, eh?"

Col leaned back in the chair and closed his eyes.

"Alright, young man, do grandmother a favor and hand her those bowls from the table."

Col lifted his head and opened one eye. "Grandmother?"

"You've been so good as to keep your names to yourselves that I see no need to burden you with the knowledge of mine. So you are simply 'boy' or 'young man' and I am 'grandmother'. And the tall one in the corner can be 'grumpy'. Unless you'd like to turn things proper for the evening?"

"Forgive us, kind mother. I am Cameron and this is my son, Colby," Caménor said.

Son? Col turned a grizzly eye on his uncle.

"My name is Ornana and I beg you, do not be afraid to use it." She ladled stew into the first bowl. "This rabbit has been cooking all day. Should be nice and tender."

She filled the remaining bowls and the three of them sat around the table. Col didn't bother letting the stew cool. His tongue paid the price for his impatience. He chewed carefully with an open mouth.

"I'm not going to take it away from you if you let it sit, Colby," Ornana said.

"It's very good. Thank you." Col replied with his tongue hanging from his mouth.

Caménor chewed quietly before speaking. "Ornana, when we met at the ravine you said you were late. Did you know we were coming? Can you see the King's Road from here?"

"Oh, no. I've known you were coming for days now. And still I was late!"

"Days? How could you know that?"

"Drinks! You need something to drink. Forgive me, it's been so long since I've had guests," she said.

"Ornana, how did you know we were coming?"

"A friend told me. He stopped in a week ago and let me know I'd be having some visitors. I was very excited."

A friend, thought Col. Perhaps it was one of Caménor's accomplices. Was he meant to be a captive here? Surely, he could overpower Ornana and, given even the dimmest chance, he knew he could get past Caménor. He looked at the old woman. She was too kindly to hold captive even a spider. He hoped so anyway. Just the same, he ate with an eye on each of them.

They spent the rest of the meal listening to Ornana talk about her garden and the birds who planted the seeds for her every Spring. She talked about the people she once knew and how they all seemed to have moved away or died, or both. It seemed to Col that perhaps Ornana was not so much crazy as she was lonely and the likelihood of any collusion with his uncle disappeared along with the last bits of their meal.

"Now that our bellies are full," she said. And indeed they were. "I'm sure you two are tired. How about some warm milk and honey?"

"Thank you, Ornana," Caménor said. "Your kindness far outweighs anything we can give in return."

"Bah," she waved her hand. "It's nothing. Now, drink and make yourselves comfortable. You two may have the bed. I sleep in my chair most nights."

Col gladly took the elixir from her. He drank it slowly before crawling into bed. He pulled the thick cover over himself but did not close his eyes. He was grateful the void in his stomach had been filled but his thoughts circled the one in his heart.

"Perhaps a story to help you sleep?" Ornana said. She snuffed the lanterns and the hearth was left to cast its low, serene glow over the room. Col could no longer see her but he heard her weathered voice as she began to speak.

—ᴥ—

Just beyond the ridge behind us there was once a large, bustling town not so different from the villages we know now. However, this town had something unlike any other. It was home to a great painter named Elim. His skill with the brush was greater than any other. He would often disappear for days or even weeks at a time and when he did so the people knew he was preparing another masterpiece.

Elim painted only the world around him. Verdant valleys and leaf-laden trees, the birds of the air and the scouring beasts. He showed people heavenly sights in new ways they'd never imagined and was sought by kings and princes alike for his work. They offered him treasures, all the wealth he could ever want, if he would only paint their portrait, but always Elim refused.

"There is nothing so beautiful as jagged peaks and tumbling waters," he would say. "People are filthy and devious, rampant with imperfection."

One day, captured by the magic of a cool Spring morning, Elim hid himself away and began to paint. He labored for seven days and by the last he knew this would be his finest work. He marveled at its magnificence. "Not even Orum, whose hand carved the land that inspires me, has ever created anything so beautiful," he said.

No sooner had the words escaped his lips then he dropped his brush and gasped in disbelief. His painting was gone.

Everything was gone.

He held his color-stained hands in front of his face but could not see them. The world he loved so much had been stricken with darkness.

"We are ended," he cried. He stumbled outside and called aloud, "Is there anyone left?"

"We are here, Elim," his friends said. "What has happened?"

He grabbed hold of the one nearest him. "The sun has forsaken us all!"

"You fool," they said. "The sun burns as bright as ever. It is your own eyes that have forsaken you." They laughed at him.

Horrified at his fate he rolled his paintings into a sack and blundered toward the hills. The jeers of his neighbors still hung in the air.

Tripping over root and rock and bouncing off unseen trunks he came to the mouth of a cave. Caked with dirt and blood he crawled in among the sharp rocks. The fragile echoes of dripping water filled the cave.

He took his paintings out and spread them around the chamber. He wept as he traced the brush strokes with his fingers. He recalled every vibrant color but was cursed to no longer see any of them. His final masterpiece, however, remained untouched. He didn't dare corrupt it with his hands.

For seven years he stayed in the cave, living where all was dark, eating worms from the bottom of a shallow pool and drinking from the same source. One night a violent storm shattered the silence of Elim's cave. It shook the hills where the cave lay. The distant murmur of the wind grew closer and closer until it took hold of the tree growing above the cave and tore it from the ground. Its tangled roots ripped open the ceiling and sent a shower of stone and dirt into Elim's chamber. He huddled in the corner as rain from black clouds washed over him.

As dawn's light broke Elim opened his eyes. For the first time in seven years he saw the crystal sheen of a clear sky.

"It's blue," he said looking up. "The sky is blue!"

A single white cloud drifted in the expanse and he ran from the cave, wild and frenzied, clutching his painting in his hand. He leapt into the air and flailed his arms about. He exalted in the lavish green and bourbon brown of the earth and danced to the blazing gold of the sun above. He unrolled his canvas and at last looked upon his prize.

What deception was this? This couldn't be the his painting. This was hideous. He raged as he realized this was indeed his work. He threw it into the river and felt only relief as the waters carried it away. How could he have thought it was beautiful?

On his way home he came across a small boy, squalid and bedraggled, with mud in his hair and mischief in the corners of his mouth.

"Who are you?" the boy said.

"My name is Elim," he said. "I am a painter."

"What do you paint?" asked the boy.

"I paint all things pure and lovely." As he said this Elim realized he'd never in all his days painted anything so true as the boy in front of him.

So Elim painted the boy in all his grime and awkward youth. This was his finest work. In the years that followed he painted the people in all their imperfection, in all their worth. At last he knew the finest beauty in all creation was not in the land but in those who dwelt in it.

Ornana's voice trailed as she finished her tale. Col watched her settle into the ragged chair and close her eyes. Even with Caménor next to him, Col felt safe for the first time in days. That was Ornana's greatest gift to him. Greater than the food or the fire or the heavy blanket that covered him so tenderly. She'd given him a haven in the midst of the cold and fear.

CHAPTER 8

UNWELCOME GUESTS

ORNANA WOKE AND PREPARED BREAKFAST before the thought of it had even occurred to Col. He rose to the smell of popping sausage, thick cream gravy and fresh biscuits. He lay there for a moment, unsure of where he was or why he was there. It was a blissful moment. Caménor stirred beside him. He looked at Col through blurry eyes. Col stared back at him, unflinching.

I'm stronger than you know, Col thought.

"I don't know what it is about sleeping that makes men hungry but I know that it does," Ornana said. "Shake those weights from your eyelids and come to the table. Let me enjoy the pleasure of your company a little longer."

Col knew that beyond his warm bed a cold day awaited.

The three of them sat down to breakfast. "We'd better see if we can find our way across the gorge," Caménor said after they'd eaten.

"Since you insist on leaving me so soon, here," Ornana pulled two small burlap bags from her cupboard. "I'm sure it won't last long but it'll be enough for a day or two." Inside the bags was some dried meat and leftover bread from the night before along with an apple for each of them.

Caménor wrapped the old woman in his arms and brazenly kissed her cheek. "May you receive far more than you've given, kind mother."

Ornana turned a bright shade of pink. "That's enough now. You'd better hurry. That bridge is fickle and if you're not there it might wander again."

"Right. You stay warm for another minute, Col. I'll take care of the horses." Caménor closed the door behind him.

"Your father is a good man," Ornana said.

Col hated that she thought Caménor was his father. His expression must've given him away.

"I've seen far worse men who were fathers to far worse children."

"You don't know him like I do." His uncle had managed to fool yet another person into thinking he was an able protector. Col winced at the thought of how quickly his father had handed him over to Caménor. Two days on and he still wasn't sure what to make of his companion.

"I'm sure I don't, but I'm a better judge of character than I let on. You have to trust somebody sometime, Colby," she said.

"I used to trust him."

"What was lost can be found again, young one."

"I'll trust myself. That will be enough." Trust wasn't something he could afford at the moment, not if he wanted to stay alive.

"If only it were. You'll need trust, especially on a journey such as yours."

What did she know about his journey? Col could only stare at her as he swallowed another bite of biscuit.

"Remember, it's up to you whether you are running from something or running toward something. Don't let what lies behind you be an anchor dragging you down. Oh, but I suppose you know all about that."

"What do you mean?"

"Why, the sea, of course. I'm surprised you could forget such a thing."

"But I've never been to the sea."

"Haven't you? I suppose I was mistaken."

"I've dreamed of the sea, though."

"The sea is a powerful thing," She leaned in close, her voice almost a whisper. "To dream of the sea is to dream of great things. Are you headed for great things?"

Col hesitated. "I don't know."

"Of course you don't! The truly great ones never do."

Caménor came back in with the cold blustering behind him. "The horses are ready."

The three said their farewells and they left the strange old woman who had so strangely appeared to them. Col was more reluctant to leave than he would have thought.

They retraced their wayward path and reached the ravine to find that where there had been nothing the day before, there now arched a bridge of stone and mortar.

"She was right," Col said.

"There is far more at work in our world than we know, Colmeron. We easily forget that."

"Do you think it's safe to cross?"

"There's only one way to find out. You go first."

"I'm not so easily lured, Uncle." His hand went for the dagger at his waist.

"I was kidding. Stay here. I'll let you know when to cross." Caménor disappeared over the arching bridge.

Col considered making for Ten Rocks but realized there was no way he would outpace Caménor. Not with two days between here and home.

"Okay, your turn!" Caménor called from the other side.

Col waited a long moment before he flicked the reins, but Salee refused his command. "Come on, you stupid horse!" He dug his heels in but still she rebelled.

"Are you coming?" Caménor called from across the bridge.

"I'm trying but this horse may as well be a mule. She won't cross."

"Cover her eyes."

"What?"

"Cover her eyes so she can't see the bridge. Then come across."

Col sliced a strip from the blanket beneath his saddle and carefully pulled the blindfold over Salee's eyes. She resisted at first, shaking her head and prancing from side to side. He whispered softly in her ear. She moved slowly over the bridge.

From the bridge their road sloped between spires of frosted pine and through fields barren beneath Winter's covering. This was the farthest from home Col had ever been and a sense of wonder at his new surroundings came over him. He would be king of this land someday, assuming he survived, but he'd seen so little of it. He had yet to see the Broken Mountains or the fields of Akeldama. He'd never even seen the Enturion Sea. Though if Ornana were to be believed, he'd be seeing it soon. Maybe that was where Caménor planned to kill Col, where his lifeless body could so easily be lost among the waves.

Just like in Col's dreams.

He shuddered. He was tired of secrets and subterfuge.

That afternoon, when they'd stopped to water the horses, Col asked, "Why the sea, Uncle?"

"What about the sea, Col?"

"Why are we heading to the sea? Are you such a coward that you hope the water will wash the blood from your hands, like it did with Tonn's?"

Caménor yanked the reins and spun hard to face Col. "You still think I killed your brother? I was with your father that night! Which shouldn't matter because you've known me your entire life. And suddenly I'm the villain? Let me tell you something you misguided whelp, I'm the only hope you have of staying alive right now. We have an enemy who seeks to destroy us. The Noflim are real, the Kheva Adem are real, and it's not a matter of if they decide to kill us — that's already been decided — but how quickly they can do it. They killed Nabal, they killed Tonn and they've taken Etau. The odds are quickly piling against us so I suggest you let this," he swung the back of his hand across Col's cheek. "knock that chip from your shoulder so we can keep going."

Col refused to show that he was hurt. The cold made it sting that much worse.

"And, yes, we are going to the Enturion. Not so I can drown you but because it's the best way for me to keep you safe. Maybe someday you'll see that."

The pain of realization swelled as the sting on his face lessened. Caménor was right. Col had no choice but to trust him. Even if he was lying, even if all the stories were just that, he was still alone, in the early gusts of Winter, in the middle of nowhere.

"How much farther are we going tonight?" Col forced the words out while trying to keep his voice steady.

"Not far. There," Caménor pointed to a tendril of smoke rising through a cluster of pines.

Their road twisted and curled upon itself down the hillside. Col smelled smoke as they drew near. They came upon the camp, a small circle of crude huts with a bonfire blazing in the middle. It danced like a woman in springtime, tempting Col with its warmth.

"Stay where you are, strangers!" A voice called from the shadows. "Who descends on us in the dark?"

Col made out the figure of a man standing at the edge of the camp. He held a spear in his hand and two dogs sat on either side of him. Their fur bristled in the firelight.

"Forgive us the late hour, friend. My son and I seek shelter for the night."

"We have no room for travelers."

"We don't ask for much."

"Something lures us in the night, tries to steal us away. How do we know it's not you?" He leveled his spear at them and the dogs gave a low growl.

"What's going on, Brin?" Another man approached.

"These two demand food and shelter for the night. Maybe more."

Caménor slid from the saddle. "We made no demands. We seek only shelter, a small kindness for the night. We mean you no harm."

The man, barrel chested with a short silver beard, looked at the one called Brin as if they were holding a silent conversation, eyebrows arching and jaws clenching. "Do you have any money?" he asked Caménor.

"We have a little," Caménor replied.

"We'll take it."

Caménor pulled two silver pieces from his belt and handed them over. "Thank you."

"You can use Norli's hut. Be gone by the time we rise."

"We will. Which hut is Norli's?"

"That one on the end."

"Where will Norli sleep?" Col said.

"He sleeps with his fathers tonight." Brin picked up a torch and lit its end in the fire. He tossed the brand to Caménor.

Caménor caught the torch. "What happened?"

"He's gone. Lured away." The man turned to his own hut but not before he gave them a final warning. "Be gone by morning or we take your horses."

Col's temper flared at the man's arrogance but Caménor took him by the arm and pulled him into their hut. "That won't help anything, Col. We'll be out of here long before they're up."

Their hut was the farthest from the fire. The inside was uglier than the out and only slightly warmer. Still, they were safe from the wind if nothing else. A small cot took up the right half of the hut. Covered in a patchwork of old skins and tattered furs, it reeked of stale sweat and urine. Caménor handed Col a chunk of bread and a few strips of dried venison.

"We should have stayed with Ornana," Col said.

"We wouldn't have been safe there for very long. We have to keep going."

Safe would have been to keep any of this from happening in the first place. Col wrapped himself in his blanket but his body shook from the cold. Eventually, somewhere amidst the shivering he managed to fall sleep.

"Prince Colmeron!"

Col sat up. The cold no longer bothered him.

"Hurry, my prince. I must speak with you."

Who could be calling him? Who even knew where he was? Had Wembus followed them?

He carefully stepped over the still sleeping Caménor and pulled aside the heavy flap to look outside. There was no one there. He stepped into the ring of huts. The fire loomed ahead. Only the man, Brin, stood on the other side of it. His back was to Col and the dogs were still at attention by his side.

"My prince." Brin turned around and Col saw it was not the gruff man from earlier that night.

"Etau?" Col walked toward the fire.

"I need to take you back to your father right away."

"My father is the one who sent me away."

"It was a mistake. Let me protect you from your uncle."

"He said you were Noflim."

"Your father waits for you, my prince. Your brothers wait for you."

"Brothers?"

"Yes, even Tonn. He's alive. Caménor's treachery failed to kill him."

"You're lying. I saw him. I touched him."

"Come with me, boy." The dogs on either side of Etau grew larger Their backs arched, limbs stretched.

Col stepped back and the animals leapt into the light. They stared at him through the fire with eyes dark like the minds of cruel men. Col saw grotesque bones twisting from the backs of their heads.

Kheva Adem.

Etau's eyes narrowed and his mouth twisted into a surly grin. "You cannot run. We will catch you. You cannot hide. We will find you."

One of the Kheva opened its mouth to reveal sharp teeth, foul and blood stained. Thin nostrils flared between sunken cheeks. A roar tore into Col's ears and burrowed in his chest. He fell to the ground and cupped his hands over his ears. The beast rose on hind legs and reached for him with six long, bony fingers. Its hand clamped around his throat.

Col gasped and squeezed his eyes shut. He opened them again. He was in Norli's hut, but he still couldn't breathe.

Someone stood over him, hand around his throat, grip threatening to tear the life from him.

So this was it. Caménor had finally shown his true self.

Col flailed and tried to find his knife but everything spun. A blade flashed before Col's eyes and burrowed deep into his assailants's gut. He was shoved and fell back outside. Col saw that it wasn't Caménor, but Brin, the man who'd given them such a warm welcome, who had tried to kill him.

Col clambered to his feet. Two more men were grappling on the floor. One of them was Caménor, who wildly swung Col's bloody dagger as the man on top of him dropped three heavy blows to his face. Caménor brought his knee up hard and fast and hit the man's groin. The hunter rolled to the ground, coughing in agony. Caménor swiftly cracked the back of his skull with the dagger's handle. The attack finally over, he met Col's eye and gasped for breath. "We have to go. Now." He wiped the blood from the dagger on the edge of the bed and handed it back to Col. "You may still need this."

They slipped from the hut and nearly tripped over Brin's body. Blood seeped from his gut. The rest of the camp still slept.

They rounded the hut to where the horses were tied. Col's stomach lurched when he saw only one of the horses. "They've taken Salee!" he said.

"Quiet, Col," Caménor came up behind him. "We're unlikely to make it out of here if any one else wakes. We still have one horse. That will be enough."

Col swallowed his anger and climbed behind Caménor in the saddle. He carefully put his arms around his uncle's waist. The two princes rode quickly away, eschewing the path in hopes of losing any who tried to pursue them.

An hour later, as the new day finally arrived, they found a clearing still boasting the vivid grass of Summer. The only bitter shadow cast was from an old shack tilting in the middle of the meadow. Beside the shack, contentedly nibbling the grass, stood Salee.

"How did she end up here?" Col said.

Caménor stared at the rundown dwelling. Its door dangled on a single hinge, The roof was nearly collapsed. A bow and quiver of arrows leaned against one wall.

Col slid to the ground and made for the weapon.

"Stop, Col. Come back here."

"Let me get her and we can go before anyone inside is the wiser."

"Just come back here."

"Let me grab them and we can go."

Caménor jumped to the ground and pulled his sword. "I don't think anyone brought her here." He slowly approached, eyes ever on the shack. "Come on girl," he carefully took her by the reins.

A voice rasped from inside the decrepit dwelling. "There's no hurry, dear boys. I have plenty to share if you'll come and sit with me."

Caménor pointed to Salee. "Get on, Col."

"Don't leave me. I don't want to be alone. You don't really want to go, do you? You don't want to go and I don't want to be alone. Come inside." A hand, wrinkled and gnarled, reached from the doorway. "The day dawn's cold and a journey is always made better by a little warmth for the stomach. Come," the hand turned with its palm up, fingers beckoning them to enter.

Caménor swung his sword in a silver arc and the hand fell limp into the snow.

"Is this how you repay a kind stranger offering a hand in friendship? You take the hand itself?" the voice hissed.

There was no blood on Caménor's sword. Neither was there coming from the hand.

"My curse upon you two travelers. Your mounts will lose all strength and whither beneath you. Your food will turn to poison in your mouths. Your sleep will be filled with horrors unimaginable. Your end may be near — oh yes, it is close at hand — but the sweetness of death will be slow in coming." Another hand reached from the doorway and took the one from the ground.

Caménor put a finger to his lips and motioned for Col to follow him. Together they fled the clearing.

Once they were free of the woods Col yelled for them to stop. "What was that?"

"That was a Piskie, one of the lesser spirits. If we'd gone inside we would have been trapped in its lair for a hundred years, until everything and everyone we've ever known or loved was gone."

"He cursed us."

"We're not cursed."

"We're not?"

"If you don't speak to a Piskie it has no power. We didn't speak to him so the curse is empty."

"How did you know he was in there?"

"I doubt Norli just disappeared and I'd be willing to bet that was his bow back there. Those hunters were afraid last night. With good reason."

"They didn't seem so afraid when they were trying to strangle me and beat your face in."

"Fear makes men do strange things." He winced and clutched his arm to himself.

In the light of the day, Col finally saw that his uncle's face wasn't all that had borne the brunt of the attack. A long gash ran down Caménor's arm, from the inside of his shoulder to his elbow. Blood caked the skin around it and the tatters of his sleeve clung to the tender skin.

Caménor followed Col's eyes. "I'll be alright. It wasn't very deep. Are you okay?"

"My throat's a little sore," he rubbed his neck and looked at his uncle before saying "And my cheek still hurts in this cold."

Caménor's eyes went to the ground. Was that shame Col sensed in him? He'd just saved Col's life, twice, and yet Col was still holding onto that. In truth, he was holding on to a lot more than that. But he was no longer convinced of those things.

"I'm sorry, Uncle Cam."

"For?"

"For not believing you."

"So you finally see, finally understand, I'm not the enemy?"

Col nodded. Tears dropped from his eyes with the motion. Nothing made sense anymore, nothing was the way it was supposed to be. "I'm afraid," he finally admitted.

"Listen to me, Col," Caménor reached a hand to him. "We are born to trials both great and small. We bend and we break and sometimes it takes awhile to put us back together. That's when we have to listen for the voice that whispers for us to get up. If you listen long enough, that whisper grows into a shout that screams at us to keep going, to not allow ourselves be slaves to fear. I promise you, Colmeron, the night will end and you will see the sun again. Listen for that voice and when you can't hear it listen for mine because I will always be here to tell you the same thing: get up, keep going."

It was the kind of advice Col had always hoped his older brother would have given him should the occasion arise. "Do you think they've buried Tonn yet?" he asked.

"Today, I would think."

"I wasn't a very good brother."

Caménor whisked away the trail of tears on Col's cheek. "What makes you say that?"

"I was always mean to him. He probably died thinking I hated him."

"No, no. You and Tonn behaved exactly as brothers do."

"We did?"

"Yes. The teasing and the chases and all the antagonizing you both did was the way you shared your love for one another. There was nothing wrong with it. And I know that someday that teasing would have turned into a deep respect. Your father and I were the same way."

"Really?"

"Oh, yes. Very much."

"I don't think I ever told Tonn I loved him."

"He knew. Remember, Col, he was a little older. He'd learned a few lessons you've still got coming."

"Do you think he'd be mad I'm not there today?"

"No. I think we've just had our own memorial."

"Yeah," Col sniffed. He sopped the rest of his tears with his sleeve before wiping his nose with it. "Do you think Mino's okay?"

"Brenna's always taken good care of him. She's an excellent nurse."

"Where are they going?"

"To the northern territories. Brenna has family there. That's where your mother was from, you know."

"I didn't know that."

"Ten Rocks holds many secrets, many stories that wait to be told."

Col had lived in that old castle his entire life. What secrets could it still hold?

"Come on, the sea awaits us," Caménor said.

Col took a deep breath and tasted salt on the wind. They rode on, leaving the wilds behind. It was a move of which Col was thankful. He'd never been so terrified as he was that morning.

They stopped beside a spring a few hours later to rest and water the horses. It was while Caménor was using the heel of his boot to break through the ice that Col realized something else his uncle must have been right about.

"What do you think happened to Etau?" Col asked.

"I don't have an answer to that question that hasn't kept me awake at night, Col." He wagged his foot and the icy drops fell from the leather. "He was either killed or escaped. I don't think one of the Noflim would allow itself to be captured."

"How long do you think he was, you know..."

"I've been asking myself that for days."

"And?"

"I don't know."

"So it was Etau that killed Tonn?" Col wasn't sure he wanted to know but asked anyway.

"More likely it was one of the Kheva. They exist to serve the Noflim."

Col imagined one of the creatures attacking his brother, holding him underwater, and suddenly wished he hadn't thought of it. "Tonn must have been terrified."

"I think your brother was a lot stronger than any of us realized."

"He tried to tell me something was out there but I didn't believe him."

"You couldn't have known, Col. There was so much happening that none of us knew about. We were all fooled. Even me. Even your father."

Caménor took Col in his arms and held him close while he wept for his brother. At last there was safety here, a comfort Col could accept without reservation. He remembered crying so many nights into his father's arms after his mother had died. Tephall had let him mourn but his arms were always stiff, rigid with unbelief at what had been lost.

Now, Caménor wept with Col and his tears served as a balm over Col's wounded heart.

That evening they camped on a high ridge. "Just beyond those hills lies the Enturion Sea," Caménor pointed into the distance. Late the next morning they crested the final ridge and saw the town of Edlin sprawling ahead of them. Its edges were littered with the crumbling remains of what was once a thriving seaport. Now, most of what remained — haphazard and uneven rows of shops and houses — clustered around the docks. And just beyond them lay the glimmering waters of the Enturion Sea with the masts of a dozen ships swaying easily at anchor.

CHAPTER 9

THE GRIM CAPTAIN

King Tephall walked wordlessly down the corridor. The foot of his robes swished with his quick, soft footfalls. He entered his rooms and closed the door behind him.

He couldn't keep sitting there. Not today. He couldn't stand his own people today. Didn't they understand he'd buried his son only yesterday? Still, they came before him one after another. Condolences were given, but only as a precursor to whatever they came to beggar from him.

So many voices sought something from him. So many faces, but all he could see was the face of one who sought nothing.

No, that wasn't true. Tonn's memory begged for itself. It pled that he should never be forgotten.

Safe within his chambers, his knees clapped on the floor and his hand muffled the cries pouring from his mouth. He quickly crossed the room to his bed chamber and shut himself even further away. With that door closed he allowed himself the anguish he'd held back. None would see their king unravel.

"How could I have let this happen?" he said aloud. He saw again Tonn's face as it was in life, before he was laid beside his mother. How he wished that face would smile and soothe his guilt. He needed it to tell him he was not to blame. But the face he saw now was not of the son made with his body but one made of his mind. And his mind could not forgive him for failing to protect the boy.

Etau had claimed him as he had claimed Nabal.

Etau!

This was the villain they had sought? A man who for years Tephall had entrusted everything? Once this treachery came to light Tephall's grief had turned to rage. Etau's body was burned as a traitor.

Tephall wet his hands in the basin and splashed tepid water on his face. He smoothed his beard and ran his fingers through his dark hair. He dried himself with a cloth, taking special care around his eyes. He couldn't be gone long. The people needed to see strength. He looked at the painting over the hearth.

Cyntara.

Tephall's wife had always shown such resilience. In many ways she'd been his strength. Her passing had been different. It had been simple, in a sense. Simple, but by no means easy.

Now, everything was an illusion. As far as everyone else knew Caménor was still held in the castle's lowest chamber. The guards still stood at their post and once a day Tephall took a plate of food in. He would say a few words and drop the food into a cold hearth. The guards would watch him leave, the plate cleaned by a silent prisoner.

Tephall stepped into the corridor and nearly collided with Wembus, who was preparing to knock on the oak door.

"A moment, your highness?" Wembus said.

He looked so much like his brother. If anyone could have been Etau's accomplice it would have been Wembus. Any doubt cast on Wembus disappeared, though, when he stumbled from the forest with Etau's body over his shoulder. His brother's own blood ran down his chest.

"Walk with me, Wembus," Tephall said.

"I know you are grieving, my king. And I grieve with you. Both for the prince and for my own brother. I know that at the end he was not himself."

"I wish I could believe that, Wembus."

"You don't understand, your majesty."

Tephall turned on his servant. "I don't understand?"

"It may have been my brother's hand at work but it wasn't him that moved it."

"What are you saying?"

"It was Noflim, my lord."

"I will not ease your grief by indulging in a faerie tale, Wembus." He resumed his pace.

"My brother's ashes were tossed to the wind like a criminal. He was a good man, a loyal man. He didn't deserve that."

"What was undeserved was that my son would die alone and afraid and will never grow to succeed his wretch of a father!"

"I'm sorry, my lord, but I cannot bear the thought of Etau being remembered this way."

"We are all remembered for what we do," Tephall looked into Wembus' eyes. "And the deeds at our end are remembered most. We cannot undo Etau's deed, but we can see that our own are worth remembering. I know your loss, but we will not speak of this again."

"Yes, my lord." Wembus nodded and walked away.

It pained Tephall to see him so broken, but there was no argument for Etau's innocence. He was sure in time Wembus would recover some measure of his former self. Whether or not he did was of little concern to Tephall at the moment.

A bell clanged in the distance. It was as much a comfort to Col as the thought of a warm bed. He itched to push Salee into a full run, but the old horse was tired. Her slow steps reminded Col how far they'd come. He looked at Caménor, who gazed at the coming seaport as they ambled down the only road into town.

"What's wrong?" Col asked.

Caménor looked at Col for a moment as though he were a stranger. "I haven't seen Edlin in many years. I can't help but think what life was like then."

"What was it like?"

"I was a few years older than you are now. One of your grandfather's lords was leading an insurrection so your grandfather sent your father and me into hiding. A trusted guard took me to his family in the south. We passed through Edlin then."

"Is that where we're going? To see the guard?"

"No. He died before you were born but his family still farms the same land. That's where we're going."

"And we'll be safe there?"

"I hope so."

"How long were you gone when Grandfather sent you away?"

"A couple of months. The lord was killed by one of his own men and the threat was over."

Months? Col wasn't sure he could stand hiding that long.

"It was while your father was in hiding that he met your mother. When the time came for him to return home he knew he couldn't leave her behind."

"What did he do?"

"What could he do? He told her he was the NéPrince. She thought he was a fool."

"She didn't believe him?"

"Not even a little," he laughed. "A month later I went back with your father. This time he took a company of the king's finest men. Etau was with us. But Cyntara still didn't believe."

"How did he convince her?"

"He didn't. She said 'Ask me to marry you. It doesn't matter whether you are a prince or a scoundrel as long as you love me.' I don't think she really believed him until they reached Ten Rocks. Over the years I would catch her looking at your father with that same look in her eyes, as though she still thought he was crazy."

"Why didn't you ever marry, Uncle? Wasn't there ever someone you couldn't leave behind?"

"Once."

"So why don't I have an aunt?"

"It's a long story, Col."

"We've got time." The horses seemed to move slower than ever. "Tell me about her."

Caménor's eyes remained on Edlin as he spoke, "She had a birth mark shaped like a crescent moon on her neck. She would always try to hide it, as if it were a blemish. I'd tell her she must've been kissed by the moon as a baby and that was why she looked so lovely in the moonlight. She was captivating. There wasn't a moment I didn't want to be with her, nothing I wouldn't have given for her, but in the end she chose another."

"What? How could she refuse you? You're a prince!"

"I never told her who I was."

"What good is being royalty if you can't use it to get what you want?"

"Some things in life aren't worth having if you have to take them, Col. Some things you have to be given. You'll learn that. Besides, my life became very full soon after. Your grandfather died a few years later, Tephall assumed the throne and I became an uncle."

"Oh."

"Being there to watch you and your brothers grow has been more than I could have asked for, Col. I have no regrets."

They reached Edlin's border and passed the broken down walls of long abandoned buildings. Day old snow covered stairs leading nowhere and blew over floors exposed by absent roofs. The scattered footprints of children ran between the derelicts.

"Arnoc once thrived by the sea," Caménor said. "Edlin was one of many ports, far from being even the greatest but it is one of only a few that remain. Now, we reign from the north. The sea and her life are all but forgotten."

"Nobody talks about Arnoc the way you do. You're a little strange. Do you know that?"

Caménor laughed. "It's not the first time I've heard such rumors."

A minute later it was as though they'd entered a different world. The streets teemed with life and the smell of fish hit Col like a punch in the nose. The clamor of Edlin's market was like nothing he'd ever seen. Men carted the morning catch from the docks as fish mongers hawked golden-eyed whitefish. Buying, selling, trading, this was the heartbeat of Edlin and Col was in the middle of it.

"Watch out, there!" A small man driving a large wagon glared at them as he passed by.

"Keep going, Col. We need to reach the docks," Caménor said.

They made their way through the throng and came to the docks. Water lapped and swirled around posts reaching into the cold earth below. It made Col dizzy.

Five ships anchored in front of them. Three were busy with men loading supplies, tossing ropes and spitting names at one another. A fourth noisily hoisted anchor while its sail billowed with a snap and the sudden creak of tightened ropes. The fifth ship sat silent. A lone man stood behind the wheel with his hands clasped behind him.

"I'll be right back." Caménor dropped from his horse and walked toward the first ship.

Sitting on the dock, Col began to see the order among the chaos of the market. Men and women moved from one vendor to the next or to and from the docks while children dodged between them. The fisherman either sold their catch themselves or brought it to a vendor whose stands were always bigger and busier.

These were his people. He would be their leader, their guardian, someday and he didn't know why he should be. He looked at them as they passed, a hundred strange faces, and felt nothing. These people were strangers. He was an alien among them. He was afraid they were beginning to notice. He slid from the saddle and hid beside Salee.

"What's your name?"

Col turned to see a young girl looking up at him. Her light hair was braided into a single tail that tugged at the edges of her smudged face. A white and orange kitten burrowed in the crook of her arm.

"My name is Col — Colby."

"Do you want to play with me?"

"I can't. Don't you have someone else to play with?"

"Only my brother and he always throws rocks at me."

"My brother used to do that, too."

"Why can't you play with me?" she asked.

"I just can't. Why don't you play with your cat?"

The kitten mewled and tried to climb its way onto the girl's shoulder. She pushed out her lower lip and scrunched her forehead. "I'll go find my brother. Maybe he won't throw rocks at me this time." She pulled the kitten from her shoulder. Its claws stuck to the fabric of her dress.

Caménor returned a few minutes later rubbing his hands together and blowing on them. "We're in luck. I found a ship that will take us south. Who were you talking to?"

"I don't know. It was just a girl and her cat."

"What did you say to her?"

"Nothing. I don't know why she was talking to me."

"You've got a friendly face."

"You think so?"

"Sure. No one's ever told you that?"

"Not that I can remember."

"Well, you do. Come on, our ship sets sail soon, with or without us, and we've still got to find the captain."

They left the docks by a road that wound along the coast. To their right the road dropped into the foaming sea.

They stopped where a skewed wooden post marked the edge of a field. "This must be our turn," Caménor said.

They trudged toward a farm on the far side of the field. A crooked fence led to a stout barn. Behind that smoke curled from the chimney of a sturdy house. A dog, more mongrel than anything, ran up to them. It yipped and snapped at Col's feet.

"Get away." Col kicked at it.

A large man with a thick beard and smooth, dark hair appeared from inside the barn. "You're kicking my dog while trespassing on my land. Consider this a warning. You won't get another."

"Tell your dog to leave me alone and I'll stop kicking it," Col said.

"He's doing exactly what he should. Why don't you do the same and leave?"

"Are you Captain Vylsom?" Caménor said.

"I am."

"Deel sent us." He handed the Captain a small square of paper, folded several times. "I'm Cameron. The boy is Colby."

Captain Vylsom looked over the scrawled letter. His lip curled before he spoke. "Deel is an idiot, but I'll agree to this." He turned his head toward the house. "Yntor! Take these horses into the barn."

Before Col could question which horses he was talking about the Captain lifted him from the saddle.

"What are you doing? Let go of me!" Col twisted in the man's grip only to be dropped in the snow.

A boy only a few years younger than Col took Salee's reins from the Captain.

"Thief! Give me back my horse!"

"You'll teach your boy some manners," the Captain said. "I won't be accused of stealing." He yanked Col back by his collar.

Caménor freed Col from the Captain's hand and pulled him aside. "How did you think we were going to pay our way, Col?"

"I don't know. I didn't think about that. But you can't just sell Salee. She's mine!"

"I didn't think you even liked that horse."

"I don't. I mean, I didn't."

"Don't worry. I don't think they're going to eat her or anything."

The Captain stomped between the house and the barn. "Yntor! Get the wagon hitched. We leave as soon as we eat."

The mention of food snapped Col's attention from Salee to his stomach. The food Ornana had given them was already gone and the gnawing in his gut was becoming all too familiar.

The Captain must've known what Col was thinking. "Not you two. You'll stay with the wagon until we leave."

A stocky woman appeared in the doorway of the house. Her chest and stomach were only separated by the apron string tied tightly across her midriff. "We've got plenty of food for your guests, husband. Let them come in and eat."

"They're not guests, Tymna. They're sorry excuses for a crew and they're fine where they are."

"New crewman, eh? Well then, when they get on your boat they'll be under your command, but right now they're guests at my house and I'll feed them if I want to," she said.

The Captain grunted. He motioned for them to come inside, Before Col could cross the threshold the Captain stopped him.

"My name is Captain Vylsom. You'll refer to me as 'Captain' or 'Sir' once we're aboard my ship. If you do anything to disturb the order on my vessel I won't lose any sleep after tossing you overboard. Your father can jump in after you if he wants."

Col's hands balled and he felt the blood rush to his temples. "You wouldn't dare."

"My ship is my kingdom, boy, and I don't suffer treason. You seem like you're going to be trouble. We're not going to have any trouble from you, are we?"

Caménor eyed Col from inside and shook his head.

"No," Col said.

"No?" the Captain waited.

Col gritted his teeth. "No, sir."

"Good." He stepped aside and Col took the chair beside Caménor. The Captain sat in the big chair at the head of the table and slapped two hairy arms on the wood. "Where's the boy? I won't wait while he dawdles."

Yntor joined them a moment later. Tymna set bowls in front of them and dipped a ladle into the kettle. Thick sides of flaky white meat drenched in a heavy tomato and cream sauce slid into the bowls. Col greedily ate the sweet fish.

"It's lucky you found us before husband casts off. Luckier still he agreed to take you on." She sat down but before she could take a bite she was up refilling the Captain's cup. "Yntor will be glad of the company, though. Won't you, son?"

Yntor only nodded in response.

"He's a shy boy, but he'll warm up as soon as you're on the water. Husband says that's where he finds his tongue."

"What kind of fish is this?" Col asked.

The Captain scraped the last of the food from his bowl and slurped it between his lips, catching sauce in his mustache. "Enturion Whitefish."

"It's our livelihood here by the sea," Tymna said. "That's what husband catches — brings it in by the boatload to sell at the markets. He's the best, you know. He knows all the secrets."

"That's enough, Tymna," the Captain said.

"If they'll be sailing with you they'll find out soon enough. Oh, that reminds me," she disappeared into the next room and emerged a minute later with two heavy coats on her arm. "You'll be needing these if you're going to sea this time of year. Those cloaks you have now would be about as good as a spider web. These will keep you warm and dry as long as you don't fall in." She made Col and Caménor stand as she slid the coats over their arms and onto their shoulders. "They're made from seal skin and wolf hide. A good mix, I've always found."

"Where did you get those?" the Captain said.

"Don't worry. They're two years old. One was yours and one was Deel's. I patched them up when you were through with them. You didn't think I'd toss them, did you?"

"I'd have taken more than the horses if I'd known we were dressing them."

"Settle down. I'm sure you'll make them work for their coats, husband."

"You can be sure of that. We're losing time talking like this," the Captain said. "That wagon better be ready."

"It is," Yntor quietly replied.

Outside, the wagon was hitched to two horses as thick and cantankerous as their master. "In the back, you two," the Captain said.

Col and Caménor found their seats after climbing over small casks of ale and sacks of potatoes. If the Captain was this amiable now, how pleasant would he be after a few drinks? Col's foot rested against one of the casks and he toyed with the idea of rolling it from the back of the wagon.

He felt a tap on his other foot and looked up to see Caménor slowly shaking his head.

"Watch the drink back there, you two. Your fate will be the same as theirs," the Captain said.

"You're going to drink us?" Col said.

Captain Vylsom turned his head and looked at him with eyes Col was sure were about to spit fire. "I thought you said you weren't going to be any trouble?"

"Once we cast off how long until we reach one of the southern ports?" Caménor stepped in.

"Three weeks. So long as the nets are holding."

Three weeks? Col wasn't ready to spend another minute with the man let alone three weeks at sea.

The wagon's pitted wheels seemed to hit every hole and jutting rock along the way. Col held tightly to the side of the wagon lest he should be bumped onto the road or worse. They reached the docks and came to a stop next to one of the ships Col had seen earlier. The name "Flapper" was painted in a fading yellow across her stern. It wasn't as sleek or as large as the other ships but looked sturdy enough. It had a single mast and a slender prow. At the stern, a short ladder led to the quarterdeck where the wheel awaited Captain Vylsom's command. A thin man with a mane of hair that shone white in the sunlight hailed them from the deck.

"Ahoy, Captain Vylsom. I see our guests found you."

"Deel, you overstep your authority by taking on new crew again and I'll be searching for a new first mate," the Captain said.

"What about young Yntor? He'll make a fine first mate someday," Deel said.

"Don't be a fool." The Captain jumped from the wagon to the gangway. "Let's get those supplies on board. The fish are waiting." He jabbed a finger at Col. "Your horse got you on board, now you'll have to work to stay. Let's go!"

Col glared at him once his back was turned. He grabbed two sacks of potatoes. Caménor and Yntor helped with the rest. Col's first steps on the Flapper were stumbling ones and he ended up with a scraped elbow, bruised potatoes and the Captain bearing down on him. Caménor ran to help before the Captain reached him. "Be careful. This isn't like a rowboat on the lake."

"I can see that. Why'd you have to pick the boat with an ox for a captain?"

"Our choices were severely limited, Col. Just try and stay out of his way."

The Flapper's three regular crew members: Captain Vylsom, Deel and Yntor quickly pulled anchor and loosed sail. The Captain stood at the wheel and looked over the water as the sheet billowed and the wind took hold. "Don't look back," he said aloud. "The land holds nothing for us now but dirt and misery. The sea's love is fickle and she waits for no man. Let's away!"

The Flapper's prow split the waves and the dock was soon behind them. Despite the Captain's advice Col gazed across the water to see Tymna in the wagon watching her family sail away. Col observed her vigil until she was so small he was sure he could snatch her between his fingers.

He turned back to the ship. He was surrounded by water as far as he could see. This tiny vessel was now his world. There was a certain helplessness here at the mercy of the waves. That strange fear one rarely knows outside of dreams crept over him and he remembered the Noflim's warning.

You cannot run, we will catch you. You cannot hide, we will find you.

Would they find him here?

CHAPTER 10

THE FLAPPER AT SEA

Tephall and Wembus nearly filled the small rowboat. Winter's early chill hung heavy over the water. The sleeves of Tephall's thin shirt were rolled high and sweat dripped from his forehead as he pulled against lake.

"Why don't you let me do that, your highness?" Wembus said.

"I've been letting you do things for me far too long, Wembus. Just enjoy the morning. The air is different here on the water, don't you think?" Tephall breathed in and contentedly let it back out. "Our friends and loved ones are dying around us, dropping like birds in the hunt, but you and I, we are alive."

"It is a beautiful morning, my lord." Wembus said. There was certain hollowness in his voice.

Tephall leaned into another stroke of the oars. "Why us, Wembus? Why is it that you and I are still alive?"

"You are king, my lord. It's the duty of every man here to protect you."

"Every man except your brother that is."

Wembus looked to the hills in the distance. Their white crests sparkled in the morning light.

"And you, Wembus? Why are you still among the living?"

"I have wondered that through many long hours of the night. I don't know why I'm alive while my brother is not. He was the better man."

"Yes, he was." Tephall stopped rowing and let the boat drift slowly where the sun burned at the mist curling from the water. "I knew Etau for years, trusted him with everything I had. That's why he was able to take it all away."

"I can't defend his actions when I don't believe they were his own."

"There are few people left for me to trust, Wembus. You know that, don't you?"

"Yes, my lord."

"Then you'll understand why we're here."

Wembus looked around them. Here, in the middle of the lake they were truly alone. There was no one to hear their words. No one would see what was about to happen.

Tephall pulled the oars from the water. "You knew Etau better than anyone, Wembus. Better than me, even."

"He was my brother, the only family I had."

"Did you know he was a murderer?"

"Please don't call him that."

"Through these days I've had one thought circling my mind, like a vulture over a carcass. Do you know what that thought is?"

"No, my lord."

"I wouldn't think so. Why would Etau kill Nabal? Why Tonn? There was nothing he could've asked from me that I wouldn't have given him."

"I agree. You see, it doesn't make sense."

"No, it makes perfect sense if there was someone else giving the orders. Etau was only a pawn."

"You're right, my lord. There is a more malevolent force at work here."

Tephall dipped his fingers past the water's surface. He let them linger until the cold pierced their tips. "These are the same waters where my son's life left his body. I wonder, how easy was it for your brother to hold him under? How hard did he have to push as the boy he watched and protected for sixteen years struggled and kicked, fighting to breathe again?" He brought his hand up from the water, splashing drops across the boat.

Wembus wiped a drop from his face. "It's very cold out here, my lord. Hand me the oars and I'll row us back to shore."

"He wasn't alone in his villainy, was he, Wembus?" He fixed a cold stare on his servant.

"You think I helped him? I could never have --"

"Just like Etau could never have?" Tephall grabbed him by the scruff of his shirt. He held Wembus over the side of the boat so that his face touched the water. "If not you, then who? Who among us would have the resolve to drown my son?" He shoved Wembus's head under and held it there before bringing the man back up gasping for air. "I need the truth, Wembus. Tell me I can trust you! Tell me you would never betray me!"

"I won't tell you that."

Tephall reached for him again.

Wembus put his hands up in surrender. "I will not say it because I will show it."

Tephall sat back down and the rocking boat settled.

Wembus slowly reached a hand into his shirt and revealed the long blade of a knife."I have lived my loyalty for years and not even Etau's apparent betrayal could change that. This is the knife I killed him with. My own brother. I did it to save your brother and your son. If my loyalty is not shown in that," He held the knife out to Tephall. "Then take this and kill me now."

Tephall looked at the knife as though it were about to cut him. He reached for Wembus' wrist and tenderly pushed the knife down. "I'm sorry, Wembus. I know your innocence. I just needed to be sure."

"My loyalty is as fierce as it has ever been, my lord. We have an enemy that seeks to destroy us and I will not leave your side until we have found either death or victory."

"I have no one else to trust, Wembus. You are all I have left."

"Then believe me when I tell you this: the morning the princes escaped I followed them from a distance. I heard them talking to someone on the path. I approached, staying low behind a boulder. It was Etau that spoke back to them but when I looked his lips weren't moving. After he was dead I checked his mouth. His tongue was gone. Only a long-healed stump remained."

"I've seen men speak without moving their lips before, Wembus. I've even seen men speak from both sides of their mouth at once. It's a trick."

"Don't you see, my lord? If my brother was taken by the Noflim then Nabal was meant to serve as host as well. Those two were closest to you, those with the greatest influence."

"I ask you for answers and you give me fables, Wembus." Tephall put the oars back into the water. "We need to keep looking. We must keep questioning. I want every guard that knew Etau interrogated. Bring in any of my lords he was in contact with."

"We've already questioned his men. They've been relieved of their posts and new soldiers have been brought in from the Eastern Garrison. Your lords have all been home for the harvests and preparing for Winter. None have been here in months."

"Etau didn't act alone. This scheme won't have died with him." He grunted as he pulled another stroke of the oars. He rowed harder, pushing his muscles to a limit they hadn't known for some time. It was good to be moving on the water. He was getting nowhere with anything else. No matter. He would find the answers he needed one way or another.

—ꝏ—

Col slept fitfully in his swaying hammock. The blanket that Deel had given him was a coarse patchwork of old canvas and threadbare wool squares. The fabric scratched at his face like an old man's beard.

He heard a footstep behind him and countered by pulling the blanket over his head. His bed swung suddenly faster and spilled him from the net like a bad catch. The hard planks punched the air from his chest. He rolled over and futilely sucked air. He saw Captain Vylsom looking down his crooked nose at him.

"It's time to get up, worm."

"Don't ever call me that," Col said once he could finally breathe again.

"What was that?"

"Don't ever call me that, sir."

"You're a quick one. If you're so quick, you'll have no problem being up before the sun from now on. That'll save the floor some abuse. Now, get on deck."

Col's hand nursed his ribs as he pulled his coat on. Up on deck he was greeted by a cold spray from the bucking prow. The sun crested the waves, its light blushing the gray above.

Deel called from the wheel. "We've got some rough seas today, boys. I hope you can tie a knot in your stomach." He was smiling. His hair tossed in the wind, his cheeks were red, his nose was like a burning ember, and he was actually smiling.

Col wondered if the Captain wasn't the only one who liked to drink. He shivered beneath his heavy coat and looked for Caménor. He found him at the prow, looking over the dark waters.

"There you are, Col. The Captain said he was going to wake you."

"That he did." He rubbed a hand over his ribs again. "When's breakfast?"

"About twenty minutes ago. Don't worry, I saved you a little." He tossed Col a hunk of sweet bread and a handful of dried whitefish.

Col bit off a piece of the meat and followed it with a chunk of sweet bread before Captain Vylsom bounded on deck.

"Yntor!" His bellow fought the wind.

The boy appeared. "The galley's all cleaned, Captain."

"Get to work on the nets. Take the burden with you," he said nodding at Col.

Col looked at his uncle and groaned.

"Just think, soon these weeks will be only a memory," Caménor said.

Weeks. Col hated the reminder.

"A little work might do you some good, Col. Go on. Yntor's waiting for you."

Col shoved the last of his breakfast into his mouth. He joined the younger boy at the hatch over the ship's hold.

He handed Col a length of net. "Here, take this and pull," he commanded. Together they lugged a tangled mess of rope and dried fish scales onto the deck.

"Why does your father treat you like that?" Col asked.

"Like what?"

"He's almost as cruel to you as he is to me. And you're his son!"

"Not while we're at sea, I'm not. Captain says family ties don't catch fish."

"And being a pig does?"

"I'd be careful what you say about the Captain. There's nothing that happens on the Flapper he doesn't know about."

"I'll be sure and keep a close eye on my tongue," Col said. He stuck out his tongue and looked down at it. Yntor laughed at him and they hoisted another mess of netting from the hold. "Why is the boat called 'Flapper'?" Col asked.

"First of all, it's a ship. Don't ever let the Captain hear you call it a boat. And he says he named it 'Flapper' because when she gets a good wind she almost flies, like a bird flapping its wings."

Col stood with the tangled nets at his feet, unsure of what he was supposed to do next.

"You've never been to sea, have you?"

"No. There's a lake beside our home. I used to swim there in the Summers. Sometimes we would take a boat on the water."

"There's no swimming here, especially in Winter. Unless you fall overboard. If that happens swimming won't do you much good." Yntor handed Col one of the nets. "Straighten this out. I'll work on these."

Col tugged and pulled in an effort to untangle the net, but only succeeded in frustrating himself and making the knots worse.

"Here, let me show you." Yntor took the mess from Col and, with a method of familiarity, slowly laid the net out. Col felt the Captain's eyes on him as he watched Yntor work. He'd never felt so despised in his entire life.

Once the nets were straightened Yntor tried to show Col how to repair any frays or tears they found. "Even one bad cord can lose a catch. Once that happens the net's useless and we get a new hammock along with a few lashes."

Yntor talked as they worked. Tymna had been right. The boy found his tongue at sea. Enough for the both of them. He told of the woes of life at sea and the thrill of the catch. He talked about the long Winters he'd spent with Deel under the Captain's stern eye and the terror of nearly wrecking during a storm two years before.

Reluctantly, Col learned what to look for. He even spotted a few bad cords and repaired them with Yntor's help. But he soon realized that if he missed any the boy inevitably found them and repaired them on his own. And Col's task quickly became about the appearance of work rather than actually doing anything.

Captain Vylsom, however, was not so easily deceived. Before Col realized what was happening his collar pulled tight around his neck and he was hoisted to his feet. The Captain's face was right next to his own. His breath reeked of fish and stale beer. "There's a loose rope atop the mast, grub. Tighten it."

Col looked at the swaying mast and felt his stomach lurch. "I'm not going up there. I could fall."

"Just don't land on any of the crew." He shoved Col into the lower rigging.

Col grabbed onto the first swag. He looked for Caménor, but the Captain had sent him below deck.

He pulled himself up and started to climb. His knees buckled beneath him as the Flapper lurched on the waves. He clung to the rigging. The rope dug into his armpit. He reached eye level with the Captain. Vylsom stared at him with cold, dark eyes. Col put his attention back on the ropes. He closed his eyes and took a deep breath. He was a prince, the NéPrince of Arnoc, and here he was being treated like a dog by the most vile man he'd ever known. But what kind of a king would he be if he couldn't even climb to the top of a mast?

His feet were unsteady on the loose swags but he pressed on, taking care not to look down. At last, he reached the top. He breathed a sigh of relief and laughed nervously. He looked over the yard, but only saw ropes tightly lashed across its length. "I don't see any loose ropes," he yelled down.

"Are you calling me a liar?" Captain Vylsom hollered back up.

Col looked to the yardarms again. Everything was tied tight. This was all a game to the Captain. He reached over as far as he could and pretended to fiddle with one of the ropes. "I got it."

The Captain put his hands behind his back and walked away.

Col climbed down with a grin of smug satisfaction.

Yntor spoke without looking up from his work. "Captain says you're to come back to the nets, Col." Col rejoined him and they passed the hours poring over every cord of every net. By the time the sun began her descent Col was sure his back would never straighten again. He stood and stretched before helping Yntor roll up the final net. He carried it below deck where the smell of dinner escaped the galley. Col felt he was never more deserving of a hot meal. He had survived his first day at sea. He would never admit it but there was a certain satisfaction found in the work.

The crew, minus the Captain, sat down to a simple meal of stewed potatoes with carrots and more whitefish. A lantern swung from the beam above them. Its precarious light dashed across their common quarters.

"The Captain always dines in his cabin," Deel said. "I've sailed under him for nearly fifteen years and I don't think I've ever taken a meal with him. He's peculiar that way."

"Peculiar wasn't the word I had in mind," Col said. He caught a glance from Yntor and remembered the boy's warning. He pictured the Captain in his cabin above them with his ear to the floor, listening for any word of dissent.

Once they'd finished their meal Deel spoke, "I don't know about you two but Yntor and I always enjoy a story after a meal." He pulled a pipe and tobacco pouch from his pocket.

"I couldn't agree more, my friend. What did you have in mind?" Caménor said.

"Poor Yntor has heard all of my stories more times than he can count..." He stuffed tobacco in the bowl before tamping it and lighting the pipe. He blew wisps of smoke into the air and its earthy scent surrounded them.

"I see. Allow me the honor then?"

"The honor would be ours," Deel said. He clenched the pipe in his teeth.

Deel passed the pipe to Caménor who puffed on it as he thought. His cheeks puckered in and out. "You know about the Greenkind, don't you, Yntor?"

"No," Yntor said. His eyes grew wide in the lamplight.

"Ha! Old folklore told by old women to keep their children from wandering too far. They're about as real as giants, dragons and Kheva Adem," Deel said. "You'll like this, Yntor."

"I think so, too," Caménor said. "Now pay close attention..."

Far to the north, where Arnoc borders an untamed wilderness, is the territory of the Greenkind. Many years ago, before the great city of Entaramu sank below the very waves we sail on, a small family lived along that border. Their farm sat against a line of trees marking the territory. It was a dangerous place to dwell.

An old mother and an even older father watched over two young boys, Trenam and Naleer. Trenam, the older of the two, was brave but cautious; never reckless in his sojourns along the border. But Naleer, the younger, was daring and foolish in his dallies among the trees.

"Keep out of the shadows and away from the woods," Trenam would warn his brother. But Naleer would not be kept from his adventures. These woods held wonders not found anywhere else. There were strange flowers with intoxicating scents and the leaves on the trees struck such mysterious notes in the wind. While his brother was busy working the fields, Naleer would slip from shadow to shadow until he crossed into the forbidden realm of the Greenkind.

The thrill of it all was enough to keep him sneaking there time after time until one day a new shadow passed over him and he heard the footfall of the forest dwellers. He ran for the forest's edge. Beyond the trees he saw his brother working in the field. "Trenam!" he called.

Trenam looked to see him leaping across the tree line. He thought it was only Naleer showing off until a knotted hand snatched Naleer's foot from the air. It yanked him back and dragged him into the forest.

Trenam ran after his brother. He crashed through the brush and into the untamed land. He called for Naleer. He searched for any sign of him, but it was all a tangled maze. Finally, as night fell, he stumbled back into the field. He knew there was only one way of redeeming his brother. He would ride for Entaramu and beg the king's help.

But what chance did he, a poor farm boy, have of seeing the Lord of Entaramu? It didn't matter. To save his brother he would give his life, if it was asked.

While his aged parents slept he saddled his horse and was quickly away. For two days he rode with neither sleep nor food. He traveled up steep slopes and down through treacherous ravines. He rode until his horse gave out beneath him and he slammed into the dirt. As he pulled himself to his knees he saw the peaks of the great city in the distance. Leaving his horse he ran. He ran until he could no longer feel his legs and all that was left to feel was the wind rising from the sea. He reached Entaramu's gates and collapsed.

It happened then that the king's servant was returning to the city when he saw Trenam on the ground. "What terror could bring you to our gates and death's door at the same time?" he asked.

Trenam begged the servant to take him to the king. So fervent was his plea that the servant picked him up and carried him to the king's tower. He laid him on a bench outside the throne room. Two enormous doors towered over him. But Trenam would not wait to be seen and burst in ahead of the servant. The room was filled with members of the king's court. Men and women from every corner of the kingdom sat beneath brilliant banners. Around them, stone walls reached the sky itself. Sunlight poured through huge ports in the ceiling and gathered around a singular figure draped in a blazing red cloak. The king sat on a throne that looked as if it had been grown in its place at the head of the hall. Thick roots twisted over one another in perfect unison to form four legs. They intertwined to shape the seat and back of the great throne. Limbs like antlers spiked from the corners of the throne. Green leaves fluttered lightly in the breeze.

"My lord, my king! Please hear me," Trenam cried.

The entire room fell silent as the king turned to look upon him. Trenam, too, was lost for words as he gazed upon the great man. The king stood tall, taller than any other there. The king's face was a cast of solid lines and quiet power. The crown upon his head only added to his stature. Vines interwove with lacing peaks and veins of gold running through them.

"Speak and I will listen," the king said.

"O mighty king, I come from the north where two days ago my brother was taken captive. I tried to find him but it was no use. Without your help I fear I will never see him again."

"Who was it that took your brother?"

"Greenkind, my lord."

"The Greenkind have no quarrel with Arnoc. Why should they take your brother?"

Trenam could no more lie to the king than he could save Naleer on his own. "He was trespassing on their lands."

"Then their justice has been done. I cannot interfere." His words cut Trenam deeply. The servant took him by the arm.

"No, please! You must save him," Trenam wept as he was pulled from the throne room. "Tannen com sunin! Tannen com sunin!"

"Wait," the king called after them.

The servant brought Trenam before the king once more.

"Forgive me, my child. May Orum himself watch over your brother until we reach him." The king led Trenam through long, sunlit hallways to a massive courtyard filled with trees radiant with cherry blossoms. A horse waited for them there. The king mounted the steed and pulled Trenam up behind him. They rode swiftly from the courtyard.

Every second took them farther from Entaramu and closer to the Greenkind. On every path the land leveled. Hills that had slowed Trenam's journey south simply rolled away or split apart, leaving a plain trek for them. And the ravines that threatened him before rose up to give them secure passage. Branches lifted to create hallways of leaves as they pushed through the night. As dawn's light streamed from the east they reached the forest's edge where Naleer had been taken.

The king stepped to the edge of the wood. His crown came alive in the morning light. He slid his sword from its scabbard. At the sound of the blade the branches pulled back and the brush scurried away. A wide path cleared before him. He sheathed his sword and stepped over the threshold. Trenam followed in amazement. Every chain of ivy, every tangled patch of bracken pulled away from the king to reveal the ground beneath. The forest held no secrets from the Earthking. They walked for nearly an hour when the ground revealed a small boy tied to the roots of a tree.

"Naleer!" Trenam cried. He ran to his brother and pulled at the ropes only to be shoved back by the hands of the Greenkind. They stood like oaks in the stark light of morning.

"Leave the boy go," the king said.

"The hand of an Earthking has not moved us for a thousand years. Would you break that trust?" one of the Greenkind, a tall one with arms like tree bark, asked.

"I do not seek to endanger that treaty, but I will not leave without the boy."

There would be nothing the forest dwellers could do to stop the king should he choose to act, for the Greenkind are made of trees and of earth and of the breath of the wind. As such they are under the Earthking's domain. But they are also men who were given a will and minds of their own.

"Would you be so blinded by your justice that you would cause me to break the oath?" the king said.

The Greenkind gathered together to make their decision. Was one child worth the collapse of a peace they had known for a millennia? They turned back to the king and announced, "The boy is yours, but let him be warned: there will be no tolerance for such a trespass again."

"It is understood," the king said. He turned to Naleer. "Should you be so foolish to enter these lands again your fate will be with the Sons of Earth."

With the bargain having been reached, Naleer was released. He fell immediately into his brother's arms. The three of them stepped back into Arnoc and the curtains of the forest drew shut behind them. The king returned to Entaramu with Naleer swearing to never cross into the Greenkind lands again. The boys never forgot the power of their king and all the Earthkings, whose reign lasted through a thousand generations.

—ɯ—

Silence filled the crew's quarters leaving the creak of the ship and the squeak of the swaying lantern to fill the void.

"What does that mean?" Yntor finally asked.

"What does what mean?" Caménor said.

"What the boy said to the king. 'Tanning come sunny'?"

"I was wondering the same thing," Deel said.

"Tannen com sunin," Caménor replied. "It means 'Where is my deliverer?'."

"I've never heard that before. Where's it from?" Deel asked.

Col had never heard it either.

"It was of the cry of the Sons of Heaven at the zenith of the Great Rebellion. Their enemies had driven them to the cliffs of the Eternal Sea. Hope was nearly lost and the heavens would belong to the dark Numen. In their final moment of desperation they cried out, 'Tannen com sunin!' Where is our deliverer? Hearing their cries Orum stepped into the fray and struck his rod upon the ground. The dissenters, every last one of them, were hurled from the heavens and the rebellion was ended with that single act."

"Why didn't Orum come sooner?" Col asked.

"Because it's a story, boy." They turned around to see the Captain leaning on the doorpost behind them. He held a half empty cup in his hand. His hair, which Col had only ever seen pulled tightly back, hung in tangled strands over his face. "And that's all it is. That's all any of them are. Orum, the Greenkind, Earthkings," he said with a scowl. "They're all fables that do nothing but keep hands from working. Supper's over. Get back to work. And you," he poked a finger at Caménor. "Save your stories for land. They've got no place at sea."

Caménor rose from his chair and matched his height with the Captain. "I've always found that men at sea are the ones most in need of a good story, Captain."

"My ship, my rules." The Captain took another gulp before giving a lingering sneer and leaving them.

CHAPTER 11

THE LONGEST NIGHT

TEPHALL WRESTLED A LARGE ROCK from the frozen soil. He pushed it to the side and furiously heaved more dirt from Nabal's grave. At last, he heard the hollow scrape of the shovel on the casket. He dropped to his knees and swept the soil from the lid. Using the shovel like an ax, he smashed through the wooden top. The wood had softened in the moist earth and split easily. He slipped numb fingers into the hole and pulled away the rotting planks. A gut wrenching stench followed the splintering lid. Tephall held his sleeve over his face and pulled the planks from over Nabal's decaying corpse.

A crow sounded from a nearby tree. Its cackle filled the dismal cemetery. Tephall looked down at what remained of his friend: a sunken face with deep sockets staring up at him.

"I need you now more than ever, old friend." Tephall took Nabal's withering head in his hands and lifted the body toward him. "Why is this happening? I know you know! You always knew. This curse, this misery, it all started with you. Tell me why!" His screams sent the crow flapping from the tree. "You were my closest friend and when I need you the most you give me nothing." He dropped Nabal back into his grave.

Nabal's head twisted to the side and his jaw fell open. Tephall leaned close and saw for himself the torn stump where the man's tongue had once been.

The sound of hooves on the cold ground preceded Wembus' breathless call. "Your highness?" Wembus knelt beside the grave. He held his hand out to Tephall.

"He won't answer me, Wembus. He can't answer me."

"I know, my lord. He's dead."

"He has no tongue." He accepted Wembus' hand and climbed from the hole. He squinted his eyes against the sun's reflection in the snow. "You were right, Wembus."

"I'm sorry, my lord. I wish things were different."

"It may be far worse than we imagine, my friend. Far worse."

"Come, my lord. Let us leave this place. It's not good for us to be here."

"No, I needed to be here. My old friend has opened my eyes once more. We have work to do and we've wasted so much time already." He reached out a hand to Wembus. "Come close, good man."

Wembus took his outstretched hand. Tephall's other hand went like a snake to Wembus' mouth and squeezed his jaw open. "Let me see it!" he said. "Let me see that you're not one of them. Where is it? Where is your tongue?" His muddy fingers probed Wembus' mouth until he felt it. "Good."

Wembus spit the mud from his mouth and wiped his lips clean.

"I'm returning to Ten Rocks now."

"I'll see that Nabal is laid to rest again, my lord."

"No! Pull him from the ground. I want him burned. I'll not risk the Noflim trying to take him again." He untied his horse from a nearby tree and swiftly swung his leg over the saddle.

"Burn him? But he's already dead. He's of no use to the Noflim."

"Since when do you dictate what the spirits can and cannot use?"

"You don't think it excessive, your highness?"

"Our families are dead and my kingdom is under threat. Nothing is in excess. Feed him to the flames!"

—∞—

For nearly two days Col wrapped his hands around the chipped wooden handle of a coarse brush. He scrubbed every surface of the Flapper but the Captain held standards far higher than Col had met. So he scoured again only to be ordered to do it once more. After the third cleaning Col was sure the sea water had seeped through his blistered fingers and would soon pour from his ears. Every time the Captain walked by Col resisted the urge to throw the brush at his head.

The next day Col reluctantly poured himself from his hammock. He ate a quick breakfast and raced the sun to the deck. He hardly remembered what it was like to sleep as late as he wanted. Those days were dreams themselves now.

The Captain walked on deck. His dark hair was pulled tightly back and hung in a loose tail over his neck. His beard was freshly combed and for once he wasn't surrounded by the stench of liquor. "I suppose this deck is as clean as your puny hands will get it, grub."

Col glared at him but said nothing.

"There'll be time to try again." He looked at his son, who stood rubbing a bleary eye in the morning light. "Ready the nets, Yntor. Today, we fish!"

"This is it. This is our spot," Yntor said to Col as they pulled the nets from the ship's hold. "Take a look around. Do you see any other ships?"

Col dropped the net on deck and scanned the horizon. The Flapper floated alone on a sheen of blue. "There's no one," he said.

"That's because only the best sailors know this is where the whitefish Winter. And the Captain is the best there is."

"Of course he is." Col rolled his eyes. "But why do the fish come here for the Winter?"

"Only the Captain knows for sure. There's something about the water here. It makes them taste better, too."

Deel joined them and together the three of them cast the nets into the water. Deel showed Col how to hold the net for a good throw and how to cinch the ends shut as they pulled it in. Col did the best he could but his hands still hurt from days of scrubbing. When the first net was full Caménor joined them. They used a maze of tackle and pulleys as they strained at the ropes. Before long they dropped a net full of twitching whitefish into the hold. The effort caused every muscle in Col's back and arms to cry out but there would be no respite for him.

After a full day of casting empty nets and dragging in full ones Col was ready to collapse. Every part of him felt as though it had reached its limit.

He ate silently while Deel and Caménor exalted in the day's fortune. Yntor had delivered the Captain's meal but was gone longer than usual.

Col scraped the last of the mush from his plate and pushed himself from the table. He stumbled to his hammock and climbed in. He kicked the boots from his swollen feet and was just pulling the blanket to his chin when Yntor interrupted him.

"The Captain wants to see you, Col."

"Can't it wait until morning?"

"I'd hurry if I were you, Colby," Deel interjected. "The Captain isn't one to be kept waiting."

Col jumped down and pitched forward as he landed. He steadied himself and pulled his boots back on before climbing on deck. He knocked once on the Captain's door and it opened.

"Oh, it's you," the Captain said.

"You wanted to see me?"

"It looks like we've got a storm coming our way. You'll be on watch tonight."

Col felt a surge of despair. "I worked all day," he protested. "I can barely stand."

"You don't work as hard as the others, grub. Don't pretend you do. I watched you standing around half the day."

"How long will I be on watch?"

"You'll be on all night. The others need to rest."

"That's not fair!"

"And if I catch you sleeping I won't even bother whipping you. I'll whip Yntor. Think about that while you're keeping an eye out for the storm." He shut the door and left Col standing alone on deck.

Tears welled in Col's eyes. He wanted to go home. He wanted to be off this horrid little boat and away from its monstrous commander. When was this misery going to end?

He turned around to find Caménor watching him.

"I'm sorry, Col."

"You heard what he said?"

"It's not right."

"Why didn't you say anything?"

"This is his ship, Col. His word is law here. I have no authority."

"You're a prince. Of course you have authority!

"Quiet, Col. Someone will hear you."

"No, you're not a prince, are you? You're a coward. I can't believe my father trusted you to protect me. Arnoc can be glad you weren't born first or we'd have a pathetic, spineless dog for a king."

"That's enough, Col. I know this is hard, but it'll all be over soon." Caménor's eyes rested on Col for a moment before he disappeared down the steps.

Col was never more glad to be alone. It wasn't just his body that was tired. He was tired of seeing the same four faces all the time. There was so little solitude to be found on the ship and his rage only made him long for it more.

A heavy cover of clouds obscured his view of the lights beyond. With the sun gone, the already cold sea air gained a fury in its chill that forced Col to keep moving to stay warm. He'd grown accustomed to moving about the tossing ship but, now, with the sails drawn and the anchor dropped, there was only a gentle sway to the sleeping timbers. His footing felt almost steady.

An hour passed and Col was losing his battle with fatigue. He slumped against the mast and watched the door to the Captain's cabin in between bouts with his falling eyelids. He imagined all of the things he'd do to the Captain once he became king. He could have him thrown naked into the wilderness or made to dress like a woman and prance around Edlin for the rest of his life. Better yet, he could make him the lowest of the low on a ship just like this and enslave him under some other tyrant of a captain.

He drifted between daydream and sleep while he devised his tortures but those images were always interrupted by the thought of the Captain taking the lash to Yntor's back. The boy was so small and worked so hard to please his father, but the Captain never took notice.

Thinking of Yntor brought Mino to mind. Col hoped his brother was having a better time in hiding than he was. He knew Mino would never have been able to handle life at sea. And Tonn would have given up long ago.

A footstep on the deck jolted Col awake. He jumped up. A shock of terror coursed through him.

"Easy now," Caménor said. "Deel thought these might help you stay awake." He held out a sack the size of a potato. Col took it and poured out a handful of dark beans. He put one in his mouth and chewed carefully. It was bitter and crumbled on his tongue.

"Ugh!" he spit it out. "I don't think getting sick is what I need now. Why aren't you sleeping?"

"I was worried about you."

"Why should you be worried? You're the one who brought me here in the first place."

"I know you're mad at me but this was the lesser of two evils. Staying on land would have only given us a different set of hardships and as much as you hate this it doesn't compare with starving to death."

"So to keep me safe you put me in the devil's hands? I'd have been safer if I'd stayed with my father."

"Maybe, but you're here with me now and I'm doing all I can to protect you."

"You keep saying that but I don't feel safe."

Caménor sighed. “The Captain is a harsh man but he won’t harm you. I’ve got to go back below deck. If he catches me up here it’ll be bad for both of us.” He hugged Col briefly. Col remained stiff.

Col was alone again and the first flakes of the coming storm began to lay on the deck. He popped another bean in his mouth only to spit it out. He tried another one. They may have tasted awful but they might be working.

He held his arms close to his chest and balled his hands in his armpits. He chewed on the bitter beans through the night and almost came to enjoy the flavor. He busied himself sweeping the sticking snow from the deck and rails as the flakes gathered. Had he not been so frustrated he may have thought it beautiful. The clouds held a dim glow and the snow dotted the air around him. It was only Col and a million tiny ships sailing from the heavens to a cold sea.

The Captain opened his door and leered out at Col twice during the night. Both times Col stared back with eyes open wide.

As dawn approached the wind batted at the rigging. The crew stirred and Col was finally able to sit down to breakfast. Sitting was dangerous. Even for a few minutes. He felt he could fall asleep anywhere. There would be no sleeping now, though. A day’s work awaited him. The Captain would give him no reprieve from his duties. By the time he climbed back on deck the falling snow had turned to a stinging sleet.

The Captain stood at the rail of the quarterdeck. “We’ve got fish to catch, boys! Never mind the weather.”

Col thought his face looked harder than usual and his tongue seemed to bend with a slur.

Col lightly slapped himself. He needed to be alert. The rain quickly soaked him, even through the seal skin coat he wore, and he shivered beneath the heavy layers. He stumbled sideways and nearly fell into the rail. He helped Yntor cast the nets as wave after wave smashed into the Flapper’s side.

Yntor leaned in and tried to whisper over the wind. "You just help a little, Col. I’ll do most of the work.”

Col looked back at the Captain who trained a hard glare on him.

"I'll be okay," Col said.

"Colby," Deel called him. "I need you to go below and make sure the food lockers are secure. We can't afford to have our supplies dumping in this storm."

Col moved to the ladder with halting gait as the ship tilted violently. He put his foot onto the first step. A thin sheet of ice covered it. He crashed onto the floor below. Chunks of ice crackled on his coat. He painfully got to his feet and checked on the food lockers. They were fine, but he took an extra minute to sit down. If anyone asked he'd say he had to secure them.

He crawled back on deck in time to see a net slide from Yntor's hands into the water. The Captain was on him in seconds.

"You stupid piece of trash!" The back of his hand lashed across Yntor's face.

"I'm sorry! I was trying to pull it in but there was too much ice," Yntor protested.

"You never pull in a net on your own, boy! You know that." The Captain raised his knee and planted a boot into Yntor's chest. The boy flew across the deck.

"I'm sorry, Father. I didn't mean to," Yntor gasped as he tried to turn over.

"What did you call me?"

"Captain! I'm sorry, Captain." Yntor's knee slipped on the ice. He fell on his chest again. Col looked at Caménor who watched along with Deel. Both men were silent. Was no one going to do anything? Were they going to stand by while the Captain killed his own son?

Watch closely Caménor, Col thought. This is what courage looks like. This is what it is to take action in the face of evil.

Col lunged at the Captain. He howled like a madman as he drove himself into the Captain's gut, but the man was strong and used to the swaying of a ship at sea. He quickly caught himself and used the momentum of Col's force against him. He swung Col around and tossed him into the air like so many of the nets he'd thrown.

Col felt himself flying. The cry from his lips disappeared in the wind. The deck beneath him was gone. He saw only the tossing black waters. He plunged into the icy waves. He surfaced for a moment and was dragged under by the weight of his coat. The frigid water closed in on him like a vise. He saw the shimmer of the Flapper above before darkness wrapped itself around him.

CHAPTER 12

THANIR

It wasn't coarse sand or unforgiving coral under Col when he twitched to life. It was smooth marble. His hand played over the cool surface. He lay in a shallow puddle. His coat and hair were still dripping. The air around him was vibrant with warmth and light. He still shivered. He knew he was awake but refused to open his eyes. If he was dead opening his eyes would only confirm it. He lay there for some time skimming his hand over the puddle. It felt real. As real as anything he'd ever known. As real as the panic he'd felt when the waters closed in on him.

He opened his eyes and stared into a gray sky. Tree limbs craned over him. There was no breeze but something stirred. There was a busyness in the trees.

He sat up and his ears buzzed like someone had shoved a beehive into his skull. He peeled off his coat and took deep breaths. The bees ceased their swarming and left him with a dull throbbing instead. His limbs ached like he was a doll two children had fought over.

He blinked and saw he wasn't outside at all. He was in a long hallway. Trees grew along the walls, within the walls. Their branches arched and splayed to hold the ceiling up. Torches blazed between them. Their light reflected on the marble floor.

"Hello," he called. The only greeting that came was an echo of his voice.

He stood and left his coat on the floor. It'd be a starting point for him to return to. He walked down the hall. He went further and further without any sign of change. It stretched on and on ahead of him. There had to be someone around here. He ran back to his coat but neither it nor the puddle were anywhere to be found.

He pressed on until the hallway suddenly forked. Left or right? Both looked exactly the same to him.

"Is there anyone here?" he called again. He realized he didn't know who, or what, could be waiting for him here. It was best to stay quiet.

He sensed movement to his right. He chose to go left. The hallway emptied into a large room. A long stone table filled the center of the room. Rigid lines etched across the table to form twelve even strips. Its surface was glassy with swirls of white and blue swimming through it. The colors stretched along the floor and up the walls.

There was no seam between the table and the floor. It was as though the room and everything in it had all been carved from the same stone. Col looked back the way he'd come and suddenly realized what was wrong with the hallway. There were no windows, no doors. It wasn't a hallway. It was a tunnel. A tunnel under the sea?

It didn't make sense. Who else was here? Torches didn't light themselves.

The room was beginning to feel too small. He felt like the tunnel would collapse and crush him. He had to get out of here. He started to run but stopped at the sound of stone scraping over stone.

He turned around. The table had sunk below the floor. The grooved strips now formed steps leading to a chamber below. A wisp of light cast itself on the bottom step. Col descended into another room. It was larger and longer than the one above. A light shone far ahead of him. He stepped forward and his eyes slowly adjusted in the dark. Dead leaves shuffled beneath his feet and scraped along the stone floor. The sound unnerved him. The walls were bare rock. Water dripped lazily from the cragged ceiling. The light ahead of him grew brighter. It came from the wall at the far end of the cavern. Col ran to it, his feet kicking through the leaves until he stood before what was not a wall but two immense stone doors.

On each door was a spindly tree. Their trunks were carved deep into the stone but turned to living branches that grew from the door. A swirling pool was etched across the seam of the doors. Col touched the middle carving and his hand came away wet.

At the center of the spring was a small hole. This was the source of the light that surrounded him. He knelt and put his eye to it. He saw blue sky washing across the horizon. He felt the warmth of a Summer sun just seeing it. Below the white tufts of meandering clouds was a green field with long grass bowing in the breeze. The only thing breaking the solitude of the plain was the presence of two tall trees. Cradled in the ground between the trees was a small spring reflecting the blue above.

Derid's grove.

This couldn't be real. It was just a story. He considered again the possibility that he was dead. If he found Tonn wandering the halls he'd know for sure.

He set his eye back to the keyhole. A ripple spread across the pool. The sight chilled him and he trembled. Though he couldn't say why.

"He is still held there. As firm as the day he was condemned."

Col lurched to the side. The one who addressed him stood with feet silently atop the fallen leaves. His entire being shone like sunlight on water. His skin was a patchwork of translucent leaves, veins and points running together. He had no eyes, only depressions of light on either side of a thinly curving nose.

"Do not be afraid, young prince. Your line is known to us."

"Us?" Col asked.

"Yes. We are Thanir." The being motioned and Col saw that four more just like him moving about the room. Each exuded the same light.

The Thanir's appearance did little to calm Col's fear. "There was a ripple in the water. Why?" He was trembling.

"He still fights against his bonds but he will never free himself. Even with all his power he is helpless."

"Who?"

"The Unnamed One, a Numinous cast from Heaven. He is captive beneath the spring where the roots of the trees twist endlessly around him. It is his punishment for leading the rebellion so long ago."

"What if someone tries to free him?"

The Thanir looked down at him, a wave of concern spreading through the light of his face. "How much truth has been lost, young one? There are those who no longer remember the light they once possessed. The Noflim were like us once, but they were twisted and filled with darkness after the Numen fell. Their only purpose is to free their master. They and their servants, the Kheva Adem, are ever working to that end. That is why you've been brought here, to Entaramu."

"Entaramu?"

"NéPrince Colmeron, the Numen is the reason your line was given dominion over the land. The sacred duty of the Earthkings is to protect Entaramu. You must guard the sacred grove and ensure the Numen is never freed. That is your purpose."

Col stared at the Thanir. "I can't —," he began.

"You must," the Thanir said. He placed his hand on Col's head.

At the being's touch the room burst with flagrant light. Col's body flooded with warmth. Every ache, every bruise and blister he'd gained was suddenly gone. He relaxed and his body slumped sideways on the floor.

Col's feet were wet. His boots were soaked all the way through and his stockings stuck to cold toes. His spent body draped over a pockmarked rock rising from sand. The tide had reached his feet.

An ebbing wave splashed his face. He huffed and snorted. He shivered and saw he wasn't wearing his coat. He'd lost it somewhere, hadn't he?

He tried to remember where, but it was all so hazy. His feet squished in his boots. It would have been enough to make him miserable were he not so glad to be alive. There were only a handful of islands in the Enturion Sea but somehow he'd managed to wash up on one of them. A beach, rough with broken coral, stones and sand, stretched around him. Beyond the beach was a dense, steep slope of trees naked for the Winter. How odd that they should clothe themselves only for the warmth of Spring and Summer.

Behind him the Enturion consumed the horizon. The sun held itself high in a cloudless sky. The light warmed his cheeks but the wind off the water nipped at him through his clothes. He needed to get warm.

He leaped from the rock to the shore. Awkwardly splayed on the beach ahead of him was what looked to be the carcass of an animal, a wolf perhaps. He crept quietly toward it. It was his coat. He shook the sand from it. To his surprise it was dry. How long had it been laying there? For that matter, how long had he been laid across that rock? He put his coat on still convinced he'd lost it somewhere.

His memory may have been a blur but one thing was for sure: that despicable wasp of a captain had thrown him overboard. Now Col was stranded.

He turned inland and made for the trees. If he was to survive he needed to see where he was. He'd taken a stand against the Captain. He'd withstood everything the man had thrown at him. He replayed the scene in his mind as he climbed between creaking trunks of aging alders.

He would find a way off this island and back home again. He was certain of it.

He grabbed hold of a shallow ledge and pulled himself up. He stood at eye level with the treetops. Their tips pointed at him. He swatted at the one nearest him and kept up the steep side of the island's sole peak. He needed to go higher. He needed to see whatever could be seen. There had to be a way off this island.

Blisters swelled on his feet and he was sweating beneath his coat. Taking it off would do no good, though, since the higher he climbed the sharper the wind snapped.

He came to a wall of sheer rock. It didn't matter. He had to keep going. His hand found a crevice he could've sworn hadn't been there a moment ago. He struggled against his own weight and the bulk of his coat as he strained higher and higher.

At last, he reached the pinnacle and rolled onto a dry plateau. He stood with his hands behind his head and surveyed the world around him. The sea consumed the distance. He was alone, stranded like the moon on a starless night.

But even the moon found her way home eventually.

The peak was home to a small grove of thin birches. They huddled around a wide patch of bare earth like a company of men keeping guard. Their even stances spiked upward like the spires of a crown atop the island. He walked their perimeter. The branches above arched in a wide circle, like dancers reaching graceful arms. There was something strange about these trees. He touched one.

Beneath years of moss and the raging of the seasons the birches were not trees of wood but of stone.

Trees of stone.

He looked closer to find intricate patterns flitting lightly through the smooth bark. All lines led to a single shape, that of a simple tree: a curving line for roots and a single upward line for the trunk. The line split and curled into short branches. He moved from tree to tree. Every birch showed this design but one. The middle tree had a small, swirling pool carved into it. Col felt he should know this shape. Then, like a ship gliding into a slip, the thought he'd been reaching for came to him.

Entaramu.

Had it been real? He looked down at his hand. His fingers still felt wet from where he'd touched the carving of the pool. He reached for the same pattern on the tree before him, hesitated, and touched it. His fingers were suddenly dry. The image began to weep. Slowly at first until a steady stream poured from the carving. It pooled between two roots and suddenly drained. A hole the size of a man's head remained. Col bent to peer inside. He reached inside and pulled out a small iron box. It was hardly bigger than his hand.

He wiped a layer of dirt away to reveal the same symbol that was on the doors. And on the trees. The Earthkings' seal was branded onto the box's lid. He pulled at it. It resisted him. The harder he tried the more stubborn it was. He gave up and looked at the stone trees surrounding him.

The Thanir's final words rang in Col's ears. Protect Entaramu. He wasn't even sure where Entaramu was let alone how to protect it. His thoughts were interrupted by the sight of a familiar sail in the water below.

CHAPTER 13

AN UNEASY BARGAIN

TEPHALL ONLY WENT TO THE Western tower when he had to. He hated heights. His sons, on the other hand, were always venturing to new zeniths. Colmeron, especially, loved this tower.

Now, this was the only place Tephall felt secure from prying ears. He noticed ears everywhere these days. They all had them. Every one of them. They each had two, in fact. But it didn't matter how many ears they had so long as they each had one tongue. And as of yesterday they all did.

The latch clicked behind him. He grabbed the handle and yanked the hatch open. "Where were you?" Tephall demanded.

"I'm sorry, your highness," Wembus said. "It took time to ensure I wasn't seen." He climbed up and closed the hatch behind him.

"Open your mouth."

Wembus obeyed but his eyes failed to meet Tephall's.

"You think I don't trust you, Wembus."

Wembus said nothing and turned his head to look beyond their perch in the clouds. A stray blackbird swooped below them and disappeared into the trees.

"Trust is a luxury not even a king can afford. I dined on it for far too many years. Blindly. Stupidly." Tephall sat on the bench and wrapped his cloak around his chest.

"These are dangerous times, my lord. I know that."

"You never married, Wembus. Why is that?"

"My life was given in service of the crown. My family is the souls within these walls."

"I suppose I should applaud your sacrifice. If anything you were saved from a great deal of pain. As king, the whole of Arnoc are my family to watch over. But it's not the same, you know, once you have children of your own. Real children. No, there's so much more worrying, so much more agonizing over them."

"And love."

"And love. Love for my sons is the root from which all these agonies bloom. That's why I need you to do something for me."

"You have but to ask, my king."

"Bring my sons home, Wembus. I've sent them into a cruel world. And our enemy waits for them there. I will not lose another one of my children."

"Is it any safer for them here, my lord?"

"Where can they be safe if not with me? I'm their father!"

"But when you sent them away—"

"I was grieving. I wasn't thinking clearly. Besides, I know our enemy now and I want my sons brought home."

Wembus hesitated. "Of course. I'll see to it."

"And Wembus..."

"Yes?"

"Their safety and yours are one now. Bring them to me."

Col climbed down from the peak as fast as he could. His feet slid on the rock face as his hands gripped knots and crevices. The box stuffed under his shirt was cold against his bare skin. It threatened to jar loose. He jumped the last few feet to the ground. He sped down the hill and grabbed at bared trunks to keep himself from toppling forward.

The Flapper dropped anchor. A rowboat was lowered on ropes Col knew all too well.

How did they know he was here? Were they searching all the islands? Had Caménor finally taken control?

He was nearly to the beach when his shipmates moored the rowboat and jumped into the knee-high surf. Col stopped short of the tree line where he was still hidden in the shadows.

Something was wrong.

There were no shouts or calls for him. They weren't looking around. Deel's eyes were down. Yntor was crying like the little boy he was never allowed to be. The Captain looked straight ahead. His eyes were set like the steady prow of his ship. His dark hair hung in limp curls over most of his face but when his head turned Col saw it was bruised. One eye was swollen shut and his upper lip showed an ugly split.

Caménor's hands were tied behind his back and his mouth was gagged. Once they were on the beach the Captain pushed him to his knees and grunted something to Deel through a tight jaw. Captain Vylsom folded his arms across his broad chest and watched as Deel grudgingly pulled a curved blade from his belt.

The rock was in Col's hand before he knew what he was going to do. He hurled the sharp stone through the air. His foot snapped a small branch as he moved. The Captain turned toward the sound and the rock punched him on the side of the head. He stumbled to the side. Blood ran down his cheek. He charged for the tree line like a bear after a hunter.

Col picked another stone from the ground and rushed to meet him. He emerged from the shadow. He cocked his arm back but as he came into the light the Captain stopped. He wiped the blood from his face and stared at Col.

"I don't care if it takes every stone on this island. Touch him and I'll kill you," Col said. All eyes were on him now. Deel's knife fell to the sand and Yntor stifled his tears.

Caménor struggled free of the gag. "Col?"

"I'm not kidding, Vylsom. If you hurt him it'll take more than drowning to stop me this time."

"I can see that," the Captain replied.

"Captain?" Deel said.

"What is it, Deel?"

"The boy's alive."

"Yes, Deel. I see him."

"It's a second chance, Captain. There's no need for anymore of this," Deel said.

"Why shouldn't I leave them both here to die? They've been nothing but trouble from the start."

Caménor got a foot under him and pushed himself up. "Because you're a man of your word, Captain. We worked to earn our passage and let's not forget the two horses in your barn. We had an agreement and you've still got your end to uphold."

"Please, Captain," Yntor begged.

"We can drop them at the closest port," Deel said. "We could have them on land by morning if the wind's right. What do you say, Captain?"

The Captain looked up at the island's peak, exposing his bruised face to the sunlight. "Put down your stone, boy. You and your father will be our guests until morning. If we haven't reached port by then you'll swim the rest of the way. You seem to be good at that."

Caménor's bonds were cut. Col dropped his rock and the two embraced. Caménor squeezed until Col was sure his ribs would crack.

"I thought you were gone!"

"I'm alright."

"Alright? You should be dead.'"

"I'm not sure I wasn't."

The others waited for them in the rowboat. "Hurry up or I might reconsider stranding you here," the Captain bellowed over the surf.

"What happened to his face?" Col asked quietly. "Did you do that?"

"That's what they tell me. I don't remember anything after he threw you overboard. Everything went black. I woke tied up below deck. My knuckles were covered in blood. I don't think much of it was my own."

Col grinned.

"What?" Caménor said.

"Nothing. I guess I'm proud of you."

"Thanks. If you hadn't shown up today my temper would have gotten me killed this time."

They climbed into the crowded rowboat. Yntor threw his arms around Col and wordlessly held on. Deel rowed them back to the Flapper. As Col stood to grab the rope ladder Yntor whispered to him. "Thank you."

Col was probably the only person to ever come to his defense. He wished he could do more to protect him.

Something was different on board. Deel quickly lowered the sail and the canvas caught a southerly wind. The Captain shut himself in his cabin and Col could scarcely turn around without tripping over Yntor. Still, he managed to escape for a few moments to hide his treasure beneath the blanket in his hammock.

A crescent moon emerged from distant waves. Its light filling the sail as they got under way. Deel stayed at the wheel while Caménor, Col and Yntor went below deck. They sat down to the first meal Col had had since his night on watch. Food had been the last thing on his mind but sitting down to a bowl of cold stew and dry bread, it was all he could do to keep from stealing the others' food when they weren't looking.

A strange silence settled over the meal. More of the disease that permeated the ship.

"How did you survive?" Yntor asked. The words felt out of place.

"I don't know. I remember hitting the water. After that there was nothing until I woke up on the island."

"Oh."

Col hated lying but how could he explain what had really happened? Yntor yawned and stretched before excusing himself.

Caménor cleared the table and the two of them played a game of cards. Once they heard the doleful moans coming from Yntor's hammock the game ended.

"You were gone four days, Col. What aren't you telling me," Caménor said.

Four days! He'd been gone four days? How was that possible? "I wasn't on that island very long, Uncle Cam."

"You were at sea, then?"

"No."

"Then where?"

"Entaramu."

"Entaramu." The word drifted between them like the first breath after a good cry.

"I saw something while I was there."

He leaned forward. "What did you see?"

"I saw the grove where Derid fought the bear. The trees and the spring, it was all there."

"It's real! I never would have thought...," he covered his mouth with his hand.

"You didn't think it was real?"

"It's been a thousand years, Col. Sometimes you believe without really knowing and sometimes that trust proves itself."

"I saw it, Caménor. I saw Entaramu. I was there. It's real."

"What else did you see?"

"I saw—" Col hesitated. "—that was it. I saw the grove and the next thing I knew I was waking up on the island. Four days later."

"Something is happening, Col. The Kheva Adem have returned and now you tell me you've been to Entaramu. Orum is at work. You, dear nephew, are going to be a great king."

"You'll be with me, though, right?"

"I promise I will be right here as long as I can draw a breath."

A great king. A guardian to protect Entaramu. There was nothing Col wanted less right now. He wanted his life back and telling Caménor the truth about what he'd seen would only drive him further from that life.

"Get some rest, Col. We'll finally be on land again tomorrow."

Col agreed and retired to his bed. He wrapped himself in his hammock like a caterpillar in a cocoon, ready to be born anew with the dawn.

Col knew Arnoc was near as soon as he stepped on deck the following morning. The air was different. The tossing of the waves was lighter.

Deel chewed his bitter beans at the wheel. He'd guided them through the night. Soon they would part ways and he would rest. Caménor joined them on deck and breathed deep.

"It seems we've reached the end of our journey together, my friends," Deel said.

"I don't know that we would've made it this far without you, Deel," Caménor said.

"Come on, you're both sturdy sailors now. Though, I can say we've never had a voyage quite like this one. I don't think Yntor will soon forget it either," Deel said.

"And the Captain?" Col asked.

"I think the Captain has learned a thing or two. Though he may never admit it." He guided them into a harbor.

In the distance a few early risers moved about the docks. Col watched them with an odd fascination, like an old man seeing the home of his youth.

"It's called Rakken, this port," Deel said.

"I've never been so happy to see strangers," Col said.

"You'll miss the water. You'll see."

"If I live to be a hundred without seeing the Enturion again I will die in peace."

"This from the boy who became a fish when the sea should've taken him? Bah! I don't believe it."

Col laughed. "A fish? Is that what you think happened?"

"It's the only thing that makes sense."

"Then a fish I was. I suppose I should be glad I didn't end up in one of your nets."

The Flapper eased her way to an open dock and dropped anchor. The gangway was lowered and what few possessions Col and Caménor had were in sacks thrown over their shoulders. Col nearly tumbled down the board as a pair of arms wrapped around his waist.

"Goodbye, Yntor," Col said.

"I'm sorry you have to go, Colby. I wish I could come with you."

"Me too, but I think your mother would be very sad if you didn't come home to her."

"I know, but I'm going to miss you."

"I'll miss you, too, friend." Col returned the embrace. "You're a great sailor and someday you'll make a great captain."

"Do you think?"

"I've never been more sure of anything." He pried the boy's arms from his waist. Col followed Caménor onto the dock and they waved a final goodbye to their shipmates. They took their first steps on Arnocean soil with the cheers of gulls sounding above them. The market square was still empty as they followed the stone street. Col looked back to see the Captain emerge from his cabin. Not a word had passed between them since the island and Col would be content if there were never another.

"Do you think Yntor will be okay?" Col asked.

"I think so, yes."

"The Captain would've killed him that day. You know that, don't you?"

"I told you, the Captain is a harsh man but he's not a murderer. I don't believe he meant to throw you from the ship like that. He was drunk. I'd say finding you alive was more of a relief to him than any of us realize. Killing changes a man and for four days the Captain lived with the weight of ending your life."

"He was going to kill you, too. Or have you forgotten that already?"

"No, I haven't forgotten. Once he thought you were dead everything changed. I'd say for the first time in his life he didn't know what to do."

"That's your excuse for him nearly slashing your throat?"

"It's not an excuse, Col. Men can crack under such strain. They can do things they wouldn't normally do. I'm not saying what he did was right, far from it, but we've got enough to worry about without holding a grudge."

"I still hate him. He's an awful man. He should hope I never find him once I'm king."

"Hatred is something a king should never be familiar with, Col. Rail against what is evil, but rule with compassion for the wounded, mercy for the penitent, and justice for the corrupt."

"Fine. In the meantime, I'd say you gave him some justice for me."

"Another mark for my infamous temper."

Rakken was much smaller than Edlin and hibernated in the Winter. Its residents huddled beneath warm blankets in front of blazing hearths, modest though they might be. None knew of the two strangers passing through their midst.

It was good to be on land again, not just in a tunnel below the sea or on an island in the middle of it. They may have been leagues away from Ten Rocks but back on land Col felt he was home.

Their road ran beneath the shadows of evergreens on the banks of an ice crusted river. The smell of soil and tree invigorated Col. He felt like a part of himself had been starved and was suddenly at a banquet.

"Quiet!" Caménor's arm reached across Col's chest, stopping him suddenly.

"I wasn't saying anything."

"Shh! Get down. In that ditch there. Don't come out until I say so."

Col slid into a small gully by the riverbank. The low bending branches of a tall pine kept him hidden. This was it, wasn't it? The Noflim were finally going to make good on their threat. His mind raced back to the sacred grove and the Being trapped beneath it. His enemy had been patient, waiting for just the right moment. There was nothing he could do now.

CHAPTER 14
THE SWEEPS

COL TWISTED A LOOSE ROOT from the ground. He clutched it, ready to spring from his shelter. He listened for a sound, any sound, out of the ordinary. His breath hung like a ghost in the air.

The creak and croak of an oncoming wagon chased the ghost away. His concern vanished with it. Two voices grew louder as the wagon neared.

"Why do you always bring that up?" the first said.

"Because every time I invite you, you never come," the second replied.

"My cousin's wedding was that week. Was I supposed to miss that?"

Col stuck his head between bowing branches. He watched the wagon through the needles. It was drawn by two dusty mules while two equally dusty men sat side by side on the bench.

"You still could have come, Uzir. You know my little girl loves to see you. Though, I don't know why. I see you every day and I can barely stand you."

Col pushed the branches aside and stepped onto the road. The root was still in his hand.

The driver tugged on the reins and the wagon stopped suddenly. "We've got nothing of value here, young man. You may as well let us pass."

Caménor rushed out behind Col and tore the root from his hand. The men's faces were washed in fear as much as dirt.

"Peace, my friends. We're not here to cause trouble," Caménor said. He tossed the root into the river.

"You could've fooled us. Jumping out of the shadows like that! You and I seem to hold different meanings of the word 'peace'."

"My apologies. I'm Cameron. This is my son, Colby. He was told to hide until I knew it was safe." He cast an accusing eye at Col.

"He doesn't look like one for orders."

"He's not," Caménor said.

"I heard them talking," Col said. "If they're dangerous then so are the mice that scamper between the trees or the snow that falls from the sky."

"Did he just insult us?" said one of the men.

"I'm not sure. He might've meant we're as cute as mice and as lovely as snow," said the other.

"That's not what I meant," Col said.

"It's too late. That's how I take it to mean so that's what it is. Thank you very much."

"Where are you gentleman headed?" Caménor asked.

"I don't see how that's any of your concern," the first said.

"For all we know you and the funny boy are only making nice so you can rob us of our immense fortune," the second continued.

"You said you had nothing of value!" Col said.

"Friends, I assure you we're not here to harm you," Caménor said.

"So we're friends all of a sudden? And here I thought you were just two strangers leaping from the trees to frighten us," the first said.

"You don't even know our names," continued the second. "It seems to me that if we were such good friends you would know our names as well as our destination."

"Even friends of a lifetime have to learn such things at some point," Caménor said.

The two travelers looked at each other in silent conversation before giving their reply. "Well said! I don't think you are the brigand we feared so let us begin such a friendship. I am Uliz and this is my business partner, Uzir. This road takes us, and all who travel it, to the modest streets of Mondiso."

"Mondiso?" Caménor said.

"Mondiso."

"That is fantastic news!"

"Why is that?" Uzir asked.

"Because, Uzir, it is a wonderful thing to be lost only to find that you're on the right path after all. Our destination lies just beyond Mondiso."

Col was tired of standing in the cold. Someone needed to hurry this along. "How about a ride for your new friends?"

"I don't see why not," Uliz said. "What do you think, Uzir?"

"I guess we could accommodate them. Heaven knows I've already heard everything you have to say. A couple of fresh faces would be welcome."

Col and Caménor climbed into the back of the wagon. It was filled with soot caked brooms and tools that looked like porcupines on sticks. Col cleared a corner for himself and sat down.

"It's a harsh life, traveling through the Winter," Uliz commented. "Take your ease now. There's plenty of work to be done tomorrow, my friends."

"Tomorrow?" Col asked.

"Well, not tomorrow tomorrow. I mean tomorrow in the proverbial sense. The future."

"Oh."

"Don't worry, Colby. We've got a few days before we reach Mondiso. Until then, remember peace."

"What makes you think we've forgotten it?" Caménor asked.

"We all forget it somewhere along the way," Uzir said

Col leaned against the wagon's rail. The tension in his bones eased. There were no orders being barked at him or waves threatening to topple him. Neither was there any immediate cause for frantic fleeing. There was only the gentle creak of wheels turning slowly beneath them and the jovial bickering of his new companions.

He closed his eyes and tried to remember peace and the spirit of the life he'd once known. His mind hung in the gray between asleep and awake where visions spring from dreams and dreams heighten reality. When he woke his dreams vanished but a sense of them remained, like an unseen fly whose buzz is still heard.

The voices around him that had been so distant while he slept were now beside him. He opened his eyes to find the sun blooming gold in a clear sky.

"What is our friends' destination, then?" Uzir said.

"Home," Caménor said.

"Wonderful! How long has it been since you were home?"

"So long I can hardly remember what it looks like."

"That's a feeling we know very well. Life on the road can be hard but adventure is a call worth heeding. Still, home should never be forgotten," Uliz said.

"What adventure calls you to the road?" Caménor asked.

"We are skilled sweeps. The best you'll ever find," Uliz said.

"What's a sweep?" Col asked.

"A chimney sweep, lad. We clean the soot from your chimneys keeping them from catching fire and in turn saving the lives of men, women and children all across the kingdom. We are the unsung heroes of Arnoc."

"And he'll never let you forget it!" Uzir said.

Col had never known such easy going men. It seemed their cares were tossed in a sack and thrown into the back of the wagon along with their tools, left there until they were needed.

Col listened as Uliz and Uzir shared stories of their journeys.

"People have a strange habit of hiding things in their chimney only to forget about them. Then they have the poor sense of saying we're trying to steal them," Uliz said.

"What sort of things have you found?" Col asked.

"All kinds. Family valuables, old clothing, money, letters, paintings. Uzir once found a man's hand."

"The woman said it was her husband's," Uzir said. "She'd put it there as a warning to any spirits that would try to harm her or hers. It was a big hand."

"How long had her husband been dead?" Caménor asked.

"That's just it. He was standing right there, paying us for our service!"

Col laughed so hard he nearly rolled off the wagon. He was drunk with mirth and his new friends joined in his revelry. It was a refreshing day. He was filled and spent at once and though he'd done no work he was exhausted all the same. They set up camp along the side of the road. Uliz and Uzir spread a low canopy over the back of the wagon to sleep among their tools. Col and Caménor laid their beds in a small cove beneath boulder and branch. They lit the fire early and shared it until their companions retired to the wagon. Col slipped easily to sleep. Peace covered him like a fresh blanket.

The days that followed held more of the same and so much more. Col shared meals and cheer with his newfound friends.

Friends. It was the first time Col had ever called anyone by that name. He'd always had his brothers and a cavalcade of servants but that wasn't the same. The sweeps treated Col as a peer and Col treated them the same. When the mules reached the streets of Mondiso Col felt a pang of sadness tighten his chest.

"Do we have time for a last meal?" Caménor said.

"I think between friends there can never be a last meal," Uliz said.

"What do you say, Col? Do you think you can stand us for another evening?" Uzir said.

"It's been rough but I guess I could survive one more meal," Col said with a wink.

"Then it's settled," Uliz said. "I know just the place." The icy streets gleamed beneath lights from the windows of butchers, bakers and blacksmiths. The wagon turned down a narrow alley where the eaves of the buildings on either side nearly touched above them. Uliz gave a tug on the reins and they stopped in front of a plain wooden door. A pole over the door reached across the alley but no sign hung from it.

"You three go in. I'll take care of the mules," Uliz said.

"Are you sure anyone's here? It looks deserted." Caménor said.

"It always looks this way. The Sometimes Inn is known to those who need to know it," Uzir said. "Come on."

"Why is it called the Sometimes Inn?" Col asked.

"Because sometimes the food is good and the beds are clean and sometimes they're not," Uzir said. He opened the door and they stepped inside.

The bottom floor of the Sometimes Inn was a dimly lit room that served as one of Mondiso's taverns. A small fire swam lazily in the corner hearth while heavy black lanterns hung from the rafters to spread just enough light to drink. Tables were set up across the room in an order that seemed to have no order at all. A handful of people sat at two of them. If the food was any good tonight word hadn't gotten out yet. They picked a table close to the fire and were met almost instantly by a short man with a big voice.

"I hope you're here to pay your tab, Uliz!" The man's clapping jaw sent flecks of spit across the table.

"I'm Uzir, Silfen. Uliz is the one coming up behind you."

Silfen spun to the left looking for Uliz while Uliz stepped to the right and quietly took a seat beside Col.

"We'll have a sampling of your finest tonight, Silfen. We've got friends you've yet to impress." Uliz slapped his hand on the table.

Silfen spun back around. His mouth twisted and his left eye squinted. "Your fine talk has gotten you by me before, Uliz, but if I don't see some coin this time, I get Oded out here. You remember my boy, don't you? He's grown tall and strong like his mother."

"Of course we remember Oded," Uzir said. "And your lovely wife? How is she?"

"Left a year ago."

"I'm sorry to hear that," Caménor said.

"That makes one of us. A harsher woman you'd never meet."

"Well, then," Caménor stammered. "You have my congratulations."

"Beer for the three of you? I take it the boy will be drinking water?"

"Do you have milk?" Col asked.

"The wife took the cow. No milk. Beer and water."

"I'll have water, then," Col said.

"Water it is." He looked back at Uliz and Uzir. "And if the money for your tab isn't on this table when I get back," he jabbed the wood with his finger. "you two will end up on the menu tonight." He walked away. His short legs shuffled over the grubby floor.

"Do you have the money you owe?" Caménor asked.

"There's something we probably should've thought of. How much do you have, Uzir?"

Uzir fished around inside his coat before answering. "I've got 20. How much've you got?"

"Almost 30. What do you think we owe?"

"Probably close to that. Put 10 on the table and see if that's enough to cool him off. If he asks we'll say that's all we owe."

"I knew your mother was wrong, Uzir. You are a smart one." He dropped a few coins on the table, making sure their clatter was heard. Silfen appeared a few moments later with mugs in hand. He set them in the middle of the table before snatching the coins up and scampering away.

"That should be enough to get us through this meal," Uzir said. "And we saved ourselves a few coins in the process. Not a bad night."

"We didn't order anything. How does he know what we want?" Col said.

"They only serve one thing here at a time, Col. I believe tonight it's pork pies and beans," Uliz said.

Col didn't have to wonder long whether it was going to be one of the 'sometimes good' nights at the inn. Their pies were before them a minute later. The meat, spiced with sage and pepper, had cooked all day and fell apart in his mouth. The beans were sweet, simmered in sugar and molasses. Col enjoyed each bite along with every word from his friends. He dined without the heavy cloud of an impending goodbye because Uliz was right, there was no such thing as a last meal between friends.

They parted ways without farewell, as though they were going to see each other the next day. Col and Caménor walked out of the now crowded Sometimes Inn with their bellies full and spirits high. The world around them — stone walls and thatched roofs, cobbled streets and blurred panes of thick glass — was slowly steeped in shadow as evening hid the light until tomorrow.

They followed the road leading south of town. The clouds above scattered as the moon rose, fearful of her silvery gaze.

"Why didn't we stay at the inn with Uliz and Uzir?" Col asked.

"That's very simple, Col. We have no money."

"Here we are, two princes in our own land, and we can't even afford a room. Did you ever think you'd see it happen?"

"I've learned a few things in my years, Col. One of them is that much of life is unexpected and so much of that is what makes life beautiful."

"You're glad this happened?"

"No, I never wished for any of this and I still don't, but that doesn't mean we can't find some good in it."

"I could never see any of this as good."

"I know you can't right now, but the good news is after riding for days on end and sleeping on the cold hard ground, setting sail and nearly drowning and spending a few days in a wagon with chimney sweeps we are now but a stone's throw from home. Not our home, but a home."

"We're almost there?"

"Tomorrow morning we wake in warm beds."

"Yes!" Col thrust his fist into the air. The road from Mondiso passed into unfurling fields and rolling pastures. The sun had been given some days to combat the snow and peaks of stubborn grass spiked above the white.

"Are you sure you remember where it is?" Col asked.

"I don't think I could ever forget. These hills look exactly as I remember them. If you weren't here with me I'd swear I never left."

Col was glad someone knew where they were going because he couldn't tell one field from the other. Not that being lost had ever stopped him from exploring before. Right now, though, he had no desire to explore. He just wanted to be there. He wanted to finally be somewhere, wherever it was they were supposed to be.

The ground sloped into a shallow valley. "Do you see it?" Caménor said.

"I don't see anything."

"Just over that ridge." He pointed across the valley to a window peaking above the rise on the other side. A flicker of light sparked across the distance.

Col focused on it. Here it was: rest and a shelter at last. With their goal in sight Col felt the burden of the past weeks fall on him like a boulder from a cliff top and land squarely on his shoulders. He saw Tonn's body on the table, the Kheva grimacing through the flames, the Thanir with their glowing skin and the ripple in the spring beneath the trees. It seemed foolish but Col thought as long as he could reach that light those things would be powerless to hurt him anymore.

They descended the shallow valley and climbed the opposite side. At the top, a house came into view. It sat in the middle of a wide field. It was two stories with a tightly thatched roof. Four windows faced them, two on bottom and two on top.

They came to a split rail fence, ancient with long flimsy splinters. Col's foot caught on a rail and knocked it to the ground as he climbed over.

"Hallo!" Caménor called. A door creaked as it opened ever so slightly. "Hello?" Caménor called again.

"It's late for visitors," a faceless voice slipped from the doorway.

"Morning is far off and we've come a long way."

"Why should anyone come any distance to see us?"

"I'm an old friend here to see Naboth."

A candle flickered and the doorway opened.

"Naboth isn't here anymore."

The flame bobbed in the dark, moving closer to them until it revealed a face of hard lines and soft eyes.

"Tensoe?" Caménor said.

"You know my name, stranger, but you've yet to give me yours."

"Have I changed so much, Tensoe?"

Tensoe moved closer. "Cameron?"

The two men's faces showed a mix of shock and awkward familiarity.

"Cameron?" A woman wrapped in a blanket ran from the house and threw her arms around Caménor.

"Sasme!" Caménor returned the embrace.

"It's been a long time," Tensoe said.

"Yes, it has. Too long."

"What brings you to our door now?"

"Never mind that!" Sasme said. "We can hear what he has to say in the morning." She saw Col and pulled the blanket tight around her shoulders and neck. "Who have we here, Cameron?"

"This is my son, Colby."

Sasme's already pale face found a new shade of white. "Colby." She caught herself and forced a smile. "It's nice to meet you. Now, let's get you two inside. I'm sure you're tired."

They were led to a small room on the second floor. There were two beds, one against either wall, with a window between them.

They were left to settle in for the night. Col collapsed onto the straw mat and everything around him blurred save a single image in his mind: a birthmark on Sasme's neck in the shape of a small crescent moon.

—ᴥ—

Mino looked through the frost glazed window. He lay with plump covers pulled snugly around his wiry neck and watched a titmouse flit between motionless boughs. The sound of plates clattering on a wooden table and the smell of fresh eggs and baking crusty bread told him Brenna was downstairs preparing his breakfast. He considered getting dressed and saving her the trouble of coming to get him but his blankets held him captive.

Since they'd arrived at her family home in the north, Mino had come to enjoy watching his young nurse cook. She worked with such vigor that he couldn't help but laugh when she got angry with herself for ruining another meal. Her mother would always come in honking like an angry goose, and lament how no man would want a woman who couldn't cook.

Something, probably the water pitcher, shattered on the kitchen's hard floor. It sent a shiver of panic through the cottage. Mino sat up expecting to hear Brenna's mother chide her. Instead, there was a shriek and feet racing up the stairs.

Mino quickly crawled beneath his bed. His knees and elbows stirred dust into his eyes. He spun himself around and watched as Brenna reached his room. Something jerked her foot out from under her. She fell and her head hit the doorpost with a sickening crack. She landed on the floor and her arm twisted awkwardly beneath her. A thin stream of blood ran over her smooth ivory forehead, soaking a strand of red hair. She was dragged from sight. The terrified screams from below escalated along with the fearful shouts of Brenna's father and brother. Mino held his hands over his ears. He tried not to cry out at the cracks of splintering wood. He squeezed his eyes shut as glass shattered.

The commotion ceased all at once. A soft thud followed the stillness. A subtle creak on the stairs signaled someone coming. A strange pair of feet intruded his room. The toes on each foot fused together to form two distinct fins of hard, calloused flesh. Thick green veins spread over dark feet and up sinewed ankles like leaves laid tightly over a rock.

The invader stopped in front of Mino's bed and sniffed the air. He flipped the bed on end. Mino was exposed. A hand seized him. It was gnarled and pitted like tree bark. Mino was tossed over a shoulder. A tightly packed ball of leaves was shoved in his mouth. It numbed his tongue, leaving him helpless to cry out. Unyielding vines wrapped tightly around his wrists and ankles. His eyes followed the trail of Brenna's blood as he was taken downstairs. The lifeless bodies of Brenna and her family lay in a pile in the kitchen. Two other intruders stoked the hearth to a frenzy and threw in what remained of the table and chairs.

Without stopping, Mino's captor rushed him from the warmth of his nurse's home to the cold, damp Winter air. As he was carried through an icy stream Mino saw the cottage catch flame. The smoke mingled with the gray above. His captor carried him deeper into the dense wood. The ball of leaves gagging him began to have a strange effect. Moments later he was under the spell of a heavy sleep.

CHAPTER 15

A WEED IN THE GARDEN

—∞—

SLEEPING IN A BED THAT was not his own Col woke with a sense someone was standing over him. He opened his eyes in alarm, ready to spring up and fight. Or run, more likely.

What awaited him was a girl who looked near his age. Her eyes, liquid and dark like cinnamon, were fixed on him. She didn't startle when he woke but kept watching. Her dark hair fell in loose curls around her neck with a single strand running across an olive cheek to cling to her lower lip.

"You snore. Do you know that?" she said.

"What? I do not."

"You do. I thought someone was killing a boar in here."

"Who are you?" His eyes were barely open and already he was annoyed.

"This is my house. I'll ask the questions."

He was suddenly aware just how out of place he was. "Fine, but can you let me get dressed first?" He reached for his shirt.

"No, that's a question. I ask those. Who are you?"

Col shook his head to clear the fuzz inside. "Where's my father?" He needed to get out of here.

"Yet another question. You don't listen very well do you?"

"My name is Col."

"Now we're getting somewhere. Why are you here, Col? You weren't here when I went to bed last night and I wake up this morning and here you are snoring in my house."

"I wasn't snoring!"

"Of course you were. You didn't answer my question. Why are you here?"

Of all her questions this was one Col wasn't prepared for. "I'm not playing your game anymore," he countered. "Where's my father?"

"You're a grump when you wake up."

"Only when I wake to an interrogation. Is he still here or did you chase him away with your ridiculous questioning?"

"He's downstairs talking to my mother. I liked you better when you were snoring."

Col slipped his shirt over his head and filled his boots with his feet before marching past the girl.

"I'm Tinea," she called after him. "But everyone just calls me Nea."

Col ignored her and quietly descended the stairs. He heard Caménor talking to the woman he'd met last night. Sasme. That was her name.

He turned left at the bottom of the stairs and entered the kitchen. The two of them sat across the table from one another.

"I still can't believe you're here. And with a son! I didn't think I'd ever see you again, Cameron. I know my father will be so happy."

"How is Naboth? I've missed him over the years," Caménor said

"You could've come to see him. You could've seen us all. What kept you away?"

His eyes focused on her. "Some doors, once shut, cannot be opened again."

Col couldn't help but notice how deliberately his uncle spoke those words. As though they'd been practiced a thousand times over a dozen years. He'd never seen him so guarded.

"Yet you're here now," Sasme said.

"Yes, I am." He looked over and caught Col watching them. "We both are. Come and have a seat, Col."

Col sensed he was intruding on something. He looked dumbly at Sasme who snugged a scarf around her neck. He remembered the birthmark he'd seen the night before. So this was the woman who had turned down the heart of a prince. Instead, she'd chosen a simple man. A farmer.

"Breakfast is almost ready. Oat mash with a little honey. It's what Tensoe always eats. I've got some tea ready, though. Would you like some?" she said.

"That'll be fine, Sasme," Caménor said.

She set two clay mugs in front of them and poured the tea from a kettle. "You still haven't told me why you're here." She tried to hide her birthmark again as though it were proof of a curse on her life.

"There was a fire," Caménor replied without hesitation. "With nothing left and Winter bearing down on us we needed to find someplace safe."

Col took a sip of his tea. At least Caménor had given some thought to their story, flimsy as it was.

"So you came here?"

"It was the safest place I could think of."

"I'm sorry. That was rude of me. You know you're welcome." She hesitated a moment before asking "And your wife?"

"Col's mother passed eight years ago."

"I had no idea. We haven't heard news of you in nearly 20 years. You just... disappeared."

"Life has a way of ripping the reins from your hands and bolting."

"Twenty years is a long time to have life get away from you."

"Yes, it is. I see you and Tensoe took over the farm."

"Father got old faster than he thought he would, and with no son to take over we made it our home again. He has his den behind the barn. He likes it there. He still talks about you sometimes. You were like another one he'd lost."

Caménor looked down at the cup in his hands. "I'm eager to see him."

"Why don't you two wash up and have breakfast with him?"

"Thank you, Sasme. I'm afraid it's been awhile since we've had a good cleaning."

"I know. It's not hard to tell."

Caménor laughed. "You go on up, Col. I'll be along in a minute."

Col put his cup down and went back upstairs. He kept an eye out for Tinea. Avoiding her could become a new pastime.

In their room a bowl of cold water and two rags sat on the table between the beds. Col cringed as he splashed his face. His skin felt tight, like new leather. He wiped the grime away with the rag and rinsed again. Had he ever been so filthy?

He took his sack from the floor and dumped its meager contents onto the bed to find something missing. He shuffled hastily through a canteen, two well worn shirts and a torn piece of netting.

"Everything okay?" Tinea stood in the doorway.

"You took it, didn't you? I wouldn't play your stupid game so you took it!" He could strangle her.

She folded her arms tight across her chest. "I didn't take anything."

"You're lying. I know you are. Give it back!" He stepped toward her with narrowed eyes.

"I don't even know what you're talking about."

"My box. It's iron with —"

Caménor came up behind Tinea. "With a particular seal on the lid?"

"Yes," Col said, the venom draining from his voice.

"I found it last night. You dropped it while we were walking."

"Oh."

"I think you owe this young lady an apology."

Tinea stared at him, eyes lit with snoot. Col glared back at her. His jaw firmly refused to move. Her demeanor eased first. "It's okay. I'll let you go this time."

"That's very kind of you," Caménor said.

"Just this time, though." She winked and left the room.

"Is there something you'd like to tell me, Col?" Caménor said.

"I don't know."

"This box," he pulled it from beneath his bed. "is old. Very old. It's not often you see something bearing the seal of the Earthkings." He held it out to Col. "Something like this is worth holding onto."

Col took the box and carefully put it back inside his sack.

"I have a feeling this has something to do with your visit to a certain fabled city."

Col didn't answer him.

"Why don't we talk about it later? Right now there's someone I want you to meet."

Caménor led him outside past a small pond to a tiny shed built into the hill behind the barn. It looked big enough to hold a cow or two but little else. It had been painted once but was now a faded blue, chipped and cracked, with dirty white under the eaves of a slate roof. A slim stone chimney climbed the backside of the shed, growing like a tree from the hillside. Smoke drifted from its mouth like an old man puffing a pipe.

Caménor knocked once and waited. A horse stomped in the barn behind them. Col wished they were still on the road. Or better yet, home. Nothing felt right here. He was sure eyes were always on him. He felt like a weed growing in the garden of their simple life.

"You're late, Nea. I expected my breakfast nearly an hour ago," came a voice from inside.

They were greeted by an old man who leaned on a cane nearly as gnarled as his hands. What remained of his snowy hair wreathed his head like a crown. Wild eyebrows reached toward the crown as though they could complete the circle. The skin around his eyes was spotted and wrinkled. He looked at Caménor and his eyes went so wide Col was prepared to catch them should they fall out.

"I'm sorry. I think we were supposed to bring your food," Caménor said.

"Caménor! Is it really you?"

"Hello, Naboth. It's good to see you."

"Oh, my boy." Naboth took him by the shoulder and pulled him down to embrace him. "You're really here."

"It's been a long time, I know."

"Come in, come in. It's cold and the light bothers my eyes."

Col could only look at his uncle in disbelief. It was as though he had been hiding a secret life or another family from him all these years. The way the old man had reacted upon seeing him caused Col to wonder if this wasn't his uncle's real family.

The three of them huddled in the small quarters. A small bed stretched beside the hearth at the far end of the room. A table with a single chair was at the foot of the bed. The other side of the room contained two chairs both covered with a plush padding of bear fur smoothed with time and use.

"Please, sit." He motioned them to the chairs and took his own by the fire. He poked the logs with his cane. "I can never seem to stay warm these days. Now," he settled in. "what brings a prince to my door again after so many years? I've heard nothing of a rebellion."

"He knows?" Col said.

"Of course I know, young man. I don't take just anybody in. So who are you that you should find shelter beneath my roof?"

"Naboth," Caménor said. "I'd like to present to you my nephew, the NéPrince Colmeron."

"*NéPrince* Colmeron? So your brother is dead." He smacked his lips in slow contemplation. "I'm very sorry to hear that. I'm afraid news doesn't reach us here very quickly. Even something as important as that."

"He was killed nearly three weeks ago. We were away within the hour," Caménor said.

"Killed?"

"It was the Kheva Adem."

"Are you sure?"

"A man named Etau, the Captain of my brother's guard, was taken by the Noflim. They killed the king's advisor first, then his son."

"This is bad. This is very bad. An advisor murdered, the heir killed and now you are here. This is very bad indeed. I'm sorry, Caménor, but you shouldn't have come here."

"Home wasn't safe anymore. I had to protect the NéPrince."

"Don't you see? This is when your brother needed you most and the enemy has chased you away."

"No!" Col jumped from his chair. "The Kheva would've found me if we'd stayed there."

"What makes you say that, Col?"

Col felt the knot in his stomach climb into his throat. "They told me they'd find me."

"When?"

"I've seen them twice. First on the tower before Tonn died and then that night in the hunter's camp."

"You saw them?" Caménor said in disbelief.

"I was asleep both times. It was only dreams. I shouldn't have said anything."

"I assure you they are as real here as they were in your dreams," Naboth said. "The Noflim are spirits. Moving between the physical world and that of dreams is not beyond their reach." He studied Col with those compassionate eyes. "That's not all you've seen though, is it?"

Col glanced at Caménor and felt he was about to betray the man. "No. There's more."

It was as if the doors guarding Col's greatest secret were opened. "I've been to Entaramu," he confessed. "But I didn't just see the trees and the pool there, Uncle Cam. I saw a ripple on the water." He shuddered as he remembered how it spread over the surface. "I know it doesn't sound like much but it terrified me. I didn't know why. It was just a ripple, but then I turned around. Standing over me was a creature made of light with skin like leaves."

"Thanir!" Naboth bounced in his seat. "You saw Thanir? In Entaramu?" He rushed to him as quickly as his stiff legs would take him.

"Yes. It told me about the Numen."

Caménor rested his arm on the table beside him but said nothing.

"I'm sorry I didn't tell you the truth, Cam. I didn't want it to be real," he breathed out. "I just wanted to go home."

"It's alright, Col. I've been trying to protect you from something far beyond my control."

"I don't think going home is an option you'll ever have again," Naboth said. "Events are in motion that make turning back a feat even an Earthking couldn't accomplish. Don't be afraid to move ahead, though. You have good council. Your uncle was always wise beyond his years."

"Not wise enough to see this coming," Caménor said.

"There's nothing you could have done. I have a feeling we are seeing the birth of a plan conceived long before any of us were even a thought."

"What can we do now?"

"Rest. I cannot shelter you long. It's too dangerous. Both for you and for my family. Go north. If they are still there, the Greenkind may offer you protection. More than I have to give here. One thing is certain. You must keep the NéPrince safe."

Col buried his face in his hands. He didn't want to run anymore. He didn't want any of this.

Naboth laid a withered hand on Col's head. "Hush," he said softly. "I don't know why Orum has chosen one so young but his ways always prove true. There are things at play far greater than we understand, dear prince, but you do not fight alone."

"Why is this happening?"

"Why it has always happened. Do you know where the Kheva Adem come from?"

"No."

"Long before man walked the earth the Sons of Heaven rebelled but their uprising failed and Orum hurled the dissenters from his realm. Their leader, the Numen you spoke of, was brought before Orum. As punishment he took the Numen's very name from him and cast the Unnamed One apart from his followers.

"At that time there was a race of higher spirits on the earth called the Thanir. They saw the Numen fall to earth, like fire from the stars. Ignoring the warnings of their brethren, three of Thanir searched for him in hopes of learning from this falling star. When they found him he swayed them from their nature.

"When word reached Orum of this corruption he condemned the Numen and threw him into a pit with two trees growing beside it. The roots of the trees ensnared the Numen far below surface. Orum filled the pit with water gathered from the Eternal Sea by his own hands.

"Sadly, the three Thanir were no longer spirits of light, but instruments of destruction. They became Noflim and led many men into darkness. These men became what they worshipped, twisted and grotesque abominations of their true selves. They became Kheva Adem. The Noflim and their followers ever schemed to free their master. So Orum raised up the Earthkings to protect the sacred grove and keep the Numen from ever being freed. The Noflim and the Kheva have always hunted what stands in their way, what they fear. And right now what they fear is you, Colmeron."

"Why should they be afraid of me?" Col said.

"They fear what you might become."

"Why haven't I ever heard this before?" Col said.

"The enemy knows that if history is forgotten so are they. I suspect its why they vanished for so long. No one will fight an enemy they don't believe in."

"I see."

"I suspect you do. So what will you do now?"

No matter how he looked at it, he was left with only two options, flee or fight. He didn't know how to fight but he was tired of fleeing. He looked to Caménor for reassurance before turning to Naboth. "I'm going to fight."

CHAPTER 16

TO KEEP A FRIEND

WEMBUS STOOD DUTIFULLY IN THE kitchen while Martle, the king's cook, chatted excitedly about his new grandson. It was his first and he planned to spoil the child as much as the parents would allow. And then a little more.

Wembus smiled at the man's fortune. The joy was short lived, though, as a succession of screams reached the kitchen. Martle looked at him with the same concern creasing his brow.

"Stay here," Wembus ordered.

Long, terror filled shrieks echoed through the halls. They could have come from nearly anywhere. Flustered faces peered from doorways and agitated servants ducked to the side as Wembus rushed past.

He turned a corner and his foot slipped. He slammed into the wall. Not hard enough to injure him but he was sure to have a fist sized bruise. He looked down, wondering what had caused him to slip.

Blood smeared the floor. Drops pooled on the stones. He followed the trail. The cries faded. He turned another corner and saw his quarry. A tall figure draped in a black robe dragged his victim to the end of the hall. The devil paid his victim's cries no mind.

"Stop!" Wembus ordered. He ran after them. "In the name of the king I order you to stop!"

The attacker flung open the courtyard door and pulled his victim from sight. Wembus reached the door moments later. He barreled into the courtyard. The blackguard stood in front of the fountain. The silver veil of a waxing moon covered him. He clenched the limp man's shirt in his fist. Blood covered his mouth and spilled onto his chest. He still grunted for help.

"I found one, Wembus. I told you they would try again." The man in black raised his head. Wembus knew the high cheekbones and proud forehead of the king. The old Healer slumped against Tephall's leg.

"My lord, what are you doing?" Wembus said.

"This old man was to be the Noflim's next assassin. I found him out. Go on, look in his mouth." He tossed the man onto his knees in front of Wembus.

Wembus bent down to examine the him. The Healer whimpered and his eyes plead in fear as he opened his mouth. His tongue had been savagely torn out. Blood filled the cavity. The Healer spat a mouthful of the stuff on the ground.

"You see? This one's been taken. I will allow no more," the king said. "Do you hear me, Noflim? No more!" The king slid the sword from his belt.

Arnoc's ruler had blood on him. It stained his clothes. His hands were covered in it. His face was smeared with it.

Tephall raised his sword and brought it down with such speed and determination Wembus hardly had time to dodge its arc. The Healer's body fell to the side.

"Do not grieve for this body, Wembus. Our friend was already gone just as your brother was already gone. We are warriors in this timeless battle, my friend. You and I share a burden. Never forget that." He put his sword back in its scabbard without bothering to clean it.

By morning two more bodies lay in the courtyard. Martle's was among them. The king stood over them as the morning light showed him his handiwork.

"I know you think this harsh, Wembus, but I won't take any chances. We weren't prepared before. I lost my sons and you your brother. I'll not have Arnoc lose her king. Not now."

"There is still hope, my lord. The princes will yet return."

"Don't be a fool, Wembus. The riders should have been back by now. No, my sons are gone and my brother is rotting in a hole somewhere. You and I are all that remain. We are all that stands between the kingdom and ruin."

"Yes, my lord." The words meant nothing. The enemy had a face at last but it wasn't who Wembus had ever thought it would be.

—~—

After a week on the farm Col couldn't help but worry about his father.

They shouldn't have left. The thought woke him often while the moon still hung low and glowed dim through the window.

Then there was the ever intruding presence of Nea. It was habit now to avoid her but she was everywhere at once. Sleep was the only respite he had from her incessant jabbering and that was as rare as a flower in Winter.

Col was awake again before dawn. He looked at the door. He was convinced one of these mornings it would open to reveal the Kheva Adem lurking in the hallway. But not this morning. This morning the door stayed closed. Caménor slept peacefully on the other side of the room.

Col rolled the covers from him in large, heaving folds. The house was warm but Winter waited just outside the window. He slipped his boots on and grabbed his coat. He could still smell the sea on it.

He opened the door without a sound and crept downstairs. Nothing stirred in the house save himself and he wanted to keep it that way.

He wandered outside where the distant light of stars retreated from the ice. He breathed in the stark air and had just decided to go for a walk when he noticed the grey plumage coming from Naboth's chimney. With soft steps he approached the old man's den. The telltale gleam of a lantern shone through the window.

Naboth passed between flame and pane. Col wondered if he was breaking some unspoken rule by being about. He turned for the pond and would have made his escape but the door opened.

Naboth called into the twilight. "You're not as quiet as you'd like to think you are. Why not join me for a hot drink before the day begins?"

"I'm sorry," Col said.

"Nothing to be sorry for. Come in."

Col followed him into the den. "Maybe a drink will help me sleep."

"Awake too early? I sometimes wonder if we wake at odd times for reasons we've yet to understand." He put a kettle over the fire.

"Is that why you're awake, Naboth?" Col asked.

"I'm away from my bed because these old bones and cold mornings tend to do battle at this hour. Such is the price of age."

"I don't ever want to get old." Col settled into the chair by the fire, its cushion warmed by the flames.

"I pray that you do, my prince. Youth is a splendid gift but with age comes experience, and with experience can come wisdom. It doesn't always, but it can. And such a reward is well worth a few aches and stiff joints."

"I never thought of it that way."

"The sun isn't even up and already you've learned something. Now, what is it that takes you from your bed so early?"

"I'm worried."

"About?"

"I fear for my father."

"Oh? Tell me, what's he like, your father? I know of the king but I'm curious of the man."

Col thought for a moment. He'd never been asked to describe his father before. "He's a good man. Strong, but not hard. Stronger than anyone I've ever known."

"And I'm sure you've known some strong warriors."

"I have and he's braver than all of them. He's never not a king and never not a father. He's always both."

"I've heard such things about him. I'm glad to know they're true."

"I'd give up sleep for a month if I could hear him laugh right now. It was always so comforting. It let me know everything was alright."

"Does he laugh much?"

"He used to. Even after my mother died he still laughed. Only in the last few years did he stop." It had been so long since he'd heard Tephall laugh. Trying to remember the sound was like an old man trying to paint what the inside of his mother's womb was like.

"It is a brave man who can laugh after the heavy blows of tragedy. I sometimes think when we've grieved all we can only laughter remains. It's one of life's beautiful oddities."

"Do you think he'll be okay?" There was no way Naboth could know but Col asked anyway.

"I can't say, but worry changes nothing. As you say, he's a strong man. Hardship is no stranger to him." Naboth pulled the kettle from the hearth and picked a few dried leaves from a small wooden box. He dropped them in the kettle and left them to steep.

"What can I do?" Col said.

"You can trust. Trust that there is a hand at work far greater than that of the enemy."

"Do you believe that?"

"I do." He poured them each a cup of tea. "Drink this. Slowly, now."

Col blew on it and took a sip. It was sweet, like berries in Summer, with a touch of mint that cooled his throat.

"Good?"

"I like it." He drank some more.

"Good."

Col put the cup down to stifle a yawn.

"Why don't you lie down for awhile, Col? May I call you 'Col'?"

"I'd like that, Naboth."

"The day is still ahead of you and a little rest would do you some good."

Col nodded and stretched out on Naboth's bed. The old man took his seat by the fire. "Rest now, young prince. I'll be right here."

Col woke a few hours later to sunlight filling the window. Naboth still sat in his chair by the fire.

"You slept through breakfast," he said.

"Why didn't you wake me?"

"To wake you would have been a crime. Treasonous, really. I saved you some food, though." He uncovered a tray containing three thick strips of bacon that had been dredged in brown sugar before being fried. A piece of fresh bread and a hard boiled egg completed the meal.

Col greedily shoved a bacon strip into his mouth before biting off half the egg.

"Feeling better?"

"Much," Col said.

"Never underestimate the power of a good nap."

Col finished his meal and lay back on the bed. "Naboth?" he asked.

"Yes, Col."

"What happened to the Earthkings?"

"Oh, the same thing that happens to all who are too great for too long."

"What's that?"

"Pride."

"What do you mean?"

"Now isn't the time for such talk. Go, enjoy the day. We'll talk later."

Col left Naboth's den with the spirit of a new day. His earlier meanderings were only a memory of a dream. A bit of rest had cleared his mind and he was sure of what he needed to do now.

He went to the barn in search of Caménor. The air inside was warm and dry. The simple, summery smell of hay filled the cool space.

Nea looked down from the loft. "What were you doing with my grandfather?"

"Eating breakfast," he said. This was her favorite place. Col should have known better than to come in here.

"Momma said you weren't in bed when she got up. That was hours ago. Were you eating that whole time?"

Why did she always have to ask so many questions. Would it be so hard for her to just leave him alone? "No. I couldn't sleep and he invited me in."

"Did you have a nightmare? Sometimes I go see momma when I have bad dreams."

"I wasn't having a nightmare and even if I was I wouldn't go to anyone." He went for the door and prayed she wouldn't follow.

"I forgot, you're a boy and boys don't get scared."

"I didn't say that."

"So what were you afraid of?"

"I wasn't afraid of anything. I just couldn't sleep." He tried again to leave.

"Then why did you go see my grandfather?"

He turned back to her and answered quickly, hoping she'd take the hint. "He likes to talk to me."

"That must be nice," her voice dipped, as if she were talking to herself. "What do you talk about?" she said to Col.

"I can't tell you."

"Why can't you tell me?"

"Because it's got nothing to do with you."

"It never does with him." Quiet again.

"What do you mean?" He almost felt a spark of concern take flame before his indifference snuffed it out.

"Nothing. Forget it."

"Okay," Col walked outside. He hadn't even gone ten steps when the door swung behind him. Col cringed and waited for her voice.

"You don't care that my grandfather never talks to me?" She came up beside him.

"Why should I?" He tried not to notice how quickly her face seemed to fall.

"If you're my friend you should."

That was it. He turned on her. "We're not friends! I won't be here long and even if I were I wouldn't want to be around you. You annoy me so much I have dreams about throwing you over a cliff. And those aren't nightmares. Those are good dreams! I don't blame your grandfather for not wanting to talk to you! You're a pest."

Once Col mentioned Naboth, his words were like arrows from the bow. Her hand went to her mouth and she ran away.

She was crying inside the house as Col walked past. He looked the other way and kept going. He only wished it hadn't felt so good to finally let her have it.

Caménor emerged from the doorway. "Col?"

"There you are," Col said.

"You wouldn't know why Nea's crying, would you?"

"She's a girl. Girls are always crying." He walked faster, hoping the matter would fall behind.

Caménor kept stride with him. "Yes, but they usually have a reason. What did you do?"

"Nothing. I told her to leave me alone."

"How did you tell her?"

"I said we weren't friends and I could see why Naboth didn't like talking to her."

"Those are terrible things to say, Colmeron."

"She was bothering me. I had to do something."

"Let's take a walk. We need to talk."

"I was thinking the same thing. We need to talk." Col fell in step with his uncle. They came to the fence and followed it, circuiting the perimeter of the field. "I don't think we should go north," Col said. "When we leave here, I mean. We need to go home."

"We can't go back. It's not safe. You know that."

"What about my father? It's not safe for him, either. He needs us."

"My brother isn't my concern right now. You are."

"I still think we should go back." Col folded his arms across his chest.

"I know you do, but I need you to trust me."

They came to where they'd climbed over the fence the night they arrived on the farm. "Take a look at this fence," Caménor said. The rail Col knocked loose was still on the ground. "We broke this days ago and it still hasn't been fixed."

"So? All Tensoe has to do is pick it up."

"True, but what if he didn't know about it? What if it stayed like this until Spring when the cattle graze here?"

"I don't know."

"The herd could get loose. Tensoe and Sasme could lose their livelihood."

"Maybe Tensoe should be keeping a closer eye on his fence."

"That's not the point, Col."

"What is the point?"

"A family is a lot like this farm. When something is damaged and remains untended it can lead to greater and greater harm. Love and harmony are disrupted because, somewhere, there's a rift. And things will only get better if that rift is repaired. Just like this fence." He picked up the rail and slid it back in place.

"Okay, I'll be more careful with the fence."

"It's too late for that, Col. The damage is done. Now you need to fix it."

"But you just did."

"No, I didn't."

"Yes, you did. I just watched you fix it." Caménor was losing his mind.

"We're not talking about the fence."

"Of course we are. You just told me all about the fence and how Tensoe and Sasme depend on it."

"And just like a broken fence needs mending, so does a relationship. Even a new one."

"This wasn't about the fence?"

"No."

"You're talking about Nea, aren't you?" He should've known Caménor would bring it all back around to her.

"I knew you'd catch on."

"I don't want to talk to her."

"You hurt her. She wants be your friend, Col. Why don't you let her? Friends aren't always easy to come by."

"What am I supposed to say? Sorry you can't mind your own business? Sorry you bother me so much I want to feed you to a bear?"

"You've never really had friends, Col. Learning how to keep one is new to you."

"I know how to keep a friend."

"Do you?"

Col stopped for a moment. Caménor could be right. He was always right about things like this. Col hated that. "I guess I could be a little nicer. I'll talk to her later."

"Col..."

"Fine. I'll talk to her now."

"I know this isn't easy for you."

"Apologies aren't something I'm used to giving."

"They may be uncommon for a prince but a man should never be afraid to confess when he's wrong."

Col looked to the house on the other side of the field. He might as well get this over with.

"And Col?"

"What?"

"I'm proud of you. I know your father would be, too."

Col grinned and walked back to the house. He stepped inside wondering what kind of damage he'd really done. Would Sasme and Tensoe be mad at him? Would Naboth? Maybe he shouldn't have said anything about him to Nea.

Sasme's hands were busy in a bowl of dough. "Hello, Col," she said.

"Is Nea in here?"

"No, she went outside," Tensoe said tenderly stoking the fire. "I think she was going fishing."

"Fishing sounds good. Thanks. I'll catch up with her." He excused himself and went to the pond. A hill ran down the other side to the edge of a wood that stretched across the valley.

She wasn't at the pond. Of course the one time he was looking for her she was nowhere to be found.

He walked beside the water. The edges were thick with ice clinging to the shore. He turned his back to the water just in time to see Nea disappear into the trees below.

"Nea, wait!" he called, but she was already gone. He ran after her. He stopped at the forest's edge. The shadows of twisting vines and bending branches took hold of his fears. The forest had always been a sanctuary for him, every tree a friend. Now, he wasn't sure he could trust them. In his mind, the Kheva sheltered in every shadow. He took a breath and pushed on.

"Tinea!" He thought he caught her in the corner of his eye. He followed the movement and trekked with the natural path of the forest. He stopped to listen and heard the crackle of a disturbed bush ahead. He pursued her but she was always ahead of him. In his haste he burst through a cluster of low branches.

His foot swung over a long drop. His stomach cinched as he saw a ravine under him. He he caught himself on a hanging branch and pulled himself to safety. He sighed in relief that no one had seen his misstep. The deep fissure opened to a rolling river. To his left a fallen tree stretched across the chasm. Clumps of moss and decaying bark littered the top.

"That was close." Nea sat on the other side of the ravine. A pole was in her hand.

"That was nothing. I was having a little fun."

"What are you doing here?"

"Nothing," he lied.

"Are you sure you weren't following me?"

"No. I wanted to talk to you." He needed to get this over with.

"I can't hear you!" she shouted across the void.

"I wanted to tell you —"

She cupped her hand to her ear.

"Never mind. I'm coming over there," he shouted. He put one foot on top of the fallen tree. He steadied himself and brought his other foot up. He put his arms out for balance and crept forward. He did his best not to look down but his head was a weight constantly pulling chin to chest. He looked up and caught Nea smiling at him.

He had to do this. She'd managed it and he wasn't about to be outdone. He moved one foot, steadied himself then moved the other. He did this over and over until he was almost to the opposite edge.

With one step to go he relaxed. The wet moss threw his foot out from under him. He came down hard on his chest. His arms draped over the tree. His face pressed against the bark and he clawed at the moss and frail, splintering wood.

"Help!" he gasped. "Help!"

Nea's hand wrapped around his wrist. She leaned back hard and pulled him onto his stomach. He brought his leg over the tree and climbed to a knee. He leapt awkwardly onto the ground. Nea tumbled backward.

"What did you do that for?" She demanded as she got to her feet.

"I was trying to get off that awful tree."

"No, why were you on the tree at all? There's a bridge right over there."

Col looked to where she was pointing. Sure enough a bridge crossed the ravine. A contraption of ropes and wooden boards that looked so much easier than what he'd just done.

"I didn't see that."

"You're kind of stupid sometimes." She sat back down beside her pole.

Col should have been incensed by the accusation but coming from her he somehow knew it wasn't an insult. Was this what it was like between friends?

"I'm sorry," he said. There, it was out.

"What?" She looked up at him with those cinnamon eyes.

"I came to tell you that I'm sorry. I shouldn't have said those things earlier. I'm not used to having friends."

"It's okay. I don't have a lot of friends, either. It's hard to find friends when you only see your family all the time. Maybe I was a little too excited to have someone new around."

"Friends?" Col offered.

"Yeah, as long as you try not to be so mean."

"I'll try," Col said with a grin.

A blackbird, just bigger than the palm of Col's hand, landed on the fallen tree. It hopped over the soggy moss and tilted its head to the side. It stared at them quizzically.

"Look," Col pointed to the bird.

Nea turned her attention from fishing.

"It's too early for him to be here, isn't it?" he said.

"My father says if a blackbird doesn't fly south in the Winter it belongs to a giant."

"Are there giants here?" Col watched the bird, suddenly fascinated with it.

"Just one."

CHAPTER 17

THE GIANT'S HALLWAY

DINNER WAS OVER AND A fire blazed cheerily in the hearth. Col settled on the floor beside Nea. The family was all together. Even Naboth had been coaxed from his den for the evening on the condition that his chair be brought with him. He sat closest to the fire. The light flowed through the wrinkles in his face.

Caménor reclined on the floor beside Naboth. His eyes were closed and Col wasn't sure if he was sleeping or simply taking in the solace of fire and friends. Sasme and Tensoe sat close on a thick rug. She laid against his shoulder while his arm wrapped around her waist.

Col and Tinea had spent the day fishing, racing up trees and building tiny boats out of tree bark. Col had bragged about his sailing expertise only to have his boat sink as soon as it hit the water. Nea's floated amiably for nearly an hour while they'd fished.

It had been a good day and as the candles burned to replace the sun Col was content. Sasme came up behind he and Tinea and wrapped a blanket around them.

"Thank you, Momma," Nea said.

"It's still too cold at night," Sasme said. "I'll be glad when Spring arrives."

"We saw a blackbird today," Col said.

"Is that so?" Naboth said.

"It stopped and stared at us."

"Maybe Spring is closer than I thought." Sasme said.

"Nea says it belongs to the giant who lives in the woods."

Sasme laughed. "There's no giant in our woods, Col."

"Oh." Col felt the wonder drain from him like water from a punctured skin.

"What makes you say that, Sasme?" Naboth said.

"There's no such thing as giants."

"Is that so?" He arched a snowy brow.

"I've been in those woods a thousand times," Tensoe said. "And I've never found so much as an oversized footprint."

Naboth grinned and shook his head at them. "When I was a boy there was a giant that lived in the woods. His name was Thash. I never saw him but I often met people who had."

"Did they try to sell you any castles while they were at it, Pop?" Sasme teased.

Naboth ignored her and continued. "I may not have seen him but I heard him singing once. He had a deep, smooth voice that carried easily on the wind."

"What did he sing?" Nea said.

"He sang about a man who carried a lantern through the deep forests, looking for his lost love. I've never forgotten some of the words."

"What were they?"

"Feet follow feet beneath a river of stars, look for my light from wherever you are, I'll seek that hand that hides you away, for what words could you leave that would ever betray..."

"Do you think Thash is still there?" Col asked.

"It's possible, I suppose. Giants don't normally live above ground."

"They don't?"

"No, that's why we never see them. Hasn't your father ever told you about giants?"

"No."

Naboth shook his head at Caménor. "Sit back and listen, children. I have a story for you." He leaned forward on his cane and began.

—ᴥ—

A young man once followed the remains of an old riverbed. Dried and cracked, the bed was barren while the forest around it was lush with Spring rains. The young man knew this was odd but paid the mystery little mind. He intended to reach his love before nightfall and had no time for such things. A poorly placed step soon changed that.

The ground crumbled beneath him. He fell through the riverbed into a large cavern. It was washed in the turbulent orange of flames racing along the ceiling. This was what had dried up the riverbed.

His eyes adjusted in the pallid light. He saw he was not in a cavern so much as he was in a very long and staggeringly high hallway. Door after door lined either side. Each impossibly tall with a heavy brass handle. Doors made for giants, no doubt.

He jumped as high as he could but the tips of his fingers couldn't even touch the brass.

At the far end of the hallway a door opened and slammed shut again. The young man ran to the door but arrived too late to find his host. Another door opened but again he was unable to reach it in time. Each time a door opened he ran for it, but he was never quick enough. Finally, he sat in the middle of the hallway. He would wait until he was found.

A black dot appeared far down the hallway. It grew larger as it neared. Much larger. It was a blackbird, astoundingly huge, with wings that beat the air in heavy rushes. It dropped abruptly in front of him.

It's a common misconception that giants can speak with animals. This is only partly true. They can speak with birds, but so can any who will simply take the time to listen. Giants especially favor blackbirds for their intensely loyal dispositions.

"What are you doing here?" the blackbird spoke in words barely discernible to the young man. His dress of black feathers shone like silk in the light. "Who are you?"

"My name is Burnee," the young man said. "I fell."

The bird stood nearly as tall his him. "Kneehighs aren't supposed to be here. You need to leave."

"Show me out and I'll gladly go."

"There's only one door leading out and my master alone holds the key.

"Take me to him, then."

"I cannot," the bird said. "He has just gone to bed and will not wake for more than a hundred years."

"A hundred years! I'll be long dead by then. One of these doors must give me a way out."

"These doors lead only where my master wishes them to."

"Then wake your master."

"I have never woken my master."

"I said wake him, Blackbird. I will not die here." He fixed a hard stare on Blackbird.

Blackbird's head shifted left then right. His eyes stayed on Burnee. "Very well."

He spread his massive wings and the tips nearly touched the doors on either side. With a hard flap he thrust himself into the air and flew down nearly a dozen doors behind Burnee. He alighted on the brass handle. His weight turned it down and the latch clicked. The towering door creaked open. Burnee slipped in ahead of Blackbird. A hearth as big as a baker's oven held in its bosom the last embers of a once stupendous blaze. Across the room the giant slept on a sprawling bed. He snored beneath a blanket as big as a ship's sail.

"Master, wake up!" Blackbird called.

The great mound stirred. The giant's head poked out. "Why have you woken me, Blackbird?"

"We have a guest. He wishes for you to open a door for him?"

"Guest? What guest?" the giant grumbled. "I see no one here." He looked around. His shaggy mane fell over his face.

"Down here, Master. Our visitor is a kneehigh."

Burnee shrank into a corner.

The giant flung his blanket and leapt for Burnee.

Burnee tried to run but the giant's thick fingers wrapped around him. He carried him into the bright hallway. The giant moved with great, lumbering steps. Twenty doors rushed past. He flung open one of the doors and tossed Burnee inside.

The door slammed shut with thunderous finality. Burnee's flight came to an end with a surprisingly soft landing. The ground was cushioned with long feathers and the sharp bristle of straw. Burnee stood and the ground swayed. He crawled forward and reached an edge. He peered over. Only his hair and eyes were visible from below. He was met with the gray silence of the moon on water far below him. He searched but only a long fall was to be found on every side. He had landed in a nest perched high above a tossing sea.

The door the giant had thrown him through sat on a high cliff across a vast span of nothingness. He lay in his soft prison thinking of a way to escape when a sudden weight shifted the nest. Blackbird nearly planted his foot on Burnee's chest.

"Watch out, there!" Blackbird cried. "What are you doing in my nest?"

"This was your master's answer to my request."

"You see! I told you he would be angry. Now we're both made to suffer."

"You can get out though, can't you?"

"Of course I can. This is my home. I come and go as I please."

"You could carry me to the door."

"Do I look like a wagon or a boat?" Blackbird tossed a few feathers, straightened a few twigs and settled in a ball on the other side of the nest. "You may as well jump to your death now. I'm not helping you."

Burnee sat down. He would find his way to that door. His picked up a feather and strummed it as he thought. He had his answer.

"Blackbird?" he said.

"Are you still here, Kneehigh? I thought I told you to jump."

"If I were able to reach that door could I open it?"

"If you somehow made it to the door, yes. But you are down here and the door is far, far away with a mile of air and empty space between you. I'm going to sleep now. I expect you to be gone when I wake. I'm sure the rocks will make your end swift and the waves will carry you far from me.

Goodbye, Kneehigh." Blackbird tucked his head under his wing and went to sleep.

Burnee sifted through the feathers around him. He pulled out the ones whose shafts and barbs were still intact. He stuck himself with their quilled ends and his body was soon covered in feathers. All he lacked was a single tail feather. He wasted no time in plucking it from Blackbird's tail. The bird gave a short squawk but stayed asleep.

With the final feather in place Burnee walked to the edge of the nest. He spread his arms and leapt toward the rocks. He flapped wildly until his wings found their rhythm and he caught the wind. Like a baby bird, he rose in awkward flight. He glided on currents of air toward the cliff above. Rising high, he tucked his wings to his sides and dove toward the ground. He landed with a tumble and a roll. It wasn't as nice as landing in the nest but he had made it.

The door wasn't set in a wall. It stood alone in the middle of a grassy plain and was, thankfully, not giant-sized on this side. Burnee shook the feathers from his body and tucked the one he'd stolen from Blackbird into his pocket.

He opened the door and stepped back into the fire lit hallway. He was back where he'd started. There had to be another way out.

The fast, high creak of a door opened down the hall. Rather than run he set himself in the middle of the hallway. He waited.

The giant was upon him. He blustered through his tangled beard and shaggy locks. "How did you get back in here, Kneehigh?"

"I am not so easily dispatched, giant. Throw me through another door and I will escape again and again until you open the door that leads me home."

The giant loomed over him. "Why should I free you? I could throw you into the ceiling and watch your ashes drift down like snow."

"True, but if you do that Blackbird will be lost to you forever."

"What've you done with him, Kneehigh? Tell me!"

"I've made Blackbird a captive in his own nest. He's as flightless as an egg."

"How could such a puny thing manage such a feat?"

"I'll tell you once you open the door that takes me back to sunlit lands."

The giant's beard swished as his mouth twitched in contemplation. His great, droopy eyes peered over his round nose. "Very well, Kneehigh. Follow me." The giant led Burnee to a door far down the hallway. He swung the tall door inward. Inside, an enormous staircase climbed a narrow tunnel. Arrows of sunlight pierced the top.

"Now tell me how to free Blackbird or I'll close the door on your neck, leaving you to see the light but never reach it."

Burnee pulled the tail feather from his pocket. "Here you are, giant."

The giant took it between his thumb and forefinger, examined it and tucked it in his shirt. "Never return, Kneehigh, or I'll make a quick snack of you."

"Take Blackbird's feather and return to your slumber. I won't bother you again." The door closed behind Burnee. He climbed the huge steps to the surface where trees and sunlight welcomed him home like old friends.

Naboth finished his tale. Only the crackling of the fire and the slow breaths of a slumbering audience remained. Col alone sat wide eyed. Tinea slept with her head resting on his shoulder. Her hair fell carelessly onto his arm. Raven tresses that brought to mind Blackbird's smooth feathers. He looked down at her afraid to move lest he should wake her.

"I didn't think it was a boring story," Naboth said. "Did you think it was, Col?"

Col shook his head slightly.

"You'll have to wake her sometime, my boy."

"But not now," Col whispered.

"No, not now."

Outside the castle walls the long, sullen Winter nights fell away like scales from a dying fish. While inside everything was rank with fear.

Bodies piled in the courtyard. More were added each day. Tephall forbade Wembus from burying them. They were to be a show of brutality to the Noflim.

The king held inquisitions throughout the day. Guards filed every servant, stablehand and soldier through the great hall. Invariably, Tephall found one that roused his suspicions. He didn't bother to check their tongues anymore. Those suspected were taken to cells far below. Tephall would question them later. The result was always the same.

The vibrant banners that once adorned the hall had been torn down by Tephall himself. "There's nothing to celebrate anymore," he'd said.

The guards moved in perfect obedience to the king. Any hesitation would be seen as an act of treason. Their armor gleamed in the torchlight like warriors facing a dragon.

Wembus held the unfortunate post at Tephall's side as each subject was brought before the king. Wembus held his hands behind his back and his head up. It was a forced stance. He wasn't sure how much longer he could be a player in this awful game where there were no winners.

A young girl no older than six Summers was brought before the king. Wembus recognized her as the daughter of a stablehand who had been killed two days before. Her blonde hair hung in a neat braid that reached her shoulders. Her clothes were clean for a child her age. Her face, too, had been scrubbed free of dirt. Her small fists were balled. She glared at Tephall, who towered over her without a note of compassion.

"What's your name?" Tephall said.

The girl pursed her lips. Her eyes narrowed.

"Answer me, child."

She shook her head.

Tephall grabbed the girl. Her mother rushed forward but the guards held her.

"Why don't you speak?" Tephall said. "Or is it too difficult to do so without a tongue?" His fingers squeezed her jaw open.

"Her father is dead," the mother cried. "Leave her alone."

"Do you grieve for your father, child? Tell me, then. Why are there no tears on your face? What child doesn't weep for her parent?" He dropped her on the ground and took the sword from beside his chair.

The girl's eyes finally showed fear.

Wembus put his hand on the king's arm. "She's just a child, my lord. She doesn't cry because her grief is found in anger."

Tephall kept his arm steady but slowly turned his face to Wembus. "And why should she be angry with me? Am I the one who stole the life from her father's body? No! That was the Noflim."

"Does that make any difference to her? She's no threat. Just a little girl who has lost her father and her way." Wembus knelt beside the girl. "It's okay," he assured her. "Open your mouth, just for a moment. Please?"

The girl looked at him. Her gaze softened. She kept her eyes on his and opened her mouth. She stuck out her tongue.

"You see, my lord?" Wembus said.

The girl's tongue retreated.

Tephall lowered his sword. "Thank you, my friend." He looked at the girl. "Go back to your mother now."

The girl fled into her mother's arms.

"You may all leave," Tephall announced. "We've pursued our enemy enough for today."

The great hall cleared as relieved suspects rushed through the wide doors. Tephall fell back into his chair. His sword clattered on the floor. "You're right, Wembus. I've been too focused to see what's in front of me. Thank you for reminding me."

"I serve the king, ever and always. I'll have dinner brought to you and a hot bath drawn for after."

"Thank you, Wembus," he covered his face with his fingers. "You are a servant in more ways than I know."

Wembus bowed and left the hall. He spoke to the new cook about the king's meal and took a pitcher of ale and a cup back to the great hall.

"I've brought you something to drink, my lord." His words echoed through the empty room. A guard entered behind him.

"The king requests you join him atop the Western tower."

Wembus dismissed the man and set the pitcher and cup beside the king's chair. He moved quickly through the halls and up the winding stairs to the tower. He shoved the hatch open and climbed into the cold air. Dusk settled around the castle and the shadows on the tower stretched. The king sat erect. His eyes were closed.

"You asked to see me, my lord?"

The king opened his eyes. "Come, sit beside me, Wembus."

Wembus sat on the bench next to him.

"How long have you served me, Wembus?"

"Over fifteen years, my lord."

"And how many more will you serve?"

"As many as there are."

"I wish that were true, my friend. More than you know." He struck Wembus with a stone hidden in his closed hand. Wembus fell to the side. Blood trailed down his face.

"I wanted to believe it would never be you, Wembus. I showed you mercy time and again waiting for you to either prove yourself or betray me."

Wembus's head spun. His ears rang. The cold grasp of iron manacles closed over his wrists.

"We were brothers in arms, warriors in this battle, but now I see I fight alone."

Wembus tried to give a defense but the words tangled in his head.

Tephall opened the hatch. "Signal your masters if you can. Tell them you've failed. Tell them to try again. I await them." He left Wembus chained to the wall atop the tower.

Wembus strained at his confines but he was a captive now. He shivered and cried into the coming night.

CHAPTER 18

THE BLACKBIRDS' TRAIL

—∞—

Col and Caménor crowded in Naboth's den. With Spring nearing it felt smaller than during Winter's bitter days. Naboth still nursed the hearth and the warmth still chased what cold remained. Col was glad for the old man's company. He'd been a quiet and reassuring support and Col no longer felt like a weed in the garden.

"Nea and I are going to build a fort today. I've got it all planned out in my head," Col said. "She says she's never built one before."

"Is that what she said?" Naboth asked.

"Yes, why?"

"That's odd. I'm sure I've seen her build quite a few over the years."

"Why would she tell me she's never built one before?"

Naboth smiled and the corners of his mouth pushed his wrinkles into bunches on the sides of his face.

"That's not important right now, Col," Caménor interrupted. "There's something we need to discuss."

Col and Naboth looked at him expectantly.

"We've been here too long. We need to leave. Tonight."

"We're leaving?"

"You knew we weren't staying long."

"The Kheva aren't going to find us here. I could barely find us if I wanted to. And I'm already here!"

"You're getting too attached, Col."

"I'm not attaching myself to anything. I don't want to flee anymore. I like it here. I have a friend. That was your idea, remember?"

"The longer we stay the more danger we're putting everyone in."

"What danger? I feel safer here than I ever did at Ten Rocks."

"Feeling safe and being safe are two different things, Col."

"I'm not leaving."

"You don't get to make that decision."

"I'm the NéPrince. You can't tell me what to do. All you've done is push me for months and now that we're finally here you're going to keep pushing? I'm not going anywhere."

"You won't be prince of anything if you're dead."

"I would think you'd want to stay more than I do," Col said.

"What are you getting at?"

"I've seen the way you look at Sasme. You've been gone twenty years, Caménor. Don't you want more time to be near her?"

"You've crossed the line, Colmeron. Watch your tongue!"

"Don't you threaten me!" Col jumped from his chair.

Caménor jumped to meet him and turned the table over sending bowl and cup clattering to the floor. "You wouldn't be alive if it weren't for me, Col. Try to remember that."

"You know I'm right!"

"Sasme is a married woman. If you think I'd ever try to come between her and Tensoe then you don't know me at all. I'm disgusted you would think that."

Col felt his reasoning shrink like a slug under salt.

"Above all, your safety is my concern. Do you really think I would ever put anything before that?"

Col sulked in his chair.

"Answer me, Colmeron."

"Fine!"

"Good."

"Did you ever think you don't know what's best for me?"

"Every day. Now, gather your things. We're leaving tonight." Caménor left without looking at him.

"Do you think we need to leave?" Col asked Naboth.

Naboth leaned forward and put his chin on his cane. He thought for a moment before giving his answer. "You've become family to me, Col. And that makes telling you this so very difficult." He pursed his lips and took a breath. "You can't stay here. I'm sorry. Your presence draws danger to the rest of the family."

"I was hoping you'd changed your mind."

"When all of this is over — and it will be over someday — you would be more welcome here than Summer rains after a drought. Whether you come as a prince or otherwise you will always have a place here."

"I'll come back. I promise."

"I hope you do."

"When Caménor left all those years ago, did he promise he would come back?"

"He did at one time, but when he left I knew I wouldn't see him again. He was too hurt."

"You knew about him and Sasme?"

"Oh, yes. It was as clear as a blue sky he was in love with her. And she held a certain affection for him, but it was Tensoe she really loved."

"Do you think she would've felt differently if she'd known who he was?"

"I'm afraid, if anything, she would've felt betrayed. Your uncle was himself with her. If she'd loved him, his being a prince would have meant nothing. I think it's been difficult for him to be here again."

"Maybe, but he seems happier than I've seen him in a long time. Like he's finally home."

"This was a very special place for him and he was very special to us."

"Then why does he want to leave?"

"I don't think he wants to, Col, but he knows he must. Putting someone else's needs before your own, whether you're a parent or an uncle or a friend, is what love asks of us. You'll learn this in time." He leaned back and stamped his cane on the floor. "The day is getting away from you. Go and find your friend."

"One more thing?"

"Of course."

"Will you tell me what happened to the Earthkings before I leave?"

Naboth hesitated. "If that's what you'd like, yes."

"Good. I'll see you tonight."

Col was glad to leave the den. It was a good day to be outside and revel in Winter's passing. The air felt clean and the sky filled with a radiant light that rained down on the thawing land.

Nea came up behind him. "Talking to my grandfather again, I see."

"So what?" he flashed a grin at her. He liked that he could tease without upsetting her.

"Your father was in there too. What were the three of you talking about?"

"Not much. Just our plans for the Spring. We can't stay here forever." It was nice to tell the truth for once, to not have to think on his feet to ensure his secret was secure.

"Are you leaving soon?"

"No, it'll be awhile," he lied.

"Can I ask you a question?"

"You always do."

"What's inside the box?"

"What box?" Col knew what she meant but didn't let on.

"The one you thought I stole."

"Oh, *that* box! I don't know. It won't open." They wandered past the pond and down the slope toward the tree line.

"Where did you get it?"

"I found it."

"Where did you find it?"

"On an island in the middle of the sea," he mused.

"No, you didn't!"

"Fine. Don't believe me." He loved the way her eyes went wide with mock fury. He loved seeing her like this, playfully exasperated. It was a dance and he was realizing he knew the steps very well.

The ground squished like a sponge from drinking in the melting snow. One at a time they crossed Tinea's bridge. It was sturdy enough for them but would've been a danger to anyone much bigger.

"Sometimes I think you make things up," she said when they reached the other side.

"Maybe." He smiled. They stopped where an outcropping of boulders slathered in moss perched over a shallow gully. "These rocks are perfect. We'll build here. We'll put the door here and the drawbridge there. Up there can be the lookout. Start collecting branches. Big ones that we can use for walls." He gave the orders but Nea had already collected an armful.

Col saw the finished bastion in his mind. It was better than anything he'd ever done. It was going to be magnificent. But as noon neared only one wall was up and even that had fallen down three times.

"You're not very good at this, are you?" Nea said. She sat with her palms pressed against the rock she was on.

"It just takes a little while, that's all. Hand me that big one." He pointed to the branch next to her. She handed it to him and he planted it in the soft terrain. He picked up one roughly the same length and placed it a few feet from the first. He set a shorter one across the top, stood back and declared, "See, we've got a door!" The frame slid in the mud and tipped over.

"You're hopeless," Nea said. "Let me show you." She set up the doorway the same way Col had but used two more stout branches to support the frame from behind "There. That should hold it until we get some more walls done."

"Your grandfather was right. You have done this before."

"He told you that?"

Col nodded. "He often talks about you."

"He does?" Her face lit.

"Of course. Why shouldn't he?"

"Sometimes I think he doesn't even like me."

"He does. Very much." It was a stretch, but it was bound to be true in some way. Wasn't it?

"Did he say that?"

Col tried to think back through all the conversations he'd had with the old man. There weren't many that had revolved around his granddaughter but there had never been an unkind word spoken against her either. "I can hear it in his voice."

Col wasn't sure if his response could be considered a lie or not. It didn't matter. It had made her happy and that was enough of a reason for him to believe it.

"You know you're lucky you have me helping you today. I'm fairly certain you'd die if you ever had to survive in the wilderness."

"I've survived things you wouldn't believe."

"Oh, really? Like what?"

"I was almost taken by a Piskie once."

"A Piskie?"

"It's an evil, dreadful spirit. It captures you and imprisons you for a thousand years. When it finally releases you everyone and everything you ever knew is long gone. I'm lucky I escaped."

"And how did you manage that?"

"I cut off its hand when it grabbed me." He puffed his chest in an effort to look fearsome.

While he talked she built a wall on either side of the door, weaving smaller sticks and twigs between the larger branches. "that must have been scary." She was less than impressed.

"Not for me."

"Are you done telling stories or are you going to help? This fort was your idea."

Col looked at her handiwork and then at his own. This wasn't as much fun as he thought it would be. "I think I'll start the tower," he said.

"Okay. I'll help once I finish down here."

"No, I got it." He didn't need her help. He just needed a little space to work, that was all.

"Okay," she sighed.

Col climbed around the edge of the outcropping and mounted the highest crag. He was deciding the best way to build his tower when he noticed a blackbird gripping the branch above him. It called a quick series of shrill chirps and stared at him. A second blackbird landed beside it. The first chirruped twice and they both stared at Col.

Col moved around looking for a branch to start with, but their eyes stayed on him. He looked up. "What do you want?"

"I didn't say anything," Nea replied from below.

"I wasn't talking to you."

The first bird hopped to another branch and the second called before following. They waited a minute before repeating the action. From the third branch they both sang to Col. He put down his stick and walked under them.

"What?"

The first tweeted at him and flew ahead. Col followed as the birds moved from branch to branch, tree to tree. He was quickly lost. He didn't care once he saw where he was. The mouth of a cave yawned from a hillside. The maw was partially concealed in a curtain of old vines. Cold air hit Col's face as the cave exhaled.

He peered into the dark hole, but his eyes pulled nothing from the black. The birds watched him and waited.

"I'm not going in there," he said.

The first bird warbled another long series of cheeps before both birds glided into the cave.

Col paused a moment and considered what he was about to do. He pushed aside the draping vines and with his first step tumbled down a steep bank. The cave's jagged bottom stabbed at him. He coughed and gently rubbed the bruises on his back and arms.

The cavern opened wider the deeper he went. The dark swallowed what little light the entrance let in. The echoes of his footsteps traveled farther and farther. He heard the distant plop and splash of dripping water.

"Is anyone there?" he called. Wings flapped ahead. With his arms stretched in front of him he moved forward. Why had he even followed those stupid birds? He thought to leave but he had no idea which way was out.

A soft grunt came from the far end of the cavern followed by the sharp scraping of stones. A spark exploded. Another quickly followed. The sparks took to tinder and a tiny flame soon illuminated the cave. A massive form blew gently on it. The flame grew and the tinder was gingerly set beneath crisscrossed logs. The arsonist turned his head and revealed a mane of shaggy hair and a beard braided into two ropes below his chin.

"My apologies, my lord. I meant to have this ready before you got here. Rees and Wurt worked faster than I anticipated." Col's host stood up. He rose and rose until his head nearly touched the cave's high ceiling.

"You're a giant!" Col gasped.

"It's the way I was born. You get used to it after the first few years. My name is Thash," he bowed. He spoke slowly with a deep voice that rumbled off the cave walls.

"You called me 'lord'."

"You are a prince, aren't you?"

"Yes. I'm Colmeron, second son of Tephall and NéPrince of Arnoc. How did you know who I was?"

"A little bird told me. Two, in fact." He twisted to show two blackbirds perched on his shoulder. "Rees and Wurt. The finest companions I've ever known."

"Did you send them to find me? Is that why they led me here?"

"When they told me a prince of Arnoc was on my land I thought they were teasing me, but they insisted and I knew I had to give you a proper welcome. So, welcome. Please, sit down." He pointed to a large cushion of straw and fur.

Col sat down and crossed his legs. The light from the fire reflected off the walls. They were in a large room that Col thought must have seemed small to the giant. Thash sat across the fire from him. Next to him was a table. A few utensils were scattered on it and two large wooden bowls were filled with potatoes and mushrooms the size of Col's fist. Thash sat in an enormous wooden rocking chair that creaked steadily as he tipped back and forth, back and forth. Rees and Wurt contented themselves on his shoulder and only occasionally gave a peep.

"My uncle was here a long time ago. Did you meet him, too?" Caménor had never mentioned meeting a giant. Then again, there was a lot his uncle had never told him.

"You're the first prince I've met. I was probably asleep when your uncle was here. Though I'm sorry to have missed him. I suppose I miss a lot while I sleep."

"Is it true that giants sleep for a hundred years?" Col asked.

"A hundred years? I'd have to be pretty tired to sleep that long. No, we giants usually sleep for 50 years or so at a time. Though, my father once slept for 72."

"How old do giants live to be?"

"Oh, some of us live to three, sometimes four thousand, years old. I'm still young though. Only 749 this Summer."

At such an age Col realized Thash must know more about the Earthkings than anyone he'd ever met. "Thash?"

"Yes, my prince?"

"Were you alive when the Earthkings reigned?"

"No, I can't say that I was. That was before my time. Before my father's, in fact."

"Do you know what happened to them?"

"You mean you don't? I should think that Arnoc's royalty would be well versed in their own history."

"The Earthkings were always regarded as faerie tales in my house. Not history."

"How can you learn from what you don't know?"

"Will you tell me? Naboth said it was because of pride."

"Aye, but first how about some dinner? It would be unforgivable if I let a prince in my house without feeding him." Thash dipped a handful of potatoes and mushrooms in a dark, pungent sauce he said was made from honey and ginger root. He skewered the food and turned it over the fire as he began his story.

"King Urion was the last of the Earthkings and pride was indeed his downfall. He was powerful and ruled well just as his fathers had. But Urion grew too concerned with his own legacy, with how he could be even greater than all the Earthkings before him.

"Blinded by his own arrogance, he failed to notice the change that took place in the members of his council. One by one they were taken by the Noflim. They spoke lies and fed Urion's pride until he was so brimming with himself he didn't oppose what they suggested. They said if he really was the greatest of the Earthkings, why shouldn't he go where the others had not?

"He opened the doors and entered the Sacred Grove. The place all Earthkings had guarded but none had entered. He saw that which should not be seen and walked where feet should not tread.

"With the doors to the grove open, the Noflim attacked. Armies of the Kheva Adem rushed upon the city. Wave after wave of monstrous beasts filled the streets. Thanir appeared in the grove and warned Urion of the invasion. Urion sealed the Sacred Grove and left the Thanir to guard it. He rushed to stem the onslaught, but before he could lift a hand he was overtaken. His power was gone. His pride had robbed him of his strength. Orum had withdrawn his blessing from him.

"They bound Urion in chains. The faces of his once trusted advisors sneered at him with the venomous eyes of the Noflim within. They threatened him and tried to coerce him into opening the doors, but he could not. They killed those he loved in front of him and left their bodies before him. He howled through the nights and moaned through the days as the enemy pounded at the doors to the Sacred Grove.

"In the darkest hour of the night Urion cried out to Orum. He cried out for his people, cried out for his shame. He had failed. He had proved himself not the greatest, but the least worthy of the Earthkings. His head hung low and the rhythms of his body stilled. Death was upon him.

"His heart beat once. The pulse flowed to the walls he was chained to. It beat again and they cracked. The screams around him fell silent. A noise like thunder came from his cell. The Kheva leapt upon him.

"His body contorted with rage as he fought the beasts. His chains clattered to the ground and he rose with a loud cry. Entaramu shook with the king's fury. The streets split and the walls crumbled. The Kheva Adem clamored upward as the sea churned and swallowed the city. Entaramu and all those in it — men and Kheva, King Urion and the Noflim, even the Sacred Grove itself — sank below the sea. Entaramu, the City of Kings, was gone. The heart of Arnoc had been destroyed and along with it passed the power of the Earthkings. The sea came to be called 'Enturion' in memorial for the city and her final king.

"And as you said, Prince Colmeron, what was once history became legend." Thash rotated their meal over the flames.

"I never knew there was such darkness in my heritage," Col said. "It's horrible!"

"You are not your ancestors, my prince."

"I'm not even king and I don't want to be. That was my brother's role, not mine."

Thash tested the potatoes with the tip of his finger and nodded to himself. He pulled the food from the spits and dropped a heavy portion into a bowl for Col. "Life rarely hands us the roles we would choose for ourselves. We all have secrets that darken our past but that doesn't mean we let them cloud our future."

Col blew on his food and picked up a mushroom. He bit into the soft flesh and tasted the sweet, smokey flavor. He tried not to think about what he'd just learned.

"I'd venture to say you've never had those before. They grow only underground. They're giant food."

"Tell me more about giants, Thash," Col said. "You're the first I've met."

"Such a shame. There was a time when giants were found all over Arnoc. We've been here from the beginning, you know. But our time passed long ago."

"Was it because of men?"

"No. It was because of the Numen. It was giants that dug the pit Orum condemned the Numen to. Did you know that?"

Col shook his head with his mouth full.

"It's true. Once men were turned by the Noflim — once they became the Kheva Adem — Orum knew something had to be done. For men are of both spirit and flesh and could have proved the undoing of all he had made. So he decided it would be through men he would sustain his creation. He brought Derid to Entaramu and gave him the power to protect the Sacred Grove. To keep the Numen trapped for all time."

Col put his bowl down. He wasn't hungry anymore.

Rees and Wurt, seeing that Col was done with his meal, hopped from Thash's shoulder and picked at the scraps.

"That's not for you, little ones," Thash swiped at them. They flapped and squawked but kept their distance.

"It's okay," Col said. "I'm done with it. They can have the rest." He nudged the bowl toward them and they returned to their feast.

"I forget how small men's stomachs are," Thash said.

"It was the best meal I've ever had in a cave."

"I hope it won't be the last. You've been an excellent guest. The first I've had in many years."

"Thank you, Thash. I can't imagine meeting a kinder giant."

"Nor I a gentler prince. I'll have Rees and Wurt lead you back to the farm."

The blackbirds trilled in protest.

"Alright, alright," said Thash. "They say it's late and far too dark for them to get you anywhere but lost. I've been a terrible host."

"It's night?"

"As soon as dawn breaks I'll see you safely home."

Col smiled to himself. He'd told Caménor he wasn't leaving tonight. "Thash, it would be my honor to spend the night in a giant's lair."

"You are very kind. Thank you. Now, lie back and be at peace."

Col spread out on the pile of furs. Let Caménor worry for a night.

Thash began to sing. His voice held the words gently, like a newborn baby.

Feet follow feet beneath a river of stars
Look for my light from wherever you are
I'll seek the land that hides you away
Where wings are free from the weight of day.

Ever between the trees I'll roam
Calling your name, calling you home
Ever through nights I'll search you out
Never to question, never to doubt

Taken on the wind like a curl of smoke
Like a dream fallen far and broke
No eyes, no hands, no voice left to sing
Only words whispered in the flap of a wing.

Feet follow feet beneath a river of stars
Abandon your flight from wherever you are
I'll forget the land that hides you away
For you've returned home this blessed day.

Col slept soundly as the words of Thash's song drifted over him. They flitted in his ears and formed the dreams he dreamt that night, of a man searching for his love with a lantern in hand.

—~~—

Wembus tugged at his chains more out of habit than conscious effort. It was futile but somewhere in his mind he prayed for a miracle. For two days he languished at the top of the tower. His wrists were bruised and cut where the manacles dug in. He wasn't asleep or awake. He slumped forward. His spirit was drained and without that the body is useless.

The hatch moaned sharply as it flipped open. Still Wembus didn't stir. He didn't want to face anyone.

A voice called to him. He hummed to drown out the noise.

"Wembus!"

The chains fell from his wrists and his arms dropped impotently at his sides.

"Wembus! I need your help."

Wembus inspected his wrists. They were free. Was this his miracle? He reached out and grabbed the collar of his deliverer. He opened his eyes. It was the king who had freed him.

"All is at an end. I've failed," Tephall said.

Wembus closed his eyes. "The failure is mine, my lord."

"No, you succeeded. Your allies are here."

"Who is here?" Wembus rose on weak legs.

"Kheva Adem. They've come to take me. You were my servant once. My friend. Don't let your masters take me. Remember your first loyalty." He held his sword out to Wembus. "Kill me!"

"You are the only master I serve, my lord!"

"Take my sword and end this before they find me. Do it or I'll leap from this tower."

Wembus took the sword from him. He pulled him down through the hatch.

The agonized cries of those below reached the tower and grew louder as they descended. The screams were followed by the awful, sickening roars of the Kheva.

Wembus peered around a corner. The evening pall cast itself through the windows. Torches burned low in their sconces, the light retreating.

"Don't let them...," Tephall whispered softly.

The screams came from the eastern end of the castle. By the gardens. There was still time.

"If we can get to the western yard before the enemy, we may have a chance of escape," Wembus said.

How much more confident Etau would be if he were here. But he wasn't here. He was dead like so many others. Wembus pushed the thought from his mind.

They only needed to manage a few hallways to make it to the outer wall. From there it would be a dash to the stables. Their escape was simple enough as long as the enemy remained distracted to the east.

The cries of the castle staff rose higher. The enemy was nearing.

The two of them reached one of the outer doors. The western yard lay just beyond it. Wembus pushed. Something blocked it.

"I need you to help me," Wembus leaned into the door.

Tephall gazed at the heavy wooden frame as though by taking in every grain and memorizing every line it would open to someplace else. He blinked and joined Wembus. Together they bullied it enough for a man to slip through. Tephall went first.

"Wait!" Wembus cried and squeezed through after him. The bodies of the stablehands were stacked against the other side of the door. He reached for Tephall but something else took his hand. He was thrown through the air. He hit the ground hard on his right side. His ribs cracked. He gasped as the air fled his lungs.

Something stood over the king. Gnarled horns twisted down its knotted back. It huffed its breath into the cold air like ominous clouds rising over them.

Tephall stared up at the beast. His sword was lying in the grass near him. He scrambled for it and stood clutching it in both hands. The Kheva stood more than a full head taller than him and a great deal wider. Tephall raised the sword.

The Kheva growled. Its thin nostrils flared. A rumble came from its throat. "Silly man." It swung and slammed Tephall into the wall. There was a soft crunch as he hit the ground.

The Kheva eclipsed him. It reached for Tephall with long, bloody fingers.

Wembus rallied and hurled himself into it. He felt the sinews and muscles, the heavily covered ribs and heat from the Kheva's body. This nightmare was real.

They crashed into the bodies blocking the door. Wembus rolled off the beast. In that scarce second the Kheva leapt against the wall. It launched itself away from the stone and landed on all fours. It stalked toward Wembus. With its head down its horns pointed up to challenge the stars. Wembus knelt beside the king.

"You cannot save him," the Kheva said.

Wembus stared at him with wide eyes and a tight throat.

"Don't let them take me, Wembus. Don't let me be a puppet," Tephall pleaded. He slid the dagger from his belt. Wembus nodded once and took it. Hot air rushed over them. Two more Kheva surrounded them. One rose up, even more menacing than the first. The other stayed on all fours and circled them.

"Your king was right to lose hope. We watched him in the night as he wept into his pillow. He is weak. Just as his fathers were. We watched them, too. Waiting and watching as our numbers grew. Men are so easily swayed. Your end is here, stubborn man. Give us your king."

The three Kheva moved closer. Wembus could wait no longer. He drove the blade hard into the king's heart. Tephall convulsed and sputtered. Tears streamed down Wembus's face. He wouldn't let them have him.

The six fingered hand of a Kheva tore Wembus from his fallen lord. He was lifted from the ground and flung aside. They pulled the knife from Tephall's chest and held him up like a doll.

Wembus tried to rise from his slump but a foot slammed him into the mud. The face of the enemy bent close. He heard the rumbling in its throat as it snorted hot bilious breaths on his face. Its nose looked like it'd been smashed a dozen times. The creature looked anything but human, though it had once been.

"The king is dead. I killed his firstborn myself. Where are the other princes?"

Wembus clenched his jaw and grimaced.

"Tell us where they are." It pressed hard on his left arm until it snapped.

"Far from here," Wembus gritted his teeth against the pain.

"A king's servant knows everything his master does." The Kheva went to the other arm. "Where are the princes?" Crack! Wembus's right arm broke faster than the left.

"I don't know!"

The Kheva Adem towered over Wembus. It slammed a foot onto his knee. Wembus writhed as the bones were ground together.

"I'll ask again. Where are the princes?"

"They are safe," he cried

The first Kheva picked up Tephall's sword and drove it into Wembus's mangled leg. It pulled the blade down and crudely cleaved limb from body. They lifted Wembus by his only remaining good limb. Two arms dangled uselessly and a mangled stump poured blood down his chest and over his face.

"We are everywhere, fleshling. And the eyes of our masters roam freely. We will find them."

Wembus laughed and spit blood on the grass. "Your desperation shows your weakness, twisted one. Your masters will fall again. Even in the warped mind of a mad king Orum has worked to ensure your doom."

Wembus fell like a length of knotted rope. The Kheva moved swiftly over the castle walls and disappeared. Flames erupted from inside the castle.

Wembus lay crumpled on the ground. He couldn't move but he could still see. He saw the face of his king, saved from the fate he had dreaded. He thought to close his eyes and let death take him but a man kneeled over the king. He leaned close and whispered. He put his ear to Tephall's mouth and listened.

Tephall's chest rose slightly. A final breath.

He stood and caught Wembus staring at him with vacant eyes. He walked calmly toward the flames and disappeared.

CHAPTER 19

A KNIFE TO THE ROPE

In the early dawn Rees and Wurt led Col back to the farm. Wisps of pink mingled in the shadows as the world woke. Thash's companions were the only birds to sing so early and Col whistled in tune as he followed them. He bit off a chunk of the potato the giant had given him as a parting gift. It made for a good breakfast.

The rocks breaking through the forest floor thought to trip Col but he was too alert, too jubilant, to be troubled by them. He pranced over them. He jumped from one to the other like the steps to some elaborate dance. He finished his potato and rubbed his sleeve on his face.

He wasn't sure what kind of welcome he'd receive when he got back to the farm. He'd been gone nearly a day after all. Would they believe his tale? It didn't matter. He was glad he'd gotten away. He was beginning to suffocate under Caménor's strict orders.

Rees trilled overhead. Just over a hillock was the ravine and the water rushing through its belly drowned out the noise of the forest. Col put his hand up to shield his eyes from the rising sun and raced up the path to Nea's bridge. Caménor emerged on the other side. Col didn't notice the knife in his hand.

He was sorry to see his retreat come to an end. His uncle yelled but his voice was lost in the fervor of the water.

Col waved him off. "I'm coming. Don't worry." He grabbed the bridge's twisting rail.

Caménor sawed feverishly at the ropes.

Col jumped back as the bridge swung loose and smashed against the sheer wall of the ravine.

"What are you doing?" Col yelled.

Caménor's voice finally rose above the din. "Run!" Tensoe came from behind and pulled him away from the bridge.

Col froze. The branches behind the men snapped and the light from the sun blinked as a Kheva emerged from the wood.

It didn't matter how far he had run, they'd found him.

"Run!" Caménor shouted.

Didn't he understand? Col had run as far as he could and still the enemy was here.

The beast grabbed Caménor by the neck and held him over of the ravine. Caménor's legs swung uselessly as he kicked at the Kheva.

"No! Don't!" Col screamed.

Tensoe stepped to the edge and called out to Col. "I think it's time you came back. Don't you, young prince?" His lips didn't move. Tensoe's jaw was slack while the spirit spoke through him. What was worse was that it still used his voice.

Col felt the Kheva's eyes on him. He tried not to shake.

"Come across that tree and your uncle's life won't end here," Tensoe pointed to the tree where Col had slipped the day Nea saved him.

Col went to the tree.

"Don't do it, Col. You have to run!" Caménor gasped. The Kheva squeezed tighter.

"Do you think I won't kill him?" Tensoe's head tilted to the side as the Noflim spat the words from his mouth. "Run and he dies. I promise you."

"Your lies are thin, spirit," Caménor said.

"You think you are wise, fleshling, but your ignorance runs deep."

Col's eyes met with Caménor's. He couldn't let him die. He stepped to the tree.

"No!" Caménor brought his knee up, reached into his boot and slid out a knife. He jammed the blade through the Kheva's arm without hesitation.

It roared in surprise and released him. Caménor fell free and dropped down, down, down into the river.

"Bring the prince to me," Tensoe said to the beast.

The Kheva stepped onto the fallen tree.

A blackbird trilled overhead and the ground suddenly trembled. Thash burst from behind him. He seized the fallen tree and heaved it into the river. The Kheva tumbled down with it.

The giant's arm wrapped around Col and he whisked him away. He cradled him as though he were an infant. Helpless against the world. Col struggled to free himself. He had to go back. He had to help Caménor. But as the day dawned so did the realization that his protector was gone. Col hid his face in the giant's chest.

Thash carried him to the top of a high hill. The bare trees around them offered scant cover. He gingerly set Col on the ground. Rees and Wurt sat on the giant's shoulder in silent company.

"I always feared they might return," Thash said.

"They came for me. If I'd left sooner they wouldn't have taken Tensoe and Caménor wouldn't be dead."

"You cannot blame yourself, little one."

"They told me they'd find me, Thash. They were looking for me and I led them here."

"Something terrible has happened. I believe they would have come soon enough whether you were there or not."

"What should I do?"

Thash picked him up and stood him on his shoulder. "Do you see that ridge across the valley?"

"Yes."

"There's a village just beyond it. Find help there." He lowered Col to the ground.

"You're not coming with me?"

"I can't take you any further. You need to stay hidden and fleeing with a giant would only draw attention. Wurt will guide you from here. Stay off the roads and close to the trees. Let the shadows be your ally."

Col took in the valley that stretched between him and the village. He'd never gone that far by himself. He turned to beg Thash to stay with him but the giant was gone.

Wurt perched on a branch above him. Col looked back. Back to where he was happy. Back to where his uncle was still alive and he was just a boy building forts with his friend. He wanted to go back to the farm and find that everyone was okay and this was a bad dream, something the mushrooms had given him.

He looked ahead. A shadow filled the valley. It seemed so lonely, so empty. Wurt called ahead of him. He had to go. He had to move forward. Going back would change nothing.

He stumbled down the long slope into the great valley. Large wooded patches spread into the distance. The gaps around them were filled with swirling seas of grass, brown and filthy from the Winter.

Col staggered through the day. He moved from tree to tree in constant awareness. At the sound of every startled deer or wayward rabbit he ducked beneath one of the ancient oaks that filled the valley. He tried to listen beyond the sound of his heart pounding in his chest. Each time he was sure would be his last. The Kheva had found him at the farm. What chance did he have of leaving the valley alive?

That night Col burrowed himself in the crook of a burly oak root and covered himself in leaves. He tried to think of all the good things he had come to know. He saw again the light in the far off window and felt the slip of the fur covering Naboth's chair. He heard Nea's voice mocking him and Sasme offering him breakfast in her sweet tones. But the memories turned sour. Those things would never be again.

He saw the fresh blood staining Tensoe's lips, his jaw loose as the spirit spoke through him. He wretched as the Kheva's eyes stared into him. They twisted his guts around the tips of his ribs. He cried out as he helplessly watched Caménor slip from the monster's hand and fall forever into the swift current.

Col woke with the moon low on the horizon. A layer of frosty leaves covered him. His face was wet from crying in his sleep.

Wurt nervously scraped his talons on a rock beside Col. The sound set Col's teeth on edge and he swatted at the bird. Wurt squawked at him and flapped away.

Col stayed in the oak's embrace. Why should he get up? Why shouldn't he just stay here and die? There was nothing left for him. All he'd ever had — all he'd ever known — was gone. The Kheva Adem had come. Col would never be able to go home again.

He laid his head back against the root. Let Mino be king.

Mino.

Col sat up. The sodden leaves tumbled from him. He had to survive. It wasn't a choice. He had to fight for Mino.

He stood and stepped forward. Wurt waited for him. He tried to stay close to the trees but was forced to cross roughshod sections of field. Wearily, he ran over them. Being caught in the open was too great a risk to slow down.

As the sun abandoned him to night Col stopped to catch his breath. The problem with stopping was that it gave him time to think and thinking was what he was trying to avoid. As long as he kept moving it was easier to distract himself. He had to look where his feet were, where the bird was. He had to listen for any sign of warning or call of alarm.

He caught his breath and looked for Wurt but the bird had disappeared.

"Wurt?" Col called cautiously. There was no call in reply. Only the eerie silence of the wood.

Col was alone. Really, truly alone. Lost in the middle of this awful valley. He took deep breaths to calm himself but choked on them. He gulped air again and tasted smoke on the wind.

He ran ahead. The ground rose, steeper and steeper, until he crested the ridge Thash had shown him. On the other side was a small village. Smoke rose from chimneys. Light glistened from shop windows and lanterns on carriages.

The smell of smoke mixed with the redolence of cattle and newly churned earth. It was a comfort. A small one, at least. Clouds gathered overhead and drops of cold rain hit Col's skin like nails through timber.

He entered the village square with his shoulders hunched. He looked warily at the faces around him. Who would help him? Who could?

Most of the village's residents were home for the evening but a few stragglers remained. They moved about going to and from wherever their lives took them. He watched a man and a woman walk arm in arm to a windowless building at the far corner of the square. They knocked twice and the door opened. The smell of roasting meat slipped into the night and the door closed behind them. Col crossed the square and knocked twice on the door. A mustachioed man with bushy eyebrows and squinty eyes opened it and looked down at him.

"What do you want?" he chewed on a turkey leg as he spoke.

"My father is dead," Col blurted out.

"Oh, yeah? Mine, too. What do you want me to do about it?"

"It was yesterday morning," Col said. Had it really been only the day before? He felt he'd lived in that valley for a month.

A woman, tall with a long face and even longer hair, came up behind the bushy browed man. "Who's this?"

"Just another beggar," the man said.

"I'm not a beggar!"

"Then what do you want?" the woman said.

"I just need a little food."

"Ah ha! He begs!" the man pointed at him and took another bite of turkey.

"You look healthy enough to me," long face said.

"I am not a beggar! I'm a prince of Arnoc!"

"Sure you are. Get out of here before I find my stick," the man shoved Col back into the square and slammed the door shut.

Col tried other doors but his welcome was always the same. Beggars weren't tolerated. Some didn't even bother to answer the door.

The rain fell in fat, icy drops. Col pulled his coat close around him. It was the only thing he had left to call his own.

He left the village. Just beyond its lights a cluster of rocks burrowed in a hillside. He found a cleft in them and crawled inside. It was cold and hard but at least he was out of the rain. He huddled in the back of the opening and fell asleep.

He laid there through the night and into the next day. The rain continued unabated and the cold stayed with him. How could he help his brother if he couldn't even do anything for himself?

A shriek from the village broke his solitude. He sat up and listened. Men and women cried out before being cut off. This was followed by bellowing roars that didn't come from man or animal.

They were here.

The Kheva Adem had found him again. Col pushed himself farther into his hole and covered his ears. Maybe they wouldn't see him. Trapped in the back of a hole in a rock was no way for a prince to die. Then again, he didn't feel much like royalty these days.

The cries from the village quieted. The Kheva Adem must've killed everyone. If he was lucky they would keep moving.

He turned over on the hard rock. His sides were bruised and he couldn't breathe. With every passing hour the cleft felt more like a coffin, but he didn't dare leave, not even for a minute.

Night fell over the village and thunder rolled overhead. It was so close he could feel it rumble inside of him. The tremor broke free something that had welled within for two days.

He was tired, hungry and grieving, but more than any of that he was angry. He was angry that all he'd ever known had been torn from him. He remembered Nabal's mauled body tangled in the undergrowth. He had been the pulled thread that unraveled everything. He thought of Tonn laying pale and ragged on the table.

Col raged in the dark and finally gave a voice to the fury within. He railed against everything and everyone that had brought him to this point. He hated the Noflim and their despicable servants. He despised his father for sending him away and cursed Caménor for leaving him to this world. His shouts echoed from the cleft.

His wrath spent he laid back down. His mouth was shut but the echoes continued. The sound became a wail, a shrill cry that filled the night.

But it wasn't his echo he heard. The Kheva had found another victim.

Col tried to shut the cries out, but they moved closer. A woman pleaded. "Somebody help me! I don't want to die!"

A low growl and a heavy pounding answered her.

She was hysterical now. "Tannen com sunnen!"

Col turned over with eyes wide in the dark. He waited for it to come again.

CHAPTER 20

THE BIRTH OF A KING

"Tannen com sunnen!"

Col crawled to the edge of the cleft. A woman ran toward the rocks. It was the long faced woman from the day before. The one who'd mocked him. The Kheva quickly overtook her. It grabbed her by her long hair and pulled her to the ground. She cried desperate tears. "Tannen com sunnen!"

Where is our deliverer?

The words struck deep within Col.

The Kheva crouched over the woman. It studied her as it moved close for the kill. It closed a hand over her face to muffle her sobs.

Col leaned forward. His fingers closed over the edge of the rock under him. The stone curved to fit his palm. He pulled on it as he stood. The stone didn't break from the ledge but slid free, a dagger from its sheath. It looked much like the one Caménor had given him.

Without a thought, Col leapt onto the Kheva's back. He grabbed a ridged horn with one hand and stabbed with the other. The blows glanced off the beast's thick hide. It bucked and twisted until Col was thrown off. It growled and swung wide, swiping at him with the sharp tips of its fingers. Col rolled to his feet. He slashed with the knife. The blade divided the soft flesh under the Kheva's arm. Col lunged for it again but the enemy was faster. It grabbed him and wrapped its hands around his chest. It lifted him into the air, ready to bash him on the rocks.

Col held the knife with both hands and raised it above his head. He swung down hard. The blade bit deep into its skull. The Kheva toppled backward and dropped Col into the mud. The impact forced the air from his lungs. He stumbled to his feet. He tried desperately to breathe as he looked for the next attack. But all that came was the rain.

Water dripped from the long tendrils of hair that fell over Col's face. The woman grabbed his hand. It startled him and he tore himself from her. She grabbed it again and held it to her bruised cheek.

"You saved me!" she cried. "You killed it! You killed it! You saved me!"

Col looked at the stone knife protruding from the dead Kheva's head. What had he done?

He pulled his hand free from the hysterical woman and ran.

She called after him but her words were lost in the rain.

He fled into the wilds. Branches lashed him and bracken tangled around his feet. The forest screamed at him as he ran. Every bird and beast sounded alarm.

He stumbled down a muddy slope. His hand slipped from a slick trunk and he fell. He tumbled down the hill. The ground beat at him mercilessly until he came to rest at the bottom. Hours later he woke to utter silence. Even the rain had stopped its pattering.

He tried to move but his limbs refused him.

Someone walked in front of him. Laying in the mud all Col could see were a pair of feet, bare and worn.

"There's blood on your hands," the stranger said.

Col looked at his hand. The Kheva's blood covered it.

"That's good. It's unfitting in war for a king not to know the blood of his enemy."

"I'm not a king." Col's jaw ached.

"If not you, then who?"

"Tephall is king."

"Your father's reign has reached its end, Colmeron."

"My father is dead?" His throat tightened.

"Yes. Your father is dead."

Hot tears slid down Col's cheeks.

"He also had blood on his hands. Not of the enemy, though. The blood he took brought death. The blood you spilled is a sign for the living."

"What sort of sign is that?"

"Winter ends. In Spring a new hope is found. You pulled that blade from the rock by the power I first gave your ancestors."

"Who are you?"

"You know my name."

"I'm just a boy. I'm not ready."

"You are no longer a child, King Colmeron. You left that behind when you slew your enemy. To the west, beyond the barrens of Akeldama, lies the Broken Mountains. Go there. Your people will need their king soon."

"What if I fail?"

"I know your fears, my son. You share their blood but you are not your ancestors. The power of the Earthkings is restored in you. Not only because Arnoc needs it but because you are worthy of it. The moment you put the life of another above your own you became worthy."

"I'm afraid."

"Do you think I won't finish what was begun here? Don't be afraid. I'll be with you. Neither is all lost. Your brother still lives."

"Mino? Where is he?"

"He's safe."

Col nearly wept with relief. He still had Mino.

"I give to you now the same charge I gave to each of your ancestors, Colmeron: protect Entaramu, preserve the Sacred Garden, and serve your people. Arnoc is in your hands now."

The weight of the charge terrified him and he made to say so but the words would not come, could not come, for Orum knelt beside him and placed a hand on his head. "You have all that you need now," he said tenderly. "Drink and be restored." Orum rose and walked away. His footprints filled with water.

Col put his mouth to the nearest track and drank. It was like a coat of pain and weariness was stripped from him. He stood invigorated. The hunger that ate away at him was filled and his thirst quenched. He felt the forest burst with that same life. He suddenly knew the trees and the sway of their branches. He sensed the eagerness of new grass beneath him. He was master of it all.

Orum had told him to go west. Col scarcely knew up from down at the moment let alone East from West.

He gazed at the night sky and the stars grew closer, but it wasn't the sky that drew near. The ground under him rose. It lifted him above the treetops like a father raising his child to see above the crowd. Col could see into the distance on every side. To the west the forest ended abruptly. From there the land was desolate.

Akeldama.

The ground returned to its former level and Col ran toward the plain. He reached the forest's edge as the new day dawned.

The barrens of Akeldama rolled out like a drab, thin blanket. Nothing grew here. It was a hideous scar on the otherwise beautiful face of Arnoc. Col doubted his father had ever even seen it.

He considered the distance before him. It could take days to cross on foot. What he wouldn't give for a horse! He had no food, no water and no way of knowing what to do once he reached the mountains. He wished Caménor were with him. He always had an answer at hand.

The sound of groaning wood and fluttering leaves came from behind him. Four legs rose from the ground. Not legs of flesh but of root and vine twisting over one another until they grew to form the barrel, neck and head of a horse. It was strangely grotesque, this entwining skeleton with sinews of vines. The horse nodded its eyeless head and stomped at the ground with a wooded hoof.

Col warily reached for it. He slowly ran his hand down the horse's flank. A trail of moss followed the path of his hand and spread. It covered the skeleton in a deep green coat.

Col determined the horse was his and mounted it. He ran his fingers through a mane of smooth grass. "I think I'll call you Dasha" It was an old word Col thought meant to grow green. It seemed fitting.

Dasha responded to Col's every move. She was an extension of his power. She was his to command. They broke into a full gallop and rode through the day. From time to time he passed a boulder or a patch of rocky terrain. Before he could think to ride around them they rolled away from him clearing his path.

As night fell a blue haze covered Akeldama behind him. It looked like the moon had fallen on the desert. It was still there when he stopped to rest a few hours later but when he woke in the morning the light was gone.

The ground beneath him was damp but he thought little of it. What surprised him was that he was neither hungry nor thirsty after his day of riding. The energy he gained from his drink the morning before still swelled within him.

Dasha's mane and coat were still lush though she seemed a bit more stiff today. Col gazed around him. The desolation felt endless. Dasha was the only divergent color in a sea of dust.

He pushed on with the rising sun at his back. The miles that passed beneath him seemed the same. One after the other. By day's end Dasha's limbs creaked a little more and Col felt an itch at the back of his throat. He hoped tomorrow would bring him to the Broken Mountains. Though, what was there for him he still didn't know.

The blue glow spread again across the eastern horizon. Col watched it for a long time. It was like the light of a far away city.

Dasha laid down and Col leaned back against her. He had no fire to keep him warm or food to fill his belly. He was a king without.

He'd never thought to be king. And if he had this is certainly not what he would have imagined. An Earthking? Col laughed to himself. More like king of the dirt. He picked up a handful of the stuff and tossed it into the wind.

He watched the blue haze in the distance until he fell asleep. It was gone again in the morning. The ground under him was damp again. He scratched at it hoping for something more but found only more dirt.

Much to his disappointment the day passed just as the previous two had. He was sure Dasha would fall apart soon and his own thirst was growing. After midday he pulled suddenly on her mane. They stopped and he jumped down. He kicked at the barren dirt and cursed. What was he doing? He was riding further and further from his people! Wasn't he supposed to be protecting them? Shouldn't he be doing something other than leaving them behind? Orum had told him to go west. For what? The Kheva were running rampant through Arnoc and their king was fleeing the scene.

King of the dirt, he said to himself again.

He could ride east and reach Arnoc again in less than two days if he didn't stop to sleep. He considered the idea but realized he had no idea what he would do then either. The only thing he knew for sure was what Orum had told him.

He got back on Dasha and turned west. "Let's hope we make it the rest of the way, girl."

He rode until nightfall. The light behind him seemed brighter tonight. He stopped and watched as the light narrowed. It grew brighter until Col made out the figure of a man drawing near.

He got behind Dasha. He had no weapons. No means of fighting.

The ghostly form of a man in armor stood before him. Akeldama's dust seemed to fill every corner.

"Have you come to save me?" the spirit said.

Col peered over his horse. "I don't know," he said.

"I've waited a long time for a king to come to Akeldama."

"What makes you think I'm a king?"

"A man rides Akeldama on a horse of green and springs of water appear wherever he lays his head. Who but a great king could do this?"

"I am Colmeron, King of Arnoc." The words sounded odd.

"Arnoc," the spirit said to himself. "I was once a General of Arnoc."

"You've been following me since I entered Akeldama?"

"Yes, my lord."

"Why?"

"I was afraid."

"What can I do to a spirit?" Col edged his way from behind Dasha.

"You have the power to withhold."

"I don't understand," Col said.

The General spread his hands out. "This place was once called Gennesare. It was fertile ground until it was covered with the blood of war. A war I led against my king. It was a fool's war led by an even greater fool. Upon my defeat, this land was cursed. It became Akeldama, the field of blood. I, too, was cursed. My name was taken and I was given another. I became Forgotten. For six hundred years I've wandered this plain, unseen and untouched. Forgotten."

"Why did you rebel against your king?"

"I was a man of great pride. I was corrupted by greed and the thought that I could rule. In turn, I corrupted the men who followed me. My punishment was just, but I pray that it is over now."

"What can I do?"

"Forgive me. Give me back my name."

Col wasn't sure what to do. He tried to think what his father would do. What a king would do. "My father once told me there is a trust between a king and his people. It's a sacred bond, not easily made or broken. Restore that trust."

"How, my lord? Name it and it shall be done."

"Swear to me your allegiance."

The General dropped to one knee. "I swear it." His voice filled the wind.

Now it was Col's turn to uphold trust. "Your deed is forgiven and your sentence ended."

"And my name, my king?"

"What was your name before you rebelled?"

"I can no longer recall, my lord. But I could no more wear that name than I could a coat I wore as a child. It wouldn't fit."

Col would have to give him a new name. He thought for a moment. "You are Akestell, the star of the desert. You're not Forgotten anymore."

"My king," Akestell beamed.

"What will you do now that your sentence is served? Will you fade away and finally be at peace?" Col asked.

"No. As long as my king lives I will serve him. I will be the star of the desert."

Col looked to the horizon. "General Akestell, how far are the Broken Mountains?"

"Continue west, my lord. You'll see them by morning."

"Good," Col sighed.

"Why does the king ride alone for the mountains?"

Col looked into the night sky. "Arnoc is under attack by an awful force. I'm a king without a home, an army or even a sword."

"My king rides into battle without a sword? Unacceptable!" he said. "Follow me." The General moved ahead of him.

Col dismounted and followed the General's light like a beacon in fog.

"Here, my lord." He pointed to the ground in front of them.

Col knelt to dig but decided to try something else. He put his hand out and raised it a few inches. The ground rolled over as though it were tilled by an invisible blade. He raised his hand further and the bones of the long dead General surfaced. Rusted armor held the skeleton in loose place.

"I give the king my sword as a token of my allegiance," Akestell said.

Col reached down and pulled the sword from what was left of the scabbard. The blade was pitted from hundreds of years in the ground. It had been a beautiful weapon. Across the guard were inscribed the words 'For Mercy I Hold, For Justice I Fall'.

"It was once a great weapon. It served my king before I turned it against him. Let it now serve another king." the General said.

Col thanked him and whistled for Dasha. The horse galloped over. Col slid the sword into her side. He'd have to find a scabbard for it later.

Col looked at the pale and glowing leader. "A few days ago I was just a boy. Now I'm a king at war. I'd be grateful for your counsel."

"Allow me to leave you with this, my lord. Men will follow a leader who fights for them. Not one who demands they fight for him. The enemy is strong with fear as an ally. Show your people a leader and they will fight."

"I'll keep your words close to mind, General. Thank you."

"I am ever your servant, my king."

Col turned Dasha west and the General's light faded behind them. As morning came, the cragged peaks of the Broken Mountains rose ahead of him.

CHAPTER 21

THE KING'S HAVEN

THE LOW AND JAGGED PEAKS of the Broken Mountains hinted at a former greatness. As though their crowns had been smashed with a large and terrible hammer. Over the centuries Akeldama had swallowed the range making it a barren child of the desert.

The dusty plain funneled into a tortuous passage leading into the mountains. Col navigated the winding maze for hours. Every fork in the path was another decision and every dead end meant turning around. His frustration rose with every turn. Why couldn't Orum have given him more instruction?

Dasha's leg caught on a rock. She was too dry and worn to withstand the force. The leg snapped at the knee. Her weight shifted and Col was thrown to the ground. He was too sore to fume. Instead, he led his creation to the side.

He sat on a rock and tried to decide what to do. He certainly couldn't lead Dasha the rest of the way. He'd have to leave her behind. Still, she was his and the thought of leaving her was a difficult one. While turning his options over he noticed a small enclave across the passage. It was no wider than a child. A crack in the wall, really. But there was light coming from the other side.

He peered through the opening. A large basin opened on the other side. He tried to squeeze through but the opening was too small. He stepped back and looked at the wall.

"Do you know who I am?" he said.

The wall gave no answer.

Col took a breath. "Open," he commanded.

The crack tore open in thunderous reply.

The passage now open, Col led Dasha in. High, steep walls surrounded the broad basin. It was as large as the lake back home, but was as dry as that body was plentiful. Col felt exposed in the middle of the broad space. He turned Dasha around to leave but something out of place stopped him.

Hidden in the crags was a straight line, a wall tucked in among the uneven jags of the basin's ridge.

He went to the basin's edge. He raised his foot.

A step formed.

He moved up and another rose to meet his foot. He switchbacked up the face until he reached the concealed wall.

A small hole, filled with loose rocks and sealed with dust, was cut into the wall. Col swept his hand and the rocks spilled out. Inside was a square room with a staircase in the corner. He pulled himself up and crawled through the window. He was dismayed to find the stairwell had long been caved in. Whatever mysteries it led to would remain that way. He had this room and his window. That was enough for now. From this vantage he could see the entire valley. The sun climbed over the eastern ridge and filled the basin with light, like water into a bowl.

This was his kingdom.

How unfair. From his father's tower there was life to be seen everywhere. From his own, there was nothing.

He remembered when Tephall would visit him on the Western tower, a cup of hot cider in his hand. Col looked at the darkened stairwell behind him. What he wouldn't give to see his father walk up with a cup for him.

No. He couldn't let himself think like that. There was too much to be done. Mino was safe. Right now that's what mattered. Col would find him as soon as he could.

He climbed back down to the basin floor. He needed to find water. Both for himself and Dasha.

He dug his fingers into the dust. The dirt was dry but he felt something more. He made a cup with his hands and spread his arms apart. Dirt and stone rolled to the sides until a large crater formed.

He extended his hand and raised it toward the sky.

Nothing happened.

He dropped his arm and sat in the dirt. He was glad no one was here to see him look so ridiculous.

A few minutes later a rumbling brought him to his feet. The bottom of the hole darkened and the ground swelled. With a sudden crack water surged into the air and rained down on him. He danced and shouted in triumph. He stripped off his clothing and scrubbed the dust from his parched skin.

Dasha soaked in the rain and her coat grew vibrant again. Col laid a hand to her and her leg grew back. She tossed her grassy mane in approval. Col felt he had his friend back. He laughed at the ridiculousness of the thought.

The geyser subsided and filled the crater. His spring complete, Col drank. He laid back with the sense of being full but still hungry. Food would be the next thing he needed. Once the sloshing in his stomach abated he tried summoning an apple tree. He put his hands out and lifted them upward. His command was met with a resilient void. He thought he only need wait like he did with the spring, but nothing came. He tried over and over but went to bed hungry.

The next day he was slurping his breakfast when a shadow passed overhead. A swift landed beside him. The bird dropped a seed from its beak, shrieked politely and flew off. Col picked up the seed and held it in his palm. It was only one seed, one small apple seed, but it was all he needed. He dug a shallow hole, planted the seed and drained a handful of water over it. He stood back and commanded the tree to grow.

He held his breath as a tiny shoot slipped from the soil. It reached a single green leaf to the sun. It pushed upward, invigorated by the light. Branches formed and craned outward. It shivered as leaves sprung from its tips. At last, tiny green orbs dropped to hang from the branches. They swelled until red filled their skins. Col plucked the first ripe apple from the new tree and eagerly bit into the sweet flesh.

Over the next few days more swifts arrived with more seeds until the basin no longer resembled the desolate bowl Col had found. Lush grass covered the floor and trees cropped up everywhere. The bright blossoms of apple, pear, peach and plum transformed the basin. Thick, tangled bushes vibrant with berries lined the edges of his garden.

Hunger and thirst no longer troubled him but loneliness plagued him. It had been nearly a week since he'd seen another living soul. The solitude was taking its toll. The shadows between the trees startled him and he was beginning to think he understood the birdsongs that passed through the branches.

This problem came to an end on his sixth day in the mountains. Voices carried to the tower where he slept. Young and old alike entered the garden. Men, women and children. They looked wearied. Afraid.

They ran to the trees. Their faces were transformed at the miracle they'd found. They feasted on fruit and satisfied their thirst at the spring.

Col wanted to run down and meet them but he was terrified. What would he tell them? He listened as their voices carried to him.

The group was made up of three families. They were from Lubin, the village below the Southern Garrison. Hearing the screams of the soldiers they'd hidden in a cellar until the attack was over. Even then they barely managed to escape.

Two long gashes ran down one of the men's cheeks. His wife tenderly tried to mend them. There were more injuries to be found but the greatest damage was to their spirits. Their needs were met in the garden but they had lost something no amount of fruit and water could replace.

Once night fell and their fires dimmed Col came down from the tower. He stayed far away for fear of waking them. He quietly drank from the spring and picked a handful of blackberries before sneaking back.

More people arrived the following day and were followed by even more the next. From his tower Col searched their faces in hopes of finding

Mino. But it was only strangers that he saw. By the end of the week nearly three hundred people occupied the basin. None of them were his brother.

The more people that came the more afraid he was to reveal himself. Wouldn't they hate him for being here while they fled for their lives? How would they receive Tephall's second son?

Despite his fears he knew he couldn't hide forever. Early one morning, while the people still slept, he came down. When they woke no one questioned who he was. Everyone assumed he'd come with one of the other groups. Fires were stoked and fruit was harvested. Women and children filled makeshift jars from the spring. Some of the men had been hunting and the smell of roasting meats mixed with the drifting smoke.

His people were surviving but there was an aimlessness to their activities. Even the jovial spirit of the children was dampened. They were a people without direction, without hope, and their wanting stares pricked Col's conscience.

"Col!"

Col jumped at the sound of his name. An arm waved at him from behind a low canvas tent. He knew that tent and scolded himself for not seeing it earlier.

"Colby!" Uliz came from behind the tent and wrapped his arms around him. "You're alive and I'm alive! Finally, a reason to celebrate!"

"Uliz!" Col was surprised by his own relief. He tried to hide a tear but when he pulled away Uliz's eyes glistened unashamedly.

"It's good to see you, Col." Uliz beamed. "Is your father here?"

Col shook his head. "Is Uzir with you?"

Uliz took a breath and attempted a weak smile. His eyes glistened again. "No."

"I'm sorry," Col said.

"I don't think there's anyone here who hasn't lost someone. No one was ready for the attack."

"I should've been."

"Don't be so hard on yourself, Col. Even the king wasn't prepared. The NéPrince Tonn was killed at the outset of Winter and word is the other princes were sent into hiding. No one knows if any of the royal family are even alive."

Col didn't want to talk about any of that. To everyone else it was all rumor. To him it was the life he'd been living for months. "How did you end up here?" he changed the subject.

"The same as everyone else, I suppose. Uzir and I were on the road when the attack came. It was the dead of night and I woke to, well, to take care of a pressing matter when I heard a noise coming from our camp. I ran back. Uzir was already dead. I grabbed what little gear I could and headed west. I've still heard nothing of my family."

"Why did you go west?"

"I don't really know. Along the way I found others who were fleeing as well. At the sight of Akeldama there wasn't a man who didn't think of giving up, but then the light appeared."

"A light?"

"A blue light in the distance. Through long nights it led us to water. Springs in Akeldama! Can you believe it? Then it led us here." He looked around. "It's amazing, isn't it?"

"I saw it, too," Col said.

Uliz stepped back and looked Col over. "You've grown since we parted ways. Yes, something is definitely different."

Col spent the rest of the day with Uliz. They talked to this man or that woman or helped to gather food for those who could not do it themselves.

One man was especially eager to speak to anyone who would listen. His hand was wrapped in a dirty cloth where his fingers used to be. The left side of his face was swollen leaving only one eye visible. "There's nothing left but to wait for them to find us. Don't think they won't." His outburst echoed the fears of many there.

"The king will help!" Someone shouted.

"What king? The king is dead and we'll all follow him soon enough."

"Isn't there anything to hope for?" Col asked.

"You obviously haven't lost what the rest of us have," the man said.

Col fought the urge to open the earth beneath the man.

"We've all lost more than we ever thought possible," Uliz said. "There's no need for hostility."

The man glared with his good eye, snatched a pear from the branch above him and stalked off.

Col stole away once Uliz was asleep. With more survivors arriving every day the needs of the people grew greater. He needed to make a second spring. On the far side of the garden, away from everyone, he summoned another geyser. Moonlight glimmered on the surface. Satisfied with his work he went to Uliz's tent. He raised a bed of soft grass beside it and laid down. He ate a little but his appetite was missing. He tried to sleep.

The people were angry and afraid. How much longer could he remain a silent monarch?

Morning had barely arrived when an excited shout stirred the camp.

Uliz poked his head from the tent. "What's going on?"

"They've found something," Col said.

"I hope it's good. Oh, I hope it's good," Uliz pulled his boots on. They joined the crowd at the far end of the basin.

The people gathered around the new spring.

"This wasn't here yesterday, was it?" Uliz said.

"No." Col shook his head in feigned amazement.

"There's something strange happening. How did such a garden grow in such a desolate place?"

A man kneeling by the water replied. "The answer is obvious, isn't it?"

"I've been known to be a little slow at times," Uliz said. "Maybe you could explain it for me."

"If King Tephall is dead a new king must take his place."

"Right."

"And if the Kheva have returned then a greater good must return to balance that evil."

Uliz raised an eyebrow in confusion. "And?"

"You still don't see?"

Uliz shook his head.

"The Earthkings."

"The Earthkings? I think I remember those stories."

"The Kheva were once but stories, too. Weren't they?"

Uliz's eyes widened as though he'd found a gold coin. "Two nights I saw the gleam of a fire coming from the ridge at the far end of the garden. That wall is too steep to climb, let alone start a fire up there. Maybe that's our mysterious king?"

"If the king is here why doesn't he show himself?" someone asked.

Just then another group of survivors poured into the basin. The demands for Col to reveal himself were lost in the hubbub. This pack was the most haggard yet. Most were from the eastern lands. There had been more of them but their numbers had been picked off as they fled. Still, over four hundred came.

As he did with every new group Col looked for his brother's face. He pushed through the beleaguered crowd but none of them were who he sought. The need to find Mino grew with every passing day.

Col turned around and found himself face to face with Captain Vylsom. Col held his breath.

The Captain stared blankly past him. His shoulders sagged. The ever kempt sailor had been exchanged for a disheveled and disoriented man. His wife, Tymna, who had once been so kind to Col, took the Captain by the arm and led him away. He hadn't even noticed. If he had there was no sign he'd recognized him. Not even with contempt.

Col followed them in hopes of seeing Yntor and Deel. Tymna set her husband down in the grass. The Captain leaned against a plum tree and closed his eyes.

Col made to leave but Tymna called after him. "It's Colby, isn't it?"

"You can just call me 'Col'," he said.

"I thought so. Once Yntor returned from that voyage he never stopped talking about you. It drove the Captain mad."

"Is he here?"

Tymna covered her mouth with her hand and shook her head. "He and Deel went ahead to work on the ship. The Captain came to the docks just as four of them leapt onto the Flapper. They were gone before the Captain could do anything."

"Yntor was a good boy," Col said. "He was kinder to me than I deserved."

"Thank you for taking an interest in my son. It meant everything to him."

Col looked behind her at the Captain propped beneath purple blossoms.

Tymna looked back. "I think we'd lose him, too, if he ever got his hands on some liquor."

"Do me a favor. Don't tell him I was here."

"I won't say anything," she said.

"Thank you." Col left the Captain and his wife under the tree. He was sure to add a few plums as he walked away.

With over seven hundred people now filling the garden the second spring was put to good use. And there was still room for more should there be any.

Col felt better that night. His verdant bed seemed softer. His eyes a little heavier. He put a log on the fire. He didn't worry about its light escaping through the window. Let them see it.

Something was different the next day. Everything looked the same but something had changed. He passed a peach grove and saw a young girl leaning over a frail old man. He knew her instantly.

"Nea!" he ran to them. Naboth sat up and Col hugged them both. "I thought you were gone!"

"We nearly were," Nea said.

"You have no idea how glad I am to see you." Despite the weeks of fear and desperation that weighed on her, Nea's face was still so vibrant, so alive, that Col couldn't believe he'd nearly forgotten it.

"You disappeared that day in the woods and the next morning the attacks came. I thought they got you," Nea said.

"They almost did," Col said. "What happened to you?"

"They killed Momma first and we haven't seen father since that morning. I hid in the barn for two days before grandfather found me. We heard about people heading west. We tried following but we were in the desert for days before we found the tracks. I thought we were going to die."

"When did you arrive? I didn't see you with the others yesterday."

"We came in the middle of the night. I thought it was a dream."

"It's okay. You're safe now. I'll get you some more water." Of all the people who had come to his garden — families both broken and whole — Naboth and Nea were the two Col was happiest to see. They had sheltered him, fed him, given him warmth and understanding, through the harsh Winter months and now it was his turn to care for them.

Col found a jar and filled it from the spring. Uliz joined him and they took back some fruit along with the water.

"Who have we here?" Uliz said.

"This is Naboth and his granddaughter, Tinea. They're the family my father and I wintered with."

"It's good to meet you. Any friend of Col's is a friend of mine. He's a spectacular young man. Don't you think?"

Naboth lifted his head and stared with vacant eyes before realizing Uliz was talking to him. "Yes, I'm hoping so."

"People say they've seen the king."

"King Tephall is dead," Naboth said.

"Not Tephall. The new king, the Earthking. Someone saw him come down from the ridge this morning."

Naboth climbed to his feet and leaned close to Uliz. "That's not possible. The Earthkings died out a thousand years ago."

"Do you know what they're calling this place? The King's Haven. That spring wasn't here two days ago. Whether they died out or not I believe there's an Earthking among us."

Nea looked at Col. "Do you think it's true?"

Col stammered a few unintelligible syllables.

"It doesn't matter," Uliz said. "Not yet anyway. Right now it's given us something to hope for. That's what's important."

"Why hasn't he shown himself?" Nea said.

"He's afraid," Naboth said.

"What would an Earthking have to fear?" Uliz said.

"Us."

Col couldn't bring himself to look any of them in the eye.

"What kind of a king is afraid of his own people?" Nea said.

"A new one," Col replied.

"I wish he wouldn't be. I've never seen such hopelessness," Uliz said.

"What if he's not what we expect?" Col said.

"A king's actions, not his appearance, defines him to his people."

"I would love nothing more than to meet our new king," Naboth said.

Col gave Naboth a thanking nod. "Excuse me, I have something I need to do." His friends were right. The people needed to see their king. They'd never accept him if he didn't give them the chance.

He was ready to ascend to the tower and reveal himself when a different sort of announcement came. From the Haven's entrance a horn bellowed its deep call.

Two hundred armed soldiers rode single file into the garden. Their breastplates were smooth and shone like polished glass. Silver gauntlets covered their wrists and came to a point over the backs of their hands. Their helmets boasted three sharp ridges on the top and sides that ran together to form a single tip at the back of the head. Leading them was a man with a face set like stone. The leather of his saddle creaked as he examined the ragamuffin group of refugees. He raised a muscled arm and put his hand up for silence.

CHAPTER 22
RETANA

"I AM RETANA, COMMANDER OF the Northern Garrison. Who has taken leadership among you? I must speak with him."

No one responded.

"You are a remnant. The few strong enough to survive. Consider yourselves under my guard from here on out. My men are here to protect you." He signaled to his lieutenants and the soldiers spread over the garden. They tore out the bushes and hammered stakes into the soil for their tents while the Commander examined the refugees.

He was a burly man. Broad shouldered and thick limbed. Grey dusted his temples and two keen eyes peered past a long, straight nose. He looked right past Col and pointed at three men. "You, you and you, come with me."

He selected more men and met with a total of thirty beneath the boughs of an apple grove.

Col casually sat a few yards away.

"How long have you been here?" Retana asked the men.

"Most of us have been in the King's Haven only a few days. Some nearly a week."

"The King's Haven?" Retana said.

"That's what the people have come to call it. We found it like this. A paradise in the middle of nothing. They say it's the work of an Earthking."

"It is the way of weak and fearful people to cling to such stories. Especially when leadership is lacking. It's up to us to change that. If we're going to take back Arnoc — and we are going to take back Arnoc — we'll need to strike before they realize we are still able."

One of the men spoke up. "We're farmers and fisherman. We don't know how to fight."

"Learning to fight is secondary to the will to fight. Find that and there's nothing you can't learn."

"You can't fight this foe. No amount of bravery or will can stop a force like that," another said.

"What's your name?" Retana pushed through his council and faced the man.

"Kinlin, Commander."

"It's true, Kinlin. Arnoc has been invaded by monsters, but not the beasts of myth. We've fallen to a force of men, brutal and given to madness. It's our fear that has made them more than men. See them for what they are and rob them of their power. For as long as there has been a king and a kingdom there have always been those who desired its downfall. Give all the reasons you will but madness knows reason not. Now I ask you, will you fight?"

Lawrkin and the others murmured their support.

"Are we so weak? I ask again, will you fight?" Retana held up a shaking fist.

The riled men shouted their assent.

"These are the king's men. These are the men of Arnoc!" Retana applauded them. "My men will train any who are willing but I need you to make them willing. They need to see their kindred rise. Spread courage."

Over the next day Retana's Thirty, as they became known, went throughout the Haven trying to muster their countrymen. They found their influence was minimal and their determination wavered. No one wanted to fight. They'd seen the Kheva.

That night Col sat next to Uliz as he turned a hare over their small fire. Juice dripped from it as it roasted, making Col hungry for something other than fruit for once.

"Something's not right, Col," Uliz said.

"What do you mean?"

"I fear our brash Commander and his Thirty may be doing more harm than good."

Col was glad to hear he wasn't the only one not worshiping at the altar of Retana. Everywhere he went people spoke his name with a certain awe.

"Uzir and I have cleaned chimneys almost everywhere and I can tell you the Northern Garrison was the runt of the litter. There are so few villages in the north I doubt they even came under attack. I'm afraid our protectors are full of bravado because they haven't seen what we have."

"Do you still think the king is here?"

"I don't know. I hoped he was."

"But you don't think Retana is who we need?"

"I'm not sure what we need right now. Our lives have been torn apart. It's like we've fallen from a ledge and are grabbing at anything we can to stop our plummet."

"What can we do?"

"Speak the truth. That's all we can do. I don't care what they're telling us. I know what I saw. People are afraid to say it, but I'm not. It's not maddened men we're against. It's Kheva!" He shouted the last word so that everyone around him could hear. "That's our enemy! The Kheva Adem!"

"Quiet down! That's enough of that!" the calls echoed from the camps around them.

"You see? They're too willing to believe the lie because the truth is far more frightening."

Col agreed and they ate their meal in silence. There was no use in agitating anyone tonight.

The next morning Col was up and moving before any of the Thirty could preach the Commander's gospel to him. He needed to speak to Naboth.

He found the old man sitting beside a waning fire. Nea slept soundly in the grass beside him. "Good morning, Col," he said.

Col spoke softly. "Do you think I should have revealed the truth by now?"

Naboth squinted his eyes and studied Col through the narrow openings. "Yes, you should have."

He looked to make sure Nea wasn't listening. "Do you think anyone will follow me if I do?"

"Do you think they should?"

"I know I should say yes. I was given this power to do more than grow trees."

"It's true, then? You did this?"

Col nodded. It felt good to be recognized.

"So the Earthkings have indeed returned. I've always wondered if it could happen."

"I'm sorry I didn't say anything earlier. There hasn't been much time since you arrived. What do you think I should do?"

"Retana is a fool. Let us see our king."

Col nodded and tried to rally his own courage.

"Go now, before the people fall further under the Commander's spell."

Col glanced at Nea one more time. "Tell her I'm sorry."

"She'll understand."

Col left the old man. As he walked between the trees he saw Tymna boiling a pot of water. The Captain dozed fitfully. His face was pale and sickly against his black hair.

"Has he been eating?" Col asked.

"Not much. I'm lucky to get any water in him," Tymna said.

"Has he spoken?"

"He either demands rum or calls for Yntor over and over."

"I never thought Yntor mattered much to him."

"Affection isn't something the Captain is given to. He's a hard man but no matter what anyone saw he loved our boy."

"I'm sorry. I shouldn't have said anything. How are you faring?"

"I hold on because I have the Captain to take care of. I am glad for the Commander's presence, though. I'm ready to feel safe again."

"We all are. I'll come back later and check on him."

"You're a kind boy. Yntor was right to look up to you."

—ᴧᴧᴧ—

The day was barely begun when Commander Retana burst through the flaps of his tent. He immediately called for his Thirty and they blearily stumbled to meet him.

"Time moves quickly when preparing for battle. Have we roused the spirits of our countrymen?"

The Thirty were silent.

"Well?"

Kinlin spoke up. "The people are afraid to fight, Commander. No matter what we say they know what they've seen. No amount of rallying will tell them otherwise."

"You'll never convince anyone of what you yourselves are unsure of. You're still afraid. You all are. I can smell it on you. You've drunk it in. You've bathed in it and you piss it. Sip on courage, men. Chew it with your bread and dip your meat in it. Nothing less than a diet of bravery will do. Gather everyone at the northern end of the basin. I'll speak to them. We don't have time to pander to them."

The Thirty dispersed and an hour later seven hundred people along with two hundred soldiers filled the far end of the Haven. Commander Retana rode through the crowd. He reached the front and addressed them from the saddle.

"I know the fear you feel. I know the pain that burns your spirits. Some say we are a people without a home. A people without a king and without hope. Those are lies. A fire fueled by fear. Only truth that will douse those flames." He snapped the reins and moved down the line. "The truth is we have a home. Arnoc is our home and it's time we took it back. The truth is we have hope. Hope because we are still alive. The truth is we have a king and he's not a mystical hero. He's a man who lies broken in the rubble of all he fought to protect. Don't let fear give our enemy a power they do not possess. Our enemies are men like us and they will bleed as they've made us bleed. They will die as they've led us to death. So put aside fear, my fellow Arnoceans, and put on courage. Rise with me and fight!"

Col could feel the crowd growing in awe of the Commander. "You're wrong!" he shouted suddenly.

"Who said that? Who among you is still ruled by fear?"

Col pushed his way to the front. "Lies about our enemy will not make them any easier to kill, Commander." He stared the man down. "We face an enemy Arnoc has not known in a thousand years. The Kheva are not men who bleed as we do. They are nightmares come to life. But that doesn't mean they don't bleed."

"And how do you know these things, young man?"

"Because I killed one."

"Who's boy is this?" the Commander laughed. "Who is your father?"

"My father was Tephall, King of Arnoc."

"This is no laughing matter, boy. What is your name?"

"I am Colmeron, second son of Tephall, and I am your king."

Confusion knit Retana's brow. He studied Col's face and looked for any sign of deceit. He motioned to his nearest lieutenant. "Take this boy into my tent. I'll speak with him later."

A rock tumbled from the ridge above them. A knotted shoulder and the tip of a horn disappeared behind a crag. Retana saw it, too.

Col grabbed the reins of the Commander's horse. "They're here!"

Retana's disbelief slowed him and two soldiers vanished from the saddle as a Kheva dove into them. Three more bounded for the crowd. Panic spread like fire over a drought stricken field.

Though unprepared, Retana's men were well trained. Groups of ten each singled out one of the four Kheva. The rest of the soldiers formed a wall between the people and the battle.

One of the beasts swatted two soldiers to the ground and threw a horse into the other men. It ran on all fours toward Retana, snarling with muscles taut. He screamed orders but only formed half sentences that trailed into gibberish.

Col's arm shot out. The ground in front of the enemy erupted. The Kheva was tossed onto its side. It rolled to its feet without hesitation.

Retana drew his sword, finally ready for the attack. Col jumped in front of him and spread his arms apart. The ground split under the Kheva but the agile beast hurled itself into the air. It landed and stumbled on the moving terrain. Col raised the ground around it and forced it into the fissure. He clapped his hands together and the cracked sealed shut, crushing the enemy within.

Two of the other three Kheva were killed by soldiers. One wounded enemy remained. It launched itself up the wall like a cat gaining land.

"Kill it! Now!" Retana ordered. The soldiers hurled spears only to have them bounce off the rock. "Stop that creature!" Retana looked at Col in silent plea.

Col watched the wall. The stone at the Kheva's chest heaved forward. The beast held with only one good arm.. The rock crumbled away and hit the ground with a crack and a thud. It lay there motionless. Air huffed through slotted nostrils.

Col walked toward it. He laid his hand on the rock wall. Pieces cracked and fell away, leaving him a long dagger with one razored edge. He rammed the blade into the Kheva's thick hide and through its heart.

The chaos settled and the people drew near. The boy who called himself king stood victorious.

Col raised himself up so everyone could see him. "Look upon our enemy with your own eyes and see they are not invincible."

The people knelt one by one.

Retana stayed where he was. A man walked up to him. "I think you'd better show some respect for our king." It was Captain Vylsom, the fire returning to his eyes.

Retana looked as though he'd just been shaken from a dream. He dropped his sword and slid from the saddle. He stared at the blood dripping from the dagger in Col's hand.

Col looked down at him. "You served my father. Will you serve me now?"

He knelt. "Yes, my lord."

Col looked up and addressed the crowd. "The Commander was right. It is easy to give in to fear. We are a broken people, but we will not stay that way. We are born to trials both great and small. We bend and we break, and sometimes it takes awhile to put us back together. That's when we have to listen for the voice that whispers for us to get up. If you listen long enough that whisper rises to a shout that tells us to keep going, to not allow ourselves to be slaves to fear. I promise you, my people, the night will end and you will see the sun again."

The crowd reacted with passion. The kind of passion only brought from trial. The kind of passion that gives men the strength to overcome. Col had given them the leader they needed and in return they gave him the support he was so afraid he wouldn't receive.

That night, after the waves of his revelation had settled to excited ripples, Col found Uliz sitting with Naboth and Nea. Uliz and Nea chatted, even laughed, while Naboth kept to himself by the fire.

"Your majesty," Uliz stood and bowed.

"Please, sit," Col said. He joined them, aware of the eyes all around him. After being absent so long the attention unsettled him. "I'm sorry I never told you who I was. You were my friends and I had to lie to you."

"If Uzir knew we'd had the king riding in the back of our wagon I think his head would have fallen from his neck," Uliz said.

"I wasn't king then. I was only the NéPrince and I was still new to that role, too."

"I'm very sorry to hear about your father and brother. You've lost more than we ever guessed. I'm glad you're here, though."

"We've all lost too much. I won't let us lose any more."

Naboth lifted his head from his chest. "And how do you intend to do that, young king?"

"I don't know yet. I know what needs to be done but I don't know how."

"If it means anything to you, my lord," Uliz said. "Whatever you decide, I'm ready to fight."

"I'm glad to hear you say that."

Uliz turned to Nea. "And what about you, young lady? What do you think of our new king?"

Nea stabbed at the branches burning brightly in the fire. "I saved his life once."

For the first time since before the attack Col laughed. "Yes, you did. If I had a treasure to reward you with I would but I'm afraid I'm fresh out of gold right now."

"I don't want your gold," she threw her poker into the flames and walked away.

"Nea?" Col called after her.

"I wouldn't worry about her," Uliz said. "You may be a king but she's still a woman and the moods of a woman are not subject to any reign."

"Did I say something wrong?"

"No, she just needs a little time to reconcile the truth with the boy she knew."

Col hoped a little time would be all she required. He needed a friend now more than ever. "I'm meeting with the Commander in the morning. I'd like it if you three could join us. I need people I can trust."

"I'll be there, your majesty."

"Naboth, please say you'll be there. If not for you I never would have been able to do this."

"Of course I'll be there, Col. Any council I have to give is yours."

Col embraced the solitude of the tower that night. There were no eyes to see him here, no hands to reach for him.

Soldiers were posted along the ridge. The enemy had found them once, and as sure as Nea was still mad at him, they would return. It was likely only a scouting party that found them, but killing the scouts wouldn't keep the hordes away for long.

He stoked the fire high and let its light blaze through the window. He looked over the throng spread across the Haven. He had a responsibility to each one of them. If only Orum had told him what his next step was after coming west.

He looked at the room around him, at the caved in stairwell in the corner. Which one of his ancestors had formed this? What happened here that ruined it? He ran his fingers along the stone and felt it respond to him. He wasn't sure he could form a room like this let alone anything as grand as his forebears had. How many of them had it taken to create Entaramu? How many had guarded that city before it fell?

He stopped and chided himself. Orum had told him the next step. How could he not have seen it sooner!

The next morning he found Commander Retana pacing in his tent. Uliz and Naboth followed Col in.

Retana swept an accusing arm at them. "What good do you think they'll be, your majesty? Have either of them seen battle?"

"No. That's why I have you, Commander. They're here because I trust them. It can't hurt to hear a voice other than yours."

"Of course not," he waved his hand as if to dismiss his own accusation. Before Retana could continue a commotion came from outside.

"Get off me!" Nea screamed.

Col rushed outside where Captain Vylsom's hands wrapped firmly around Nea's arms.

"I caught this one trying to sneak in."

"Let her go, Captain. She's my guest," Col said.

The Captain released her. She smoothed out her rumpled shirt and picked something from the ground. It was a box, very old and very beautiful, with two trees and a swirling pool etched into the lid. "I thought you might want this back," she said.

Col accepted the box from her. "Where did you find it?"

"Your hiding spot under the bed wasn't very clever."

"Thank you, Nea. I thought I'd lost it."

"You're welcome... King Colmeron." She gave him a wink and walked away.

Captain Vylsom crossed his arms and huffed. He was starting to resemble the man Col had feared at sea.

"Captain?"

"Your majesty?"

"Is everything alright?"

"She shouldn't talk to you like that."

"Don't get worked up over her. It won't do any good."

"Can I speak with you, my lord?" Vylsom said.

Col looked back at the men waiting in the tent. "Go ahead, Captain."

"I've lost my son and I know I'll never get the chance to make amends with him, but you're still here. I nearly killed you once and it doesn't matter that I didn't know who you were. You are my king and I've come to accept your judgement, whatever it may be."

If there was something Col understood it was what it meant to be broken. Here before him was one of the most vile men he'd ever known seeking amends. Such men do not change apart from brokenness.

"The man you knew as my father was really my uncle. He was a good man. He once told me to rule with compassion for the wounded, mercy for the penitent, and justice for the corrupt. Killing you would solve nothing. I think you could be put to much better use than death."

"You've made my wife very happy, your majesty."

"Come with me," Col said.

The two of them went into the tent where an impatient Retana lectured the others on the merits of leadership.

"This is Captain Vylsom," Col said. "I've asked him to join us."

"Another friend of yours?" Retana said.

"The Captain knows our destination better than any man here."

"You know where we're going, my lord?" Naboth asked.

"We're going to sea. The Noflim have only ever been after one thing: Entaramu. And I know where it is."

"Your majesty, I trust your knowledge," Retana said. "Now I ask that you trust mine. After seeing our enemy I must warn you we are not yet ready to mount an attack. You are powerful but you can't be everywhere on a battlefield at once."

"I agree. We need more men."

"Where do you expect to find these men?"

Uliz raised his hand. "There must be more survivors. This can't be the only refuge."

Retana cut him off. "There isn't time for us to search them all out."

"Naboth, don't you have anything to say?" Col said.

Naboth leaned forward on his cane and spoke just over a whisper. "Will any of this matter tomorrow if an army of Kheva Adem attacks tonight? What hope is there when our demise could come at any moment?"

Vylsom thrust a finger in Naboth's face. "We serve a king unlike any other. That's our hope. Never forget that. None of you forget that."

"Our seafaring friend is right," Uliz said. "The way is unclear but there is still hope."

Col's fingers played over the box Nea had returned to him. The latch within slid free. He lifted the lid and looked down. He took two deep breaths. "I know where to find the soldiers we need."

CHAPTER 23

OF LEAVES AND BLOOD

—∞—

COL RODE NORTH AND THE Haven fell away behind him. He urged Dasha to a racing gallop. He felt the twine and pull of supple green beneath him. Immersed again in Akeldama's desolate plains he longed for verdant hills.

He stopped that night if only to give himself a few hours rest. He would need it. The path before him was more uncertain than ever.

It was strange to be alone again. After a week being surrounded by so many people the solitude was unsettling and the dark isolation of the desert felt like an immense womb preparing him for a world of madness and fury.

He slipped the box from its satchel and set it on his chest. He opened the lid, shut it and opened it once more. It was so easy now. He pulled out a teardrop shaped leaf and considered the crimson streak staining its evergreen surface. The foliage curled in on itself and flexed out again.

It hadn't come from any tree or bush Col had ever seen. It felt different, too. He could sense something in it. This was Greenkind flesh. He was sure of it. As wondrous as that was it wasn't the leaf that concerned him. It was the blood on it. He was connected to it.

He stared into the distance. He didn't know how far the Greenkind lands were but he knew he had to hurry. The Haven wouldn't be safe for long.

He slept a few short hours before riding again. He passed through Akeldama and into more fertile pastures. Though they were hardly a paradise. The grass was stiff and broken, pale yellow in the light of the arching sun. The trees were different, too. They reached to take hold of the sun's feet, but their skyward path was winding and crooked. They were old with trunks that creaked in the wind and whispered ancient secrets to young leaves.

With each passing hour Col's world shrank as the forest flourished. Crickets chirped their chorus and owls began their eerie questioning as night fell. He rode as far as he could but without light he was forced to stop for the night. As soon as day broke he pushed on.

He stopped at the edge of a shallow clearing. The air around him was tense with Spring's early vigor. He sensed the men of earth. He couldn't see them but he knew they were there, like ghosts in the shadows.

"My name is Colmeron, King of Arnoc," he said aloud. "I need to speak with you."

The forest replied only with the sound of the wind sifting through the branches.

"I know you're here," Col said.

A figure stepped from the bracken. The Greenkind resembled a man — two arms, two legs, a head and neck sitting on squared shoulders — but large veins of rock and wood covered his body. His hands were knotted and sharp edges lined a stone-like face. Dark leaves grew in his twisting hair and fell over deep set brown eyes. He reached for Col. His arm was a gnarled root that met with bronze flesh at the wrist.

Col blinked and the Greenkind froze. Terror filled his eyes. He tried to recoil but Col held him firmly in place. Col stepped around him and released him.

A voice came from the trees. "You are not a king as your father was. What manner of lord are you?"

"Show yourself and I will tell you," Col said.

A low branch swung to the side to reveal the leader. He was immense, a living statue of stone, earth and flesh.

"Speak plainly, O King."

"You see more than most, Greenkind. I rule not only men but earth itself."

"An Earthking? They are legends, stories for children," he laughed.

"The same has been said of you. Yet here we both stand."

"Tell me, why has the Earthking come to Greenkind lands? We've posed no threat to Arnoc."

"An adversary has risen from our past and taken my kingdom. I need your help to take it back."

"We know the enemy you speak of. We have seen the Kheva Adem gathering in the shadows, growing their numbers."

"And you said nothing?"

"We owe nothing to the rulers of Arnoc, Earthking or otherwise. Your request is denied." He vanished into the fauna.

"I will not leave without your help, Greenkind!" The trees shook. "My kingdom teeters at the edge of oblivion. Without your help it will fall."

One of them appeared beside Col. "Mon-Tesh has spoken. Take what pride you have left and leave now."

"My pride lies with Arnoc and I will not let her come to ruin. Listen to me, Mon-Tesh! There was once an alliance between our peoples. I want to restore that alliance." He took the leaf from the box and held it up.

A hollow chirp came from above. The Greenkind beside Col mimicked the sound. "Follow me," he said.

His guide delved further into the dense forest. He cast a wary eye at Col.

"You smell like the other one," he said.

"What other one?"

"The boy. You have the same smell."

"What boy?"

"Mee-no."

"Mino! Where is he?"

Col had no sooner spoken the words than two strong hands reached down and took him by the shoulders. He was lifted to an intricate system of walkways suspended between the trees. Large green pods rested on some of the larger branches. Crude lanterns shone within.

Col's guide moved deftly over the narrow footbridge and disappeared into one of the pods.

Col's eyes scoured the trees. Mino was here.

His guide appeared at the pod's entrance. "Mon-Tesh will speak with you."

Col went inside. The lantern's dim light reflected off the pod's curved walls and filled the room.

Mon-Tesh sat in a large chair of interwoven branches. "Show me the token," he said.

Col held out the leaf and spun it so the blood was clearly seen.

"You've shown me two things today, Earthking. And one revokes the other. You say you would honor an agreement between our peoples yet you imposed your will on one of us."

"I was only protecting myself. There are no soldiers waiting behind me."

"Would you protect yourself from us if we chose to renew this alliance?"

"Would I need to?"

"What would it benefit us to agree to this?"

"Isn't peace its own benefit?"

"The kings of Arnoc have always kept us at bay, pushing our borders further and further north. A one-sided peace. You seek freedom for your people? I seek the same for mine."

"Help me and half of Akeldama is yours."

"The field of blood? Do you think me stupid?"

"I can make it fertile again."

Mon-Tesh stroked his chin. It made a scraping sound that unnerved Col. "Give us the whole of the cursed plain."

All of it? That was a lot of land for Col to give away. Still, what choice did he have?

"Come to our aid and the whole of Akeldama is yours."

"Very well. We will seal our agreement by the same token you hold."

"I have one more request, Mon-Tesh."

"You've barely been granted the first and you already have a second? Your diplomacy is lacking."

"There is a boy with you."

"You know he is here?"

"He's my brother."

"He says he is Mee-no, prince of men and hero of the Greenkind."

"Why do you have him?"

"One of our tribes took him from a family who thought to violate our borders without consequence."

"You kidnapped my brother?" The leaves above him trembled.

"We didn't know who he was. He was to be held for ransom but no one sought to claim him."

Col didn't have to wonder what happened to Brenna's family. "I've come to claim him now. Return him to me and we'll move forward with our alliance."

"You think to keep him out of harm's reach by taking him to war? Leave him here until the fight is won and we will return him to you."

"I will come for him if you don't."

"I would expect nothing less. I swear your brother will be returned." Mon-Tesh peeled a single leaf from the back of his hand.

Col could tell it was painful but Mon-Tesh remained grim faced.

He held the still warm leaf out to Col.

Col took a knife from his belt and ran the tip across his palm. He held his hand over the leaf and drops of blood met with the green.

"It is done," Mon-Tesh said.

Col took the leaf and placed it in the box beside the old one. "When will your soldiers be ready?"

"We are ready now, Earthking. We've been preparing from the moment you arrived. Why else would you have come?"

The Greenkind soldiers rode on Meugs. Creatures as ugly as their name. They resembled dogs but were taller and wider with a stout neck leading to a flat face that looked angry no matter what their temperament.

The Greenkind rode two per Meug. Each soldier had a short spear with a long head strapped to their back.

It was only when they reached the edge of Akeldama that Col saw the size of the army following him. Meug after Meug poured from between the trees. A wave of raincloud grey filling the open plain.

The Greenkind army charged south and the tremendous roar of pounding feet split the air. Only Mon-Tesh rode his own Meug. He paced a few feet behind Col, but remained at the head of his troops.

As night fell Col slowed and came beside Mon-Tesh. "Give me one more hour and we'll stop for the night," he said.

"We didn't come to rest, Earthking. As long as you ride, we follow."

Col gave a sharp nod and urged Dasha ahead. He'd been gone three days now and there was no telling what could have happened while he was away. He thought back to the morning he left.

If the people thought he was crazy when he claimed to be king they knew he was insane when he told them he was going to find the Greenkind. He couldn't make Retana understand why they were Arnoc's last hope.

"This is our kingdom and we'll fight the enemy as Arnoceans do. Give your people a chance," Retana said.

Col couldn't blame the Commander for his skepticism. The idea of finding an ally in a people nearly as savage as their enemy was absurd.

Naboth wasn't keen on Col leaving the Haven, either. "It's not right for a king to abandon his people, Col. What if you are wrong?"

But Col knew this was what he had to do as sure as he had known he needed to show mercy to Akestell.

Col contemplated leaving unannounced but Uliz reminded him that to do so would look like he was deserting the people.

After reviving Dasha, who'd been standing like a garden sculpture hidden among the trees, Col addressed the Haven's residents.

"You've all seen our enemy. We can't win this war alone. I'm going for help. We need an ally. Commander Retana and his men will protect you until I return."

With his final words given he rode from the Haven. He could hear the questions rise behind him.

The first gleam of dawn pulled Col from his recollection and back to the head of the Greenkind army. In the far distance rose the crags of the Broken Mountains. He was ready to fulfill his promise to return.

Hours later he bounded into the mountain passage. The Greenkind followed close. The tremendous sound of their movement echoed off the mountains. The passage filled with thunder. Col navigated the twists and turns and at last entered the beautiful expanse of his Haven.

He pulled hard on Dasha's grass mane and jumped to the ground. This couldn't be. This wasn't right.

There was no one here.

He called out for anyone to answer. There were no bodies lying anywhere. The people had vanished.

Col returned to Mon-Tesh. "We're too late. I wasn't quick enough"

Mon-Tesh turned to his soldiers. "Return to Akeldama. Search for any sign of the enemy."

"There were two hundred soldiers here. They wouldn't have gone without a fight. I fear the enemy was here all along."

Mon-Tesh's Meug snorted and shuffled. "Your willful ignorance leads to defeat, Earthking."

The thought of the Noflim being among them sickened Col. He'd left his people in the hands of the enemy.

A wisp of smoke trailed up through the trees at the far end of the Haven.

"Wait here," Col said. He rode toward the smoke. He dismounted as he neared and edged closer.

In the middle of a copse, sitting with his legs crossed and head bowed, was Naboth. A fire smoldered in front of him.

Col approached the old man. "Where is everyone?" He prayed it would be his friend who answered.

"They're gone, Col. The Kheva Adem came. Horde after horde. They carried your people deeper into the mountains. I fear you may never find them."

"How are you still here?"

"I hid."

"What about Nea? Did they take her?"

"They took the girl. They took everyone. You weren't here to protect them. This is your fault, boy."

"I know it is."

"Why don't you give up now? It'll be easier than fighting."

"I know."

"Good." Naboth breathed the word like a curse.

Col shook his head. "Not Naboth. Not my friend."

Naboth opened a vacant mouth and spilled a deep, hollow laugh.

The sound made Col shiver. "You took him. He did nothing but help me."

"And now he serves us."

Col's grief turned suddenly to anger. "Where are my people, Noflim? Tell me!" He pulled the old man up by his shirt.

"You're too late." Naboth wrapped his fingers around Col's wrist and pulled it down. His other hand clamped on Col's throat. "There's no man that can stand against us. You are far from the first we've dealt with. But you are by far the most pathetic!" He glowered.

He pushed Col to his knees. Col choked and fought to breathe. The pressure in his head built.

"Such a shame that Orum's chosen fall so easily."

Col reached for Dasha with his free hand. She answered his summons and he reached through her flank. He felt a steel handle inside. He tore the General's sword free and swung wide. The blade bit deep between the old man's ribs. Naboth staggered back and dropped.

Col pulled him up. "Tell me where my people are, spirit!"

The Noflim gasped. "They tumble like leaves into the fire."

Naboth's body went limp.

Col pulled the sword from his side. The old man was already gone. The Naboth Col had known had been dead since the first attack. He cradled his head in his lap until the last beats of a once true heart stilled.

CHAPTER 24

LIKE ANTS FROM THE HILL

MON-TESH WAITED IMPATIENTLY BEHIND HIM. Col was unwilling to let his friend go.

"I should've known this wasn't him," Col said.

"Heaping guilt on yourself won't win the battle, Earthking."

Col carefully laid Naboth on the grass and the body slowly sunk into the earth. A patch of lilacs spun to life over the grave.

"Have your scouts found anything?" Col asked.

"The tracks of men and Kheva lead east while those on horseback lead west, into the mountains."

Why would Retana and his men go west while the rest of the people fled east?

"Retana and his men will have to wait. The people are my concern. How far ahead of us are they?"

"A day at the most."

"Good. We leave now."

Col retrieved his stone dagger from the tower. The weight of the long, flat blade felt good as he strapped it to his waist. He mounted Dasha and rode to the desert's edge to wait. The Greenkind army came soon after. He could tell they were tiring. Rest is a luxury not afforded in war, Col reminded himself.

He pushed Dasha ever faster, but the Meugs were bred for war and not a marathon charge. The Greenkind fell farther and farther behind. Mon-Tesh raced ahead to catch Col.

"There are nearly a thousand of your people trekking Akeldama on foot. We'll catch them, but wearing ourselves out doing so will only hurt us."

"Fight with me or return home."

Mon-Tesh clenched a stone jaw. "We will honor our agreement."

"Good." Col rode on.

The Greenkind were soon out of sight. Finally, Col stopped.

He cleared a large bowl in the arid ground and slid to its center. He put his hand in the dirt and rubbed it between his fingers. It was cooler this far down. He raised his hand and clenched a fist.

Col climbed back up as a geyser burst through the ground. Water shot high and rained back down. He didn't feel the cold drops soak him.

Mon-Tesh and his soldiers arrived a few minutes later.

"You make good use of your power, Earthking. Even your green horse was in need of a drink."

"We'll rest here for a few hours."

"A spark of wisdom among the dark of ignorance. You're learning." Mon-Tesh put his face to the water and slurped his fill along with the rest of his soldiers.

As with everything the Greenkind leader said there was a mix of derision and awe. At some point he would have to decide whether he respected Col or reviled him. At the moment, Col didn't care which one it was.

The Greenkind soldiers didn't complain about their stiff pace. Though grateful for a respite, their focus was on the battle ahead. They watered their Meugs and were ready to ride again.

They rode through the night and made to catch the people as quickly as they could. The amber rays of a new day revealed a throng of people being herded by nearly a hundred Kheva.

Col and Mon-Tesh stopped on a high ridge. A thundercloud rolled overhead as rain began to fall across the valley.

"We caught them, just as I said." Mon-Tesh boasted. "Now, see for yourself the strength of the Greenkind."

"I'm sure to see it since I'll be in the middle of it," Col said.

"A dead king is no good to his people, Earthking. You should stay here."

"A cowardly one is just as useless. We fight until every one of them is dead. There are no prisoners. There is no mercy. We take them or they take us. There is no in-between."

Mon-Tesh grinned. "At last the boy is gone and a man takes his place." He raised a fist and motioned for the charge.

Col took the lead and sped down the hillside. The falling rain lashed at him as the sky gave a long, low rumble.

The Kheva saw his charge and a horde of growling death swept onto the plain to meet him. Col spurred Dasha faster. Her limbs splintered with the exertion. Bits of moss flung into the wind.

A leg snapped and she faltered beneath him. He jumped away from her and the ground rose to meet him. He pulled the dagger from his belt and ran to meet the enemy head on.

He put out his hand and the ground in front of the Kheva surged. They clamored over the swell without losing pace.

The first of the Kheva was upon Col. He dropped to the ground as it sprung for him. The only thing that hit him was the stench of blood matted fur. He wasn't going to waste time with this one. He was on his feet and running again.

The Kheva behind him wheeled around. A torrid growl came from its throat. The ground under it convulsed suddenly and hurled it into the oncoming rush of Greenkind who quickly pinned it with their spears. Meugs tore it apart before the soldiers pressed on.

Col leapt at the next beast. The ground thrust him up and he landed with his knees in its chest. His knife slashed across its face. Its jaw stretched its limits as it roared in fury. Col hacked again. The Kheva tumbled backward and landed with Col's knife plunged through its neck.

Col pulled the knife free and ran to meet his next foe but this one wasn't as unprepared as the last. It dodged Col's first slash and grabbed for his chest, ready to crush him, but a slab of stone pushed up under it. Its claws grazed Col's shoulder. Col jumped at it and used its arm as a step. He grabbed a long horn and swung onto its back. He pulled its head back, reached an arm around and drew his blade across the demon's throat.

All around Col the battle raged. Teeth and fur and claws clashed with spear and earth and stone. Meugs snorted and bellowed as they aided in the fray.

The enemy pounded furiously at the frenzied attacks of the Greenkind. Their thick arms and tendriled fingers tore at the soldiers. They flung them from their mounts and seized them to crush their ribs and everything caged within. They fought without order and without restraint.

The Kheva nearest Col tore the life from the Greenkind it was fighting. It sniffed the air, and turned on Col so fast he barely had time to duck as it lunged for his head. Col swung low and stabbed through it's calf muscle. The Kheva faltered and Col seized the opportunity. He tilted the ground and his foe fell to the mud. Three Greenkind were upon it before it could rise again.

Col hacked his way deeper into the fray. All around him the bodies of both Greenkind and Kheva fell. The fetid scent of blood mixed with mud filled the air.

Col had nearly reached his people. Only the Kheva left behind as guards stood between them. Twenty of them remained. They spread out to surround him. Col put his arms out. The desert ground swelled like a pot beginning to boil. Two steep mounds began to rise high. The gully between the hills narrowed and funneled the Kheva into a cluster. Col clenched his fist and the ground under them dropped. They tumbled over one another in attempt to scramble out. They crawled up the sides, long fingers stabbing the dirt as they pulled themselves up. They poured from the hole like ants from an anthill.

Col had to act quickly. He couldn't hesitate now. He lifted both arms into the air and the hills raised like angry bears. Two towers of earth loomed over the Kheva. He brought his arms down and the towers crashed onto them. The sky echoed the earth's thunder as if to pronounce judgement on the Kheva Adem.

With their guards now buried the people rushed forward. Men, boys and even a few furious women pulled stones from the newly turned soil. The Greenkind army had routed nearly all of the Kheva leaving only a handful to finish off. The enemy were using the carcasses of three Meugs as shields.

Mon-Tesh hurled himself into one of the Kheva and knocked it to the ground. The beast wasn't down for long, though. It tossed both the dead Meug and Mon-Tesh from itself. It stalked on all fours toward the stunned Greenkind leader. Mon-Tesh regained his footing just as it charged. He seized it by the horns and strained at them until both snapped at the base. He spun the horns around and drove them into his adversary's neck.

The Kheva's legs gave way and it crashed into the ground, pinning Mon-Tesh beneath its limp body. Mon-Tesh heaved it off and pulled the horns free.

The last two Kheva were cornered. Mon-Tesh marched toward them, a broken horn in each hand. Kheva blood covered his arms and chest. Bloodlust filled his wild eyes. He leapt over his soldiers and, in two quick motions, killed both beasts. Each fell with a horn through the bottom of their jaw.

The battle was over.

All fell silent save the rain. Bodies littered the field. Col closed his eyes and let the falling rain wash his face clean.

The people cheered but the Greenkind were muted in their celebration. The price for victory had been heavy and it was they who'd paid it.

That night they set up camp on a high plateau that hadn't been there that morning. For further protection Col summoned enormous slabs of rock from deep within the earth. They broke the surface and formed a high wall around the top of the plateau.

The people within the camp settled for the night after having food and water for the first time in days. Col walked among them, making sure to be seen and heard. He found it difficult to look any of them in the eye. He wanted to tell everyone of them he was sorry but words would never be enough.

He walked up a crude stone ramp to the top of the wall. Two men stood guard. They held Greenkind spears and stared blearily over the desert.

"It's a beautiful night, isn't it?" Col said.

The two men stiffened when they realized who spoke. "Yes, my lord," one said.

"What's your name?" Col asked.

"Eldrin, your majesty."

"Did you think it was all over, Eldrin? Did you think we'd lost?"

"I was afraid we had."

"What about you?" Col asked the other man. "Did you think I'd abandoned you?"

He shook his head. "I didn't know what to think, my lord."

"Go to your families. I'll keep watch for awhile."

The men stood still, unsure if they should so readily abandon their post.

"Go." Col repeated himself. The men nodded their gratitude and left him.

Col looked out over the vast plain. Over fresh mounds that hid the fallen Greenkind. He listened to the sounds of the camp behind him and was never so glad for something so mundane. He wondered if this was how a parent felt after finding a child who'd been lost. There were so many things about being a leader that his father never showed him. Things Caménor never told him.

What kind of ruler would he be once this was all over? What would life be like once the tides of war had settled?

Col's rumination was short lived as a small figure came softly up the ramp and tried to hide in the shadows.

"I'm sorry we haven't spoken today," he said.

Nea stepped into the light. "I need your help. I can't find my grandfather."

She still clung to some small strand of hope and it was Col that had to cut it. He took a breath. "Naboth never left the farm, Nea. He died the morning of the first attack. I'm sorry."

"What do you mean?" Her voice cracked.

"His body was taken by one of the Noflim. It was never him that was with us after that morning."

"He was acting so strange," she sniffed. "I thought it was because of all that was happening. I should have known."

"You weren't the only one he fooled, Nea. I didn't see it until it was too late."

"Is he," she tried to find the right word. "Gone now?"

Col nodded. "I buried him in the Haven."

"Thank you. He would've wanted you to take care of him. He loved you."

"He loved you too, Nea. We were both fortunate to have him."

She wiped her eyes and looked east toward Arnoc. "You're king now."

"Things are different, but I'm still me."

"What should I call you?"

"You can still call me 'Col'." He shrugged. "That hasn't changed."

"Are we still friends?"

Her words came like the pleas of a frightened child. He'd never heard her so timid. In many ways she was a frightened child. Her family was gone. All of them now. Except for the company of a friend. "Of course we are," he said.

"Good." She smiled.

"What happened after I left?" Col asked. "I trusted Retana to protect you."

"The night after you rode off the Commander received a report the Kheva were gathering in a canyon to the west. He sent half the soldiers to hunt them but they didn't return. Grandfather — or what I thought was my grandfather — told him it was his duty to find them, that he owed it to his men to go after them. He left us. He took the rest of his soldiers and left. We were afraid but you said you'd return. But the Kheva came first.

They were everywhere. Retana left his Thirty in charge but they were as useless as he was. They surrendered before most of us even knew what was happening."

"Nobody fought?"

"How could we? You were gone."

"I'm sorry."

She looked over the field. "Do you think anything will ever feel normal again?"

"I hope so. I haven't felt normal in a very long time. Everything changed after my brother was killed."

"It's strange to hear you talk about a brother. What was he like?"

"Tonn was full of himself. He always had to be right. I considered it my duty to make sure he knew otherwise. But he was also very afraid he would never be as good a king as our father. I think he never felt like he could be a real man. He would've been great, though."

"What about your other brother?"

"Mino? He's a brat. He was always getting in the way or messing things up because he didn't know any better. And even if he did, he got away with it because he was the baby. The Greenkind have been keeping him safe. I didn't think I'd ever think of anyone being 'safe' with the Greenkind," he chuckled. "I just want to end all of this and get him back."

"You will, Col. If anyone can, it's you."

Col looked at his friend with starlight shining down on her. This wasn't the same fiery girl who woke him that first morning on the farm. There was still fire, to be sure, but it had been tempered through pain and hardship. The girl was passing, a woman taking her place.

"It's awful to think I'll never feel Momma's arms around me again. I shouldn't think about it, I know, but sometimes I can't help it."

"There's nothing wrong with that. I used to think about my mother so often it almost felt like she was still there."

"What was her name?" Nea asked.

"Cyntara." The name rolled from his tongue like a foal from the mare, awkward and destined for grace all at once. It had been years since he'd said it out loud.

"Such a lovely name. I'm sure I knew it at one time, but it's been so long."

"She was the first loss of my life," Col thought aloud. "I've lost so much in the past months but she was the greatest. I miss her in a way so different from the others."

He waited for Nea's response but none came. She cried silently in the growing night. Col allowed himself the luxury of a single tear before steeling himself, lest the dam should break. "You should probably get some rest," he said.

She made to leave but turned suddenly and gave him a brief, awkward hug before disappearing down the ramp.

Col turned his attention back to the east to Entaramu. To the Sacred Grove where the water rippled with the terrifying force below.

CHAPTER 25

A CAPTIVE PORT

Morning came quickly. Col had barely shut his eyes when the light pried them open again. He'd fallen asleep atop the wall and his limbs paid the price. He shook the drowsy from his eyes, stretched, and went outside the wall to meet with Mon-Tesh.

"There's still a long road between us and the rest of the Kheva."

"Good. They have the lives of many of my soldiers to pay for. How far do we ride?"

"We ride for the heart of Arnoc, for Entaramu."

"And what of these people?"

"We can't afford to travel with them. A large group like that will only slow us down. I doubt the enemy has any more Kheva this far out. They would have come to help the others yesterday."

"They're cunning, Earthking, and I doubt they care for their own. They've already infiltrated your ranks once."

"That's why I need you to leave half of your soldiers behind. To guard my people. There will be plenty of food and water for everyone."

Mon-Tesh frowned. "Very well. Just remember your promise, Earthking. The Greenkind are upholding our end of the agreement."

"Akeldama will flourish as never before. I promise."

Col went in search of help for the journey. He found Uliz first. The two hadn't spoken since the battle and the distance between them stung Col.

"I need to ask you something, Uliz."

Uliz didn't look up from his breakfast. "What does the king require?"

"I'm going to Rakken."

"You're leaving us again?"

"I want you to come with me."

"I stood up for you in the Haven. I told everyone you were coming back but it was the Kheva who came. You made a fool of me."

"I'm here now, Uliz, and I will see this through. I can't give anymore than that."

Uliz sighed and looked up. "Rakken?"

"The enemy are looking for Entaramu. Rakken is the closest port."

"Is this a command?"

"No, I'm asking you as my friend."

"I've been to Rakken almost as many times as I've been to Mondiso. I'll go."

The next person Col sought was Captain Vylsom. The change that had taken place in the man astounded Col. There was a time he would have picked anyone else to go with him and now there wasn't anyone he trusted more.

They found the Captain trimming his beard while Tymna fussed over his hair.

"I said don't cut anymore off, woman," Vylsom waved her away.

"It's getting too long, Captain. You know you'll start complaining of it soon," Tymna said.

"Leave it. I'll worry about it later."

"Captain, I need to ask a favor," Col said.

"I'll do it."

"I haven't even asked yet."

"It doesn't matter. I'll do it."

"Alright. We're going to Rakken."

"Rakken, eh? That's my kind of place!"

"That's what I was hoping. We need sailors, though. Do you recognize any here?"

"Aye. There's a few. None I would trust with The Flapper but they'll do."

"Find them and tell them I need them."

Vylsom grinned wide. "I'd be happy to, my lord."

Col turned to Tymna and saw the worry in her eyes.

"I can't lose him, too," she said.

"You won't."

In all they found another eight able-bodied sailors. "They look wimpy, I know," Vylsom said. "But get them to the sea and their might will return. Those like us aren't made for land. Too long on it and we begin to lose a bit of something."

"I'll be glad to see you get that something back, Captain."

"What should they tell their families?"

"Tell them we're leaving to end this so they can finally go home."

A king, a handful of sailors, a chimney sweep and half of what remained of the Greenkind army rode from the plateau. Col fixed up Dasha and was glad to ride her again. Uliz and the sailors rode reluctantly with the Greenkind. Uliz clung gingerly to the Greenkind he rode with while Vylsom nearly fought his for control of their Meug.

Col rode in a wide arc around the plateau. A trail of briars and thorns followed him until they'd grown thick as a man's waist and twisted as a hermit's mind. They formed thick, high fence around his people and their Greenkind protectors.

"Are they captives still?" Mon-Tesh said.

"What else would you have me do, Mon-Tesh? They need to be kept safe."

"Then let's make them safe." Mon-Tesh raised a hand and signaled his troops forward. The horde surged forward. Col raced to the front and led the way.

It was nearly two days later when they reached the edge of Akeldama. The Greenkind seemed uneasy crossing into Arnoc's fertile hills.

"Is everything alright, Mon-Tesh?" Col said to him.

"We've never before entered these lands. It's been forbidden to us for generations beyond counting."

"Enter with my blessing," Col said. "You're not only welcome here. You're needed."

They passed through a small village some hours later. Doors were still torn from their hinges and splintered wood still littered the streets. The blackened husks of homes stood like vacant-eyed corpses. Men and women peered from broken windows and held their children close as the procession rumbled through town. They trembled with the same fear as when the Kheva had attacked. Col would have been afraid too but after losing so much he wasn't sure there was anything left to fear.

They stopped to rest and eat only as needed. They rode hard. The procession roared swiftly through the fields and scant villages of Western Arnoc. They saw no signs of the Kheva other than the devastation left in their wake.

Uliz and Vylsom eventually took to their Greenkind companions. Vylsom soon spent more time piloting his Meug than Greenkind. Both men proved their worth in advising Col on the best approach into Rakken. They would pass well north of Mondiso and approach from above the port.

On the fourth day of their ride the tall masts of ships harboring in Rakken came into view. Col and his army of Greenkind warriors stopped behind the last ridge before the village.

Col met with Mon-Tesh and his friends to discuss their next step.

"Uliz, Vylsom, I need you two to come with me. We need to get into Rakken unseen."

"I can do that. What then?" Uliz asked.

"I need to see what kind of presence the Kheva have there. Once we know the enemy's position we'll leave and return with the warriors." He nodded to Mon-Tesh. "After Rakken is taken we can focus on the island." He turned to Vylsom. "Captain, I'll need you to have the sailors ready as many ships as we can take. From there we'll sail to the island with the Greenkind."

"How are you so sure the enemy will be on this island?" Mon-Tesh interrupted.

"I know what they're looking for and I know where it is. They'll be there." Col looked at his fellow conspirators. "Mon-Tesh, if we're not back in 4 hours I want you to take the port. Show the enemy no mercy."

Mon-Tesh nodded gravely. "It will be done."

Col, Uliz and Vylsom set off for Rakken on foot. They had only a few stone daggers that Col made and stuck close to the bluffs where they were less likely to be seen.

They rounded a crag and Vylsom pulled them both to the side. He put a finger to his lips.

"Someone is following us," he said.

Col peeked over the rock. "One of the Greenkind has followed us."

"Why would one of them break ranks to do that?" Uliz wondered.

"He's awfully short for a Greenkind," Col said.

"We can't go into Rakken with someone following us," Vylsom said.

Col nodded. "Give me a moment." Their interloper suddenly dropped from view.

The three of them ran back and found their pursuer at the bottom of a pit Col had made. To Col's surprise it wasn't one of the Greenkind but a very muddied Nea who looked angrily up at them.

"Nea!" Col said. "What are you doing?"

"I came to help. Get me out of this stupid hole!"

"Our mission isn't for little girls," Vylsom said.

Nea called up. "I travelled with you for four days without you realizing it!"

"How did you manage that?" Vylsom asked.

"I rolled in some mud, threw on some moss and grass. The men all thought I was Greenkind and the Greenkind thought I was just a filthy child."

"I say we let her," Uliz said. "She could be of use. Of course, it's the king's decision."

"Please, Col. For my grandfather."

Col brought the pit back to level and handed her the knife from his belt. "Stay close."

Their trail along the bluffs came to its end and they climbed to the edge of a thicket. Rakken's border lay across a short field. Col peered between the leaves and tried to determine who, or what, could be lurking about.

A low stone wall marked the perimeter. Beyond it was a narrow alley.

"I know this alley," Uliz said. "This was one of the, shall I say, less reputable corners of Rakken. There was always something happening here. Strange to see it so quiet."

"I'll wager the closer we get to the docks the more we'll find," Vylsom said.

"I agree," Col said. "Stay mindful."

The four of them crouched low and hurried to the wall. They silently jumped over it and crept into the alley. They kept to the sides and moved a few yards in before stopping. Clawed feet scraped on tiled roofs. The Kheva were moving fast. Three shadows passed over the alley and a tile cracked as the enemy continued their patrol.

A weathered sign creaked softly in the wind.

"I don't like this," Uliz said.

"You knew what you were in for," Vylsom said.

The alley opened onto a wide street.

"What are you doing here?" The deep, growling voice of a Kheva called.

Col pressed against the wall and held his breath.

A frightened reply came from the street. "I'm looking for my son. Please, I need to find him. He has to be here."

"You won't find him if you're dead."

Col peeked around the corner and saw the Kheva lift the man from the ground.

"Get back to the docks!"

Col motioned for the others to follow him. They tracked the Kheva and the man from a distance. The man was put into a line with others. The prisoners walked slowly toward the coast.

"I know a shortcut to the docks," Uliz said. "This way."

They darted into another alley. More footfalls and grunts echoed around them. Col could hear them inside the buildings.

They came to another street. It was the same one Caménor and he had taken out of town. It felt hollow now, like the trail of smoke in a lantern after the flame has been snuffed.

One of the Kheva led a line of prisoners past them. They fell in behind the subjugated crew. Col tried to look as desperate and fearful as them. It wasn't too difficult.

The Kheva circled behind the line and snarled at the prisoners. The man in front of Vylsom began to fall. He caught him and held him up until the man could walk again.

The line stopped in front of a tall woman with golden hair. While the rest of the people were caked with dirt and sweat, she alone was clean.

She motioned to a pile of shovels and picks beside her. "You will all take a tool. You will give your life with it or you will give it now." Her lips moved out of sync with her voice. "The choice is yours."

Each of the prisoners took a tool. The Kheva that led them forced them on with a roar. They marched through more deserted streets. They joined three other lines of prisoners and were delivered to the Kheva waiting at the docks. Over a dozen ships were anchored and each was busy preparing to cast off. The Kheva were everywhere like flies on a carcass. They beat those who moved too slowly and threw them into the water to drown. The calling of the gulls was never so mournful.

"Wait!" Vylsom hissed.

Col and the others dropped behind an upended vendor's stall.

"That's my ship!" Vylsom pointed to the one on the far right.

"Are you sure?" Uliz said.

"It's her alright. I need to board her. If she's here there's a chance Deel and Yntor may still be alive."

Col peered around the corner. Vylsom was right. It was The Flapper.

"Uliz," Col said. "I need you and Nea to go back. Tell Mon-Tesh what we've seen. He'll know best how to attack."

"Why?" Nea said. "Where are you going?"

"We're going to board Vylsom's ship."

"Let me come with you. Uliz can deliver the message by himself."

"No, it'll be safer if there are two of you."

"We'll get the message to Mon-Tesh," Uliz said. He placed a hand on Nea's shoulder. "Come on."

"Be careful, Col," she said.

"I will. Now, go."

The two of them ran back the way they came. They stuck to the shadows and soon disappeared.

"Captain, we've got to get aboard and back off as quickly as possible," Col said. He held his shovel over his shoulder and they hurried to The Flapper. The Kheva paid no mind to two slaves who were doing what they were supposed to.

Col stepped onto The Flapper's familiar deck. It was like stepping into an old dream.

Four men fumbled with the ropes in an effort to drop sail and raise anchor. The Kheva pacing the quarterdeck grew impatient. A rope slipped from one of the men's hands. The sail's corner flapped wildly in the wind. Their guard whirled toward the sound but Vylsom was already at the rail, securing the rope.

Col went to the port side of the deck and checked those ropes. It was obvious these men weren't sailors. He needed to look busy anyway until they could find Yntor and sneak ashore.

The Kheva stomped a foot on the quarterdeck. A moment later the door to the Captain's quarters opened. Deel stood meekly in the doorway. The room behind him was empty.

"Ready?" he said.

"Get us moving!" the Kheva demanded.

"Yes." With his head down he took his place at the wheel. Deel had never been happier than at his post. Now, he couldn't have looked any more miserable if he'd been tied naked to it in a hurricane.

Vylsom stared at Deel. The first mate hadn't even seen them. All he saw was the sea.

"Set the sail." Deel raised his voice only enough to be heard.

Col came up beside Vylsom and grabbed a rope. "How are we going to get off now?"

"I'm sorry, my lord. We should've waited."

The sheet caught the wind and the ship slipped smoothly away from the dock.

"It's too late to worry about that, Captain. Deel's here. There's a good chance Yntor could still be aboard."

They snuck below while their guard was busy circling Deel. The hold was filled with timber, planks and posts pulled from homes and shops. It was piled high and left only a narrow passage across the hull. They searched every hole and corner but Yntor was nowhere to be found.

"I shouldn't have let myself hope," Vylsom said.

"Let's finish what we came to do. Tomorrow, we'll make them pay for Yntor."

A plank clattered from the pile. They both looked up with their hands reaching for their knives. A head of tousled hair and two wide eyes peered over the edge. "Colby?"

"Yntor!" Vylsom rushed past Col.

"Captain!" The boy fell into his father's arms and buried his face in Vylsom's shoulder.

"My son! My son!" Vylsom kept saying. He checked Yntor for injury like a cat preening her kitten.

"Is Momma okay?"

"She's fine. She's just fine. We're gonna get you back to her. She's missed you."

"How long have you been down here?" Col asked.

"Since they took the ship. I tried to fight them off, Captain. I really did."

"It's okay, Yntor. You did fine," Vylsom said.

"Deel's been sneaking me food. I don't think he's doing well."

"You let us worry about Deel," Col said. "I'll go back on deck and see how he's faring. You two stay down here a while longer. And, Yntor, stay hidden. We're not about to lose you again."

Col left father and son and returned to the deck. A stiff Spring wind drove the ship. The four crewmen slept idly by the prow. It was probably the first they'd slept in days. Deel still manned the wheel while their guard crouched atop the mast. They had several hours until they'd reach the island.

Col climbed to the quarterdeck and stood beside Deel. "Hello, old friend."

Deel slowly turned his head. "Col?"

"This is where you were the last time I saw you."

"Col." The man couldn't manage more than a word at a breath.

"It's okay. The Captain's here, too. We found Yntor. We'll get you two somewhere safe."

"Captain."

"I'm going to make this right." Col squeezed Deel's hand before leaving him. He joined the other men by the prow. He closed his eyes. It had been days since he'd really slept and being back on The Flapper brought a strange nostalgia. For the first time in weeks, Col felt as though Caménor were still with him. He missed him so much. The waves breaking against the hull let Col believe, if only for a minute, that he'd gone backwards through time. He'd hated the weeks he spent aboard this ship but would give anything now to return to that time.

A growl pulled him from his revelry. The Kheva's stench followed and there was no mistaking where Col was now.

Col had slept much longer than he'd realized. The Enturion unfurled all around them.

Vylsom helped him to his feet. "What do you think we'll find when we get there?"

"I'm afraid to answer that. How's Yntor?"

"He could use a few days under the sun and a good walk but he'll be alright. He's a strong boy."

"He is his father's son. I'm worried about Deel. They did something to him."

"Aye, they did. They broke him. He's got no will of his own anymore. If the enemy had their way every one of us would be just like him."

"Can we help him?"

"We'll try. He's a part of my crew. That will never change."

"They'll turn the world upside down to get Entaramu," Col said.

Vylsom vanished from the corner of Col's eye. Col turned to look but something struck him.

The first thing Col noticed when he came to, other than the throbbing at the back of his head, was that he couldn't move his arms. They were stretched out and tied to the deck rail. The wind had changed and the light was gone. The deck was empty, though Deel still stood at the wheel.

"Deel!" Col called.

Deel's eyes stayed on the horizon.

Col remained like this for what seemed hours, unable to move, unable to do anything but wait. At last he heard the thumping of feet coming to the deck.

One of the other men, the one who'd let the rope slip earlier, knelt in front of him.

"What's going on?" Col asked. "Where are the others?"

The man opened his mouth and a voice came from within. "They're below. I thought it might be nice if we spoke. Just the two of us."

"I've got nothing to say to you, spirit."

"We were so close to taking you that day in the woods. The day you left home, Colmeron. You thought you could hide. You thought we wouldn't know who you are, that you could hide in plain sight? I watched you and your brothers for months as the Captain of your father's guard. What was his name? Towel?"

"His name was Etau. He was a good man."

"He was a weak man. You all are. That one was," he looked at Deel. " You can thank him for letting us know you were here. This poor soul," the

Noflim motioned to the body it inhabited. "Was only too eager to let me take him so he could finally die."

"Deel wouldn't do that."

"But he did. Men have always been easy to manipulate."

"Then why haven't you won yet?"

"We are patient, but we are not without our limits. If we'd killed you sooner we could have saved ourselves all the trouble you've brought. Then again, an Earthking can give us that which was out of reach."

"I won't help you."

"Do you know how your father died?"

"Stop it."

"Slowly. Painfully. He lost his mind, you know. It was great sport for us to watch him descend into madness until the Ayshen relieved him of his burden."

"Stop it!"

"And your brother, Tonn. Do you know how he died?"

Col strained at the ropes.

"He died alone and afraid. He was so afraid," the Noflim laughed. "But not you. You are a brave little king. You may have slipped through our fingers before but you're ours now. And you will give to us all that we ask. Raise the city. Free our master."

"I will never give you Entaramu. You may as well kill me."

"Not just yet." He snapped Col's bonds. "I have something for you, Earthking."

Another ship came slowly up beside them. Standing on deck were two figures, one taller than the other.

"There's nothing so comforting as a familiar face. Don't you agree, Colmeron?"

Nea and Tensoe came to the rail. Tensoe wrapped his hand around Nea's neck and lifted her into the air. She screamed.

"Raise the city or we'll snap her neck."

"I can't," Col said breathlessly. He tried not to look at her.

"Give us Entaramu or watch as we tear her body apart. Every scream, every agonizing cry, will be meant for your ears alone."

"No."

"Kill her!" The Noflim ordered Tensoe.

CHAPTER 26

WHAT LIES BEYOND THE DOORS

—∞—

NEA BEAT AT HER FATHER's arm but the Noflim was too strong.

"Don't!" Col said.

The Noflim beside Col leaned close. "You have only one option, Earthking."

He wanted to scream, to open the earth beneath the evil before him and end it all. Despite his strength, he felt powerless in that moment.

"I know." He managed to keep his voice steady.

"Give us Entaramu and she lives."

Col watched his friend struggle to breathe. Her face twisted in agony. Col remembered Caménor in the Kheva's grasp. He remembered how his stomach dropped as he watched his uncle fall. "I'll do it," he said.

"Such a wise decision, young king." The Noflim called to Tensoe. "Bring her aboard."

They bound Col again and placed him below deck. Nea sat across from him, hands and feet similarly bound. Captain Vylsom and Yntor joined them. The Captain nursed a gash along his temple.

Col hung his head. He couldn't bear to look any of them in the eye.

"I should thank you," Nea said. "But we both know you should've let them kill me."

Col didn't look up.

"You're king now. You can't just give in every time someone is threatened."

"King?" Yntor perked up. "Colby's a king?"

"His name isn't Colby. It's Colmeron. King Colmeron," Nea said.

The boy stared wide-eyed at Col. "I always knew there was something different about you. Yeah, I knew."

"He's a powerful king, at that," Vylsom said.

Col didn't want to be reminded of his power. Even with it he had failed. Why did he have to be so weak?

"You can't give them the city, Col," Nea reminded him.

"It's too late," Col finally replied. "What else can I do?"

"It's my fault," Nea said. "When I saw my father in Rakken I ran to him. I had no idea that..."

"The fault is mine, Nea. I never should have let you come."

"What about Uliz?" Vylsom said.

"What about him?" Col said.

"You sent him back to the Greenkind, too. Where is he?"

"He was ahead of me. He had to have gotten through," Nea said.

"If the Greenkind take Rakken that leaves only the Kheva on the island," Vylsom said.

Col chided them. "They'll kill all of you if I don't raise Entaramu."

"Forget about us, Col. You have to stop them," Nea said.

"You put too much faith in me." It pained him to think how he'd let his friends down.

"I have as much faith in you as you deserve."

"I thought I could do this. I thought I was strong enough. I was wrong."

"Don't say that, King Colby," Yntor said.

"I'm sorry, Yntor. We are crushed beneath a stone even I can't move."

"Like a leaf beneath a stone?" Yntor said.

"Yes, Yntor. Like a leaf beneath a stone."

"Good," Yntor said. "Tell him the story, Captain."

Vylsom's face lit with recognition. "I'd forgotten that one."

"Tell him!"

"There was once a leaf blowing idly in the wind. It followed the breeze wherever it went until one day a stone rolled onto it. The wind came again to carry the leaf but the leaf was pinned beneath the stone. The leaf longed more than anything to glide again on the wind but, crushed beneath the stone, it was impossible.

"The leaf, however, wasn't willing to give up so easily. It wrapped itself around the stone and squeezed with all the strength something so small could muster. It held on, squeezing and squeezing, day after day until one day the stone cracked and fell away. The leaf was free to ride the wind once more."

Col lifted his head. "That's a lovely story, Captain, but leaves have no strength and stories won't save us today."

"True. Leaves have no strength but neither did you not so long ago," Vylsom said. "And you still fought."

No one said anything for awhile after that. The hours passed. The Flapper sailed ever towards their dreaded destination until at last a shout came from the deck above. The hatch over the hold opened. Dim morning light spilled through. They had arrived.

Col stood painfully on stiff legs.

"You don't have to do this," Nea said. "We'll die for you."

"You're better friends than I deserve. You truly are. But I'm not willing to let you die for me. Too many have done that already."

Tensoe came down and cut his bonds. Col rubbed sore wrists and shuffled to the deck. The sun crested the horizon and illuminated the island in the distance. The Enturion shimmered in the early light. Col had never been so mesmerized by the sea.

Or so afraid of it.

The clanging of pick and shovel echoed from the island. The vegetation had been stripped and every tree felled. Huge chunks of the peak had been cut away and a patchwork of scaffolding and ladders climbed the face. Nearly six dozen ships were at anchor, their crews at work on the island.

"What are you waiting for, Earthking?" The tall woman from the docks had arrived on another ship. All three Noflim were aboard The Flapper now. The ship rocked gently far from the island's shore.

Col could feel the City of Kings beneath the water's surface. Entaramu. The citadel he was sworn to protect. And he was about to hand it over to the enemy. He was even worse than Urion, who had sunk the city to save it. Now Col would resurrect it to save his friends. It was a selfish act of a failed king.

Col looked behind them in hopes of seeing ships laden with Greenkind warriors but the horizon showed only growing dawn. There was nothing left for him but to give the Noflim what they sought.

He reached a hand toward the island and focused on the city beneath. The air around them began to thrum. The waters surged. The beach surrounding the island crumbled and slid into the sea. The peak rose. Col felt his strength draining like a cask uncorked.

The collapsed roofs of ancient buildings broke the surface of the water. The ships anchored around the island were suddenly beached atop the decayed ruins. Their hulls split with terrible cracks that echoed over the tumult. More towers blocked the sun as the city slowly rose. Water rushed from alleys between decrepit buildings.

Col fell to his knees. He clung to the railing and forced himself to concentrate.

The sea around them burst with the glossy tails of whitefish fleeing the maelstrom. The Flapper rocked violently for what seemed like hours before the fury subsided. They drifted at the banks of the city.

Col lowered his hand.

"At last," Tensoe said. "You've done well, Earthking."

"Let my friends go."

"No," Tensoe said flatly. "Take us to the grove."

"I don't know where it is."

"But you do. You bear the fear of one who has seen the master."

The gangplank was lowered. Col and the Noflim entered Entaramu. A host of Kheva swarmed after them. Stone buildings erratically lined the streets. Colonies of coral and long, slick rivers of seaweed covered the landscape. Once majestic towers toppled onto once bustling avenues.

They pushed further into the city. The crews of the ships that were stranded clung desperately to the wreckage. The Kheva clamored over the ruins. They leapt and climbed the broken walls like spiders on a web. And Col felt like the fly trapped in the center of it all.

The three Noflim walked ahead of him in steady formation. Had any of Col's ancestors had an opportunity like this? The Three were in one place. Col tried to think of a way to end this before it went any farther. Could he sink the city again? No. He didn't have the strength for that. He couldn't run either. The Kheva would catch him. His thoughts raced but only ended up in circles. He continued to follow his captors.

The sun peeked between the ruins. They neared the center of the city. The king's palace, or what remained of it, rose ahead of them. Col felt small in its shadow. A broken archway spread over them. Its sides stood like two lovers unable to touch.

Their road curved up a hill before leveling in front of a massive empty doorway. A cavernous hall welcomed them to the home of the Earthkings.

"Give us light!" Tensoe demanded.

One of the Kheva handed him an unlit torch. Tensoe spit on the branch and breathed hot air onto it. Smoke curled and a flame burst. More torches were lit and spread among them.

Col didn't wonder at the Noflim's power but why torches were needed at all. To him the room already brimmed with light.

Scores of Thanir filled the hall. The enemy gave no sign they saw them.

The Thanir ran their hands over Col's face. Their touch was like sunlight after years of darkness. He drank it in and felt as though he was waking from a long and terrible sleep.

"The master is near," the blonde woman said. "Take us to him, fleshling."

One of the Thanir motioned Col to follow. He went after it and the Noflim followed. They passed through hallways still dripping with the sea and crossed long bridges arching over coral gardens. A wide staircase descended far into the ground below. The Thanir waited at the bottom.

Tensoe turned to the Kheva with them. "Wait here. Kill anything that moves."

The Noflim moved quickly down the slick steps while Col tried to remain standing. They waited impatiently at the bottom for Col.

Col reached them at last and recognized the long tunnel ahead of them. It seemed to go on without end. "It's this way," he said.

He led them with the Thanir ever ahead of him. The Noflim twitched and their breathing quickened the further they went. The hallway ended abruptly. It split in opposite directions.

"Which way?" Tensoe said.

Col knew the Sacred Grove lay to the left but that hallway was dark. His guide had gone right. "It's down there," Col pointed to the right.

They came to a room with a long stone table in the middle. It was identical to the one Col had found before.

The Noflim turned on him. "There's nothing here!"

"Wait!" Col said. He put his hand on the table. Stone ground against stone. The table dropped and became stairs leading down.

"What you want is down there," Col said. "I've done as you asked."

"You have more to do, little king."

"I've already handed you the city, spirit. What more do you want?"

"Go down and open the doors so that our master may receive us. He's waited a long time."

Col looked across the room to his guide. The Thanir stared at Col with eyes like the stars and nodded.

Col descended wordlessly. The Thanir did not go ahead of him and Col was soon surrounded by darkness. The three Noflim waited at the top of the stairs. "I need light," Col said.

A torch was tossed down to him. He held it out. A large cavern opened ahead of him. It was nearly identical to the one he'd been in before. This room was cold, though. No trees lined the walls either. Only bare stone.

Two large doors stood at the far end of the room. While the doors to the Sacred Grove were carved with the trees and spring in them these doors showed a much different scene.

Col held his torch up.

On the doors in front of him was a hideous creature. Its face was covered in eyes and four arms stretched from a bloated and twisting body. Its victims were held tightly in its hands. Its mouth gaped open. It stretched past the borders of its face. Both man and beast fell into the creature's mouth.

Col closed his eyes and put his hands to the door. The seam in the middle split with a terrible crack and the sound of rushing wind. Stale air rushed past him. The doors swung out and revealed only black beyond them. There was something in the darkness. No, it was the darkness.

The Noflim were next to Col before he could call to them.

"There. Your master awaits you," Col said.

"Do you feel his power?" The Noflim moved toward the open doors. Col crept backward as they passed him.

The Darkness swallowed the light from their torches. "A trick?" The Noflim shouted. "Now you and your friends will die, Earthking."

"It doesn't matter. I won't let you enter the grove."

Something moved behind the Noflim. The Darkness wrapped itself around them. They tried to run but hands tore at them and dragged them toward the doors. They gave a final shriek as the Darkness swallowed them.

The shadow reached for Col. He ran for the stairs. A blinding light flashed past him and the Darkness retreated. The echo of the doors slamming shut shook the chamber.

A Thanir stood beside Col. "Come away from here, O King. You do not yet belong to death."

Col climbed toward the light. "Are the Noflim dead?"

"They are spirit and cannot die as men do, but the bodies they dwelled in are gone."

"Won't they find new ones?"

"That is up to you. The Kheva Adem are the tools the Noflim use to prepare new hosts. Only a few remain. Without them the Noflim remain spirit without flesh."

Col ran back to the long corridor. It wouldn't take the Kheva long to realize their masters were gone. He needed to stop them before they had time to hide.

He bounded up the wide staircase. Each step lifted to propel him onward. The towering pillars in the entrance hall rushed by as he made for the gates. The Kheva that had followed them in were gone. He didn't see any as he ran through the streets either. At the city's edge he ascended a high cliff. He scanned the water. What remained of the Kheva Adem swam away from the city. They sped like shadows beneath the waves.

Col had to act quickly. He tore a piece of the seaweed that tangled around his feet. He held it before him and concentrated. The water around the Kheva grew murky. The powerful strokes of the Kheva slowed. Tendrils of seaweed wrapped around limb and horn. The beasts began to disappear beneath the green. Soon, the Kheva Adem were no more.

It was finally over. Arnoc and her people were free once more. The clouds above scattered like frightened squirrels, leaving the sun to pour light on Entaramu. Col scanned the city he'd raised. Even in ruins it was still beautiful. Caménor would have been proud.

CHAPTER 27

WAITING FOR HOME

Col rode on a horse. A real horse. A good horse. Col had been a week in Akeldama. Each day more of the barren land turned lush and Col was that much closer to having his brother with him again. It seemed a lifetime since he'd seen him.

The horse slowed to an easy amble through the tightly grown wood. Col didn't know its name. The farmer who'd given him the steed hadn't mentioned it and Col hadn't thought to give it one. Maybe Mino would name it. It could be his horse. A gift to welcome him home.

Col reached Akeldama's edge. The myrtles he'd grown creaked and their leaves clamored in the wind. It was no longer a field of blood, cursed to desolation. It was something else now. Something full of promise. He supposed it should be renamed, but he would leave that to its new denizens.

He clucked his tongue and the horse crossed onto Arnoc's fertile ground. He was ready to return to Entaramu. The city was a strange, hollow place. Not like a corpse. More like a cup waiting to be filled.

He rode for Rakken, taking care to feed and water the farmer's horse. He gave himself time to rest as well. He slept better these days. The constant fear that had buried itself in his gut like a worm in an apple was gone.

When Col didn't return from the port Mon-Tesh had attacked Rakken as planned. The battle between the Greenkind and the Kheva lasted into the night. Mon-Tesh nearly tore the port apart hunting down the last of the enemy. The Kheva Adem were gone.

After the battle, Col left Captain Vylsom in charge of Rakken. The village, as well as most of Arnoc, would need time and guidance to find its footing again. Word was slowly reaching those in hiding that freedom had come. More of his people emerged from their holes every day.

Col sensed a change in the devastated port before he even set foot on the streets. Those he passed ceased their busyness. Some bowed. Others just stared. Men working on rooftops halted their hammering to shout greetings. Col smiled back as he rode by. To them he was no longer a prince, Tephall's boy. He was king now. Their king. King Colmeron.

"Get back to work! This town will never be rebuilt with you gawking all day!" Vylsom yelled at the men. He marched toward Col with his head held higher than ever. "Ah! I've missed having a crew under me," he said.

"I can tell," Col said.

"I trust my lord had a successful journey."

"Akeldama is unrecognizable. The Greenkind should be pleased."

"And Prince Mino will finally be able to join you."

"Has there been any word of their arrival?"

"Not yet. It'll come, my lord."

"The Greenkind have earned their reward. Their losses were heavy in a battle that wasn't their own."

"Arnoc won't soon forget any of the sacrifices that were made."

Vylsom was right. The Greenkind had not been the only ones to suffer. The enemy's invasion had spread quickly. Many of those who weren't deemed solid enough to be slaves were slaughtered along the way. Arnoc would never be the same but it would never again forget either.

"Yntor will be glad to hear you've returned. I think he's still sore he couldn't go with you. The wife hasn't let him out of her sight."

"He'll be lucky if she ever allows him to leave home again," Col laughed. He left Vylsom to his duties and went to the port's southern corner. A wide bridge that pushed above the waves led to Entaramu. He wasted no time putting Rakken behind him. It would be a full afternoon's ride. The waves lapped harmlessly at the bridge's sound walls as he rode.

Ahead of him his city rose like a man from a dream. Entaramu had been born of the earth and looked like it had been hewn from a mountain. It had once been vibrant with life. Filled with lush vegetation and sprawling gardens. The entire city was a testament to the power and glory of the Earthkings. It was a glory Col hoped to restore in time.

For now the city was barren, like a tree without leaves. Those left without homes filled a few habitable corners of the city.

Col rode quickly through the empty streets and passed beneath the broken archway. A torch flickered at the gates of the king's palace and a beat up wagon sat outside rusted iron gates.

Nea and Uliz waited inside the hall. Its walls had been scraped clean and firelight filled the space making it feel less alien.

"Welcome home, your majesty," Uliz said.

"You did this?" Col asked.

"You didn't think we'd let the king return to the cold, dark hallways he'd left, did you?"

"Thank you, my friends. This is as much your home as it is mine, though."

"Good, because we have nowhere else to go," Nea said. "Follow us. There's something we want to show you."

They led Col through labyrinthine passages littered with sand to a window-lined room larger than the great hall in Ten Rocks. Col looked at Nea for an explanation.

"These are the king's quarters. At least that's what we think. There could be more." Two chairs and a small table sat forlornly in the middle of the sprawling room.

"That's all we've been able to bring so far," she said.

"It's perfect," Col laughed.

"We'll leave you to rest, my lord. I'm sure you're tired," Uliz said.

Col was still for the first time in days. The sun's fading light slipped through the windows. It gave the room a drowsy glow.

He heard his friends' voices echo through the halls. He smiled. This was his now and once Mino was here it would be home.

There was no bed in the room so he sat down and laid his head on the table.

He woke to the delicate chirps of a golden finch hopping happily along a windowsill. Col shook his head and rubbed his face. He remembered where he was and stood up so fast he nearly knocked the table over. The frightened bird flew away. Col ran from the room and down a long, curving staircase to the palace's main passage. After several wrong turns and carefully skipping through a hallway full of mussels he found the tower. He sprinted up the spiral stairs. The peak was a mess of rocks and soil. He took a step back and charged up. The debris rolled away like frightened minnows fleeing a salmon. It exploded out as Col reached the top sending a shower onto the city far, far below.

Col climbed into the early light. He was surrounded by the thin stone birches of what was once the small island's peak. He grabbed two trunks and leaned over the edge. The wind rushed through his hair as the city spread below him. Beyond that, a ruffled sea greeted his eyes. He looked to the bridge. He could nearly see it reaching the coast. There was no sign of the Greenkind. He stepped back. Perhaps tomorrow, he resigned. But the next morning only held the same.

More people made their way to the fabled city and Col busied himself helping them settle into various districts. The distant glow of lanterns soon dotted the city at night. It was a pleasant sight that eased Col. It reminded him to hope for better news with the morning.

Weeks passed until one morning Col did not ascend the tower. He stayed in his room. A bowl of weak stew sat cooling in front of him.

Nea came in. She didn't bother to knock anymore. "Another group arrived last night," she said. "Do you want to greet them?"

Col stared silently at the bowl in front of him.

"He'll be here soon. Mon-Tesh won't falter on his promise."

"Then where are they? Why haven't they brought him yet?"

"It's a long journey. Be patient."

"I've been patient, Nea. I've moved earth and sea and now I want my brother back!" He shoved the table away from him. Hard. The stew spilled.

"At least you have a brother to have back. My entire family is gone. I'll never see any of them again."

Her words stung. "You're right. I'm sorry. But that doesn't make the waiting any easier."

"I know. If I did have someone left, there's nothing I wouldn't do to get them back. So don't be too sorry."

"Thanks, Nea."

She started for the door. "Are you coming?"

Col tore his eyes from the cold broth. "Yes."

They went to the throne room. Nea and Uliz had labored for days on it and Col was proud of what his friends had accomplished. This would be the first time he greeted any of his subjects there.

It was a long room with windows at even intervals along the sloped ceiling. Pillars shaped like trunks rose from floor to ceiling with stone branches arching into the roof. Long, wrinkled blades of seagrass hung from them like the leaves they could never grow. The room felt alive. Like a part of every Earthking before Col remained.

The city's newest residents crowded from wall to wall. They strained to see him as he entered through a tall archway and fell silent as he walked down the long aisle. He stepped onto the dais where a defunct remnant of the throne sat. It was little more than a stump of stone with a cracked back.

He lowered his hand and raised it a few inches. The stone pushed up. The crack sealed shut. An arm rose on either side of the wide seat and four legs reached under it. Col turned and faced the awestruck crowd.

"My people," he said. He stopped and realized what he was saying. "My people. That is what you are. You are my countrymen, my brothers. Today, let us celebrate the victory of Arnoc. We are at peace once more but that peace does not bring with it the comfort of the past. Instead, it is a new order, one not born of our fathers' sacrifice, but of our own. It's a peace that leads us ahead. Let's not look back but walk the road before us. For along that road we have found a new home. Your home. Welcome!"

The crowd cheered but their applause quickly died out. It was replaced with gasps as a party of Greenkind entered the hall. Mon-Tesh walked at their head.

"Earthking," he began. "We come not only to honor you but to honor our agreement."

Col fought the urge to run to them.

Mon-Tesh stepped aside to reveal a small boy of nine Summers. Mino's time among the forest dwellers was evident.

"Mino!" Col ran to him.

"Col?"

"It's me, Mino. You're finally here!"

"Col." He garbled it like a foreign word.

"Yes!" Col wrapped his arms around all that remained of his family. "It's okay now. You're home."

"Home? This isn't my home."

"It's a new home, Mino. Our home."

"No, I live in the forest. My family is there."

"No, Mino. This is your home. I am your family."

"I don't want to stay here. I want to go back." He pulled himself free of Col's arms.

"I told you the boy was not mistreated," Mon-Tesh said.

"Thank you, Mon-Tesh. Your reward awaits you and your people."

Mon-Tesh signaled those with him and they turned to leave. Mino ran after them. He buried himself in their midst.

"Mino! Come back," Col pleaded with him. His brother ignored him. "Mon-Tesh, bring him here."

The Greenkind leader turned back to Col. "He thinks himself one of us and just as I would not give you any of my people against their will, I will not force him to stay. Mee-no is free to choose."

"He's not one of you, Greenkind. He's my brother!" Col reached a hand to Mino. "Come back, Mino. It's me, Colmeron. I'm your brother."

The boy shook his head and disappeared into the arms of one of the soldiers. Col flexed his hand open and the soldier released him.

"What are you doing?" Mon-Tesh demanded.

"Bring him here," Col said. The soldier pulled Mino to Col.

Col took his brother and released the soldier. "I won't let you take him. Not after everything else that's been taken."

Mon-Tesh stiffened. He raised himself up. Long limbs of flesh and earth creaked like an oak in the wind. His broad stone jaw set and his eyes narrowed. "You've forced your will over us, Earthking. You've broken your oath."

"You and your soldiers can leave now, Mon-Tesh."

The Greenkind leader looked at the gathered crowd. "Bear witness to your king's fading honor."

"Go! Enjoy the paradise that awaits you," Col said.

"What follows will be on your head, Earthking!" Mon-Tesh declared. The Greenkind stormed from the hall. Their curses buried a seed of fear in every man there.

Every man but Col, who looked intently at his brother. He saw traces of their father around his eyes and chin. And he had their mother's cheeks. There was even a trace of Tonn in the curl of his lips. Col smiled. He pulled his brother close and held him tight. Mino slowly returned the embrace.

Col was home at last.

THE END

EPILOGUE

Commander Retana motioned for his men to stop. Weeks wandering through the Broken Mountains had left him with only a portion of his troops. There were no Kheva to be found here. There never were. There was only thirst and hunger. Those who fell behind disappeared. Their numbers dwindled. He was beginning to think these mountains were cursed.

Today was different though.

The smell of food — roasting meats and steaming breads, creamy sauces and sweet pastries — lured them through the mountain pass like a groom to his bride.

They came to a barren ravine. Gravel crunched underfoot and a sharp wind whipped the dust into blinding dervishes. Up a slope of jagged rocks gaped the mouth of a cave. The smell was coming from there. Retana was sure of it. The men knew it too. They fought over one another to reach it.

He pulled two of them apart. "Enough! We'll all get a taste soon enough."

He steadied himself with one hand while the other held his sword. "A feast fit for a king," he said to himself. His feet barely lifted as he climbed the slope. He moved slow but he could feel himself speeding toward death.

A figure appeared at the mouth of the cave. Retana startled and stumbled back.

His men clamored to pull him to his feet. The rocks had torn his skin and he was sure his arm was broken.

"Captain?" One of the men pointed to the cave. Retana followed his gaze to the figure standing there.

A wild man, covered in dust and blood, looked down on them.

"If this feast is for a king should the king be the only one to table?" the man said.

Retana knew that voice. He knew who it should belong to but this couldn't be him.

"Come and eat with me, Commander. You and your men have come far."

There could be no mistake. This was him. This was their king.

This was Tephall.